Niamh O'Connor is one of Ireland's best-known crime authors. She is the true-crime editor with the *Sunday World*, Ireland's biggest selling Sunday newspaper. Her job, in which she interviews both high-profile criminals and their victims, means she knows the world she is writing about. *If I Never See You Again* went to number one in the Nielsen Heatseekers chart when it was released in the UK in January 2011 and was nominated in the Best Newcomers category of the Irish Book Awards in November 2010. Her follow-up novel, *Taken*, was a number-two bestseller in Ireland in June 2011.

For more information on Niamh O'Connor and her books, see her website at www.niamhoconnor.co.uk

www.transworldireland.ie

www.**transworldbooks**.co.uk

Also by Niamh O'Connor

Non-fiction
BLOOD TIES

Fiction
IF I NEVER SEE YOU AGAIN
TAKEN

and published by Transworld Ireland

Too Close For Comfort

Niamh O'Connor

TRANSWORLD IRELAND

TRANSWORLD IRELAND
an imprint of The Random House Group Limited
20 Vauxhall Bridge Road, London SW1V 2SA
www.transworldbooks.co.uk

TOO CLOSE FOR COMFORT
A TRANSWORLD IRELAND BOOK: 9781848271395

First published in 2012 by Transworld Ireland,
a division of Transworld Publishers
Transworld Ireland paperback edition published 2013

Addresses for Random House Group Ltd companies outside the UK
can be found at: www.randomhouse.co.uk
The Random House Group Ltd Reg. No. 954009

The Random House Group Limited supports The Forest Stewardship
Council (FSC®), the leading international forest-certification organization.
Our books carrying the FSC label are printed on FSC®-certified paper.
FSC is the only forest-certification scheme endorsed by the leading
environmental organizations, including Greenpeace.
Our paper-procurement policy can be found at
www.randomhouse.co.uk/environment

Typeset in 11/15pt Sabon by Falcon Oast Graphic Art Ltd.
Printed and bound by CPI Group (UK) Ltd, Croydon, CR0 4YY.

2 4 6 8 10 9 7 5 3 1

TOO CLOSE FOR COMFORT

Author's Note

This book was partly inspired by events surrounding the demise of the *News of the World*, and the shocking tactics used to get stories. Events in *Too Close For Comfort* are fictitious, but inspired by the truth, which in this case really is stranger than fiction. To recap on what actually happened: Sean Hoare (48), the whistleblower in the *News of the World* phone-hacking scandal, was found dead at his flat in Watford, Hertfordshire, on 18 July 2011, having spent most of his last weeks living there as a paranoid recluse, keeping the curtains drawn, convinced someone from the government was out to get him.

Shortly before his death, he'd revealed to the *New York Times* the practice of 'pinging' people via mobilephone signals, in exchange for payments to police officers. The going rate was three hundred pounds sterling, he'd claimed.

The scandal culminated in the 4 July 2011 revelation that mobile-phone voice messages left for murdered schoolgirl Milly Dowler had been intercepted by the newspaper, leading her family to believe she was still alive and listening to them.

A public inquiry under Lord Justice Brian Leveson was set up to examine the ethics of the press and, on 7 July 2011, the *News of the World*, once the biggest-selling English-language newspaper in the world, and which was selling almost three million copies per week in 2010, was shut down, and senior members of staff arrested. The former editor Rebekah Brooks was the tenth person to be held in custody, on 17 July 2011.

Subsequently, a post-mortem examination revealed that there was no third party involved in the death of Sean Hoare, and his inquest found he'd died from alcoholic liver disease. He had 76mg of alcohol per 100ml of blood, an amount under the drink-driving limit of 80mg at the time of his death.

All other characters in this book are entirely fictitious and any resemblance to actual persons, living or dead, is purely coincidental.

Monday

Prologue

The hospital room was ten feet by twelve. The man delivering the bouquet to the Central Maternity Hospital in Dublin had put heel to toe to measure out the steps last time on the recce. He'd noted the contents – bed, bedside locker, meal tray, Perspex baby cot with wood-encased storage area underneath – in the notebook in his back jeans pocket. He'd scored the words 'all on wheels' underneath, and had measured the precise dimensions of the press under the cot in which the baby was currently sleeping. There would be no room for a margin of error. If he'd learned one thing from his previous line of work, it was that research was everything. He knew exactly where the panic button was located, for instance, thanks to the sketch he'd made of the room from photos taken with his phone. An 'x' on his map marked the approximate point where it dangled from a wire over the bed.

The reward would make the risk worthwhile. He'd come a long way from his previous life, but he didn't regret a minute of the years he'd spent actually working for a living. It had given him a set of skills that were about to earn him a small fortune. The devil was in the detail.

The three pictures in front of him were fixed to the wall with screws. The first was an illustrated guide to good hand hygiene; the second, a bland print of pressed flowers; and last, but by no means least, a black and white floor plan of the entire third storey. A red arrow pointed to a spot, declaring: 'You are here.' Dots mapped the route to the nearest fire escape. He'd memorized it.

He moved to a corner of the room and pressed the pedal of a narrow, rectangular, white, hazardous-waste metal bin, three feet in height. The lid rose, and as he lifted his foot, began to lower gently, exactly as he remembered. It was operated by a silent closing mechanism, and the perfect size for his purposes.

His notebook contained a verbatim description of the notice on the bin, which gave a pager number for the environmental officer of the hospital, who, according to the notice, was responsible for ensuring only tagged, clear bags were placed inside the bin, and later disposed of in a green wheelie container. He'd also jotted the details of the supplier and the address for customer support – a zone in an industrial park on the north side of the city. He'd established the uniform the crew wore, and the company logos for their visitor ID . . .

He closed his eyes and noted today's sounds: seagulls screeching; metal rattling, which turned out to be a trolley being wheeled by a bread man; and the zizz and beep of an ambulance ramp lowering at a set of open doors directly underneath.

Sunlight streamed in through the sliding sash window, which he was aware locked at six inches. The sill was the only shelf in the room, and the pungent bunch of lilies he'd brought were giving off an over-powering, distinctly funereal smell that he'd realized last time could mask even the cloying smell of dis-infectant. It was doing the same job on the chloroform . . .

He glanced at the bathroom door, behind which the new mum was lying on the floor. She'd gone voluntarily when he'd handed her a vase to fill for the bouquet he'd brought. He checked his watch. She'd start to come to in a couple of minutes. He needed to get moving.

The CCTV camera attached to the outside wall of the adjacent wing had not proved to be the obstacle he'd feared. It was old and it pointed in only one direction – away from the room and towards the staff car park. His gaze lit on a stocky-looking nurse barrelling across the lot towards the entrance, one pudgy arm crossing her chest to reach into a handbag. She pulled out a can of Sure Extra – useless for any kind of hit – and tucked it under one arm of her blouse, then the other, without any change of pace. If there was one thing he had learned from his years spent staking out subjects, it was that most people never even noticed what was going on right in front of their noses.

To the right of the car park was a staff smoking shelter. That had been his biggest worry during the planning phase. It was much more likely that someone on a fag break would spot something untoward unfolding right in front of them. Luckily the fire alarm going off would provide the perfect distraction.

He reached for the cord of the blind and gave it a tug. It lowered straight away, revealing the details of its Norfolk-based manufacturer on a sticker that he could recite word for word – yet another contractor who could enter the room legitimately. He'd been spoilt for choice. Even the TV was pay-as-you-go, one of those touch-screen computer jobs where the sound and lip movements were never in sync. It was suspended on a smart swivel arm. A notice said the use of the TV cost five euro a night and required a card bought from a vending machine outside. He could easily have blagged his way in by pretending it needed servicing.

The only group he'd steered well clear of impersonating were the staff members, though their uniforms would have been the easiest to get hold of. Their shirts varied according to profession, but were all worn with black trousers and Hush Puppies or Crocs. The nurses had white short-sleeved tunic tops with black trim, and upside-down watches pinned to the breast. The matrons wore navy, the catering staff speckled tunics and hairnets, the cleaners purple. But the banter he'd witnessed between them meant they probably all knew each other. He couldn't risk them realizing that he wasn't one of them.

All things considered, he was happy he'd made the right choice in his plan to arrive with a delivery of flowers, and leave as a bin man. Underneath his overalls was the uniform of the hazardous-waste company that disposed of the contents of the metal bin.

He opened the bathroom door to check on the mum. The room was half the size of the bedroom, but had presented him with just as many possibilities. The same firm provided the soft soap in the dispenser, paper bath mats, tissues, pump-action alcohol rub for hand hygiene, toilet brush and toilet rolls. There was a sanitary disposal unit, which he'd noted required daily emptying. The mum was still conked out . . .

Time to get a move on. He turned to the cot where the sleeping infant was all swaddled up and warm and safe, innocent of the world and its vices and predators. He moved to the bin, whipped off and dumped his outer layer of clothing in a plastic bag, knotted it and stuffed it down to the bottom.

He plucked the baby out of the cot and placed it in the bin. Snug as a bug, cushioned by the clothing padding. It started to cry a bit, but that sound was *expected here, and he was aware it was so muffled it was really only audible to him. As long as nobody saw the baby in his arms, he'd be safe enough. He headed out the door with the bin under his arm, just as he'd watched it carried out before. One arm brushed against the flowers on the way, his shirt picking up an annoying rust-coloured pollen stain. Out in the corridor, he glanced left towards the nurses' station at the far end and then right to the double doors fifty feet away, which separated the private wing from the public ward and the stairs to the exit. Ironically the public ward had not been an option for the snatch. Women turned into busy-bodies when they were together. But in a private ward they were isolated from each other in the name of comfort, and more likely to doubt their instincts.*

The objects he passed on the corridor were as he had memorized them last time: a water dispenser, and a sizeable steel refrigeration unit on wheels, about five feet high by three. There was something new this time – a blood-pressure monitor, but it was on wheels. It would be possible to shove it out of the way if he had to run, or to use it as a weapon, if needs be. If things went pear-shaped, he could grab the fire extinguisher on the wall beside a box dispensing latex gloves and throw it at anyone who tried to chase him. One press of the panic button at the nurses' station would cause all the doors in the maternity unit to seal shut in three seconds. However, the fire alarm would prevent the lockdown command from working.

He walked steadily past three doors on the right leading to private patients' rooms, a fourth to the laundry storeroom, and a fifth to a kitchen, which bore a sign that read: 'No Unauthorized Personnel Beyond This Area'. He passed the sixth door, a locked cupboard he'd seen a nurse restock with medicine, and the seventh, a baby-changing area. He felt a surge of adrenalin as he passed the last door on the right. It was open and the room was glowing blue from the UV lamps treating the jaundiced infants. He was almost home and dry. He pushed through the set of swing doors, under a globe camera fixed to the wall above, which could not see below the peak of his cap.

Behind him a nurse was shouting that a mum had collapsed and she needed assistance. Three seconds to lockdown, which he reckoned would be approximately two seconds too late. Pulling out his keys, he smashed the glass panel to trigger the fire alarm, and as it shrieked into life, he took the stairs two at a time, forcing a woman to step sideways, and tighten the dressing-gown belt around her bump.

Once out on the street, he climbed into the back of his white van, and transferred the baby from the bin to a Moses basket.

No question about it, those years in his old job had stood him in good stead. As he climbed into the driving seat and gunned the engine, he thought back to his first day as a copyboy. The year was 2000, the place Wapping in London's Docklands, and he had just stepped on to the lowest rung of the newspaper ladder . . .

Three days earlier: Friday

1

Amanda Wells was so sorry she'd parked in a multi-storey car park. She'd lapped seven of the nine floors already – positive her Beamer wasn't on the ground or top levels – but there was still no sign of it. It was a cold April night, but she was clammy all over. The car park closed at midnight, in about fifteen minutes. She could barely see ten feet in front of her, the lighting was so bad and the floor space so vast. A car alarm burst into life, making her start and drowning out the clicking of her heels.

Amanda bent down and scooped off her expensive shoes: they were too good for this place, and her feet were killing her. She'd blisters on her toes and the backs of her heels. If she stepped on broken glass, she was going to threaten whoever managed this car park with legal action; she'd sued for clients over a lot less in her time. It was bloody well dangerous to expect a woman to wander around like this, on her own, at this hour of the night. The lifts hadn't been working either, and the stairwell, which ran straight up from an open door on the street, was like an invitation to every social inadequate to come on in and shoot up – or rob the vulnerable blonde woman with the big flash bag and expensive jewellery. Amanda couldn't wait to get home and write this day off. A pulse struck up in her temple. Where was her bloody car?

'Bastard, bastard, bastard,' she said under her breath, each time with more conviction. Two and a half hours earlier, she had walked up to a dark-haired man in a denim jacket standing in a crowd on the main street in Temple Bar watching a busker with a bushy beard play a guitar, harmonica, and drum simultaneously. She had tossed some loose change into the musician's cap, and had linked arms with the cute guy, zigzagging past a gaggle of women in tutus, grinning when they'd wolf-whistled at him. She'd walked him purposefully around the corner to a dingy hotel, stifling a giggle at the desk as the pretty receptionist took in the age difference.

'I booked a room for Mr and Mrs Kutcher,' she'd said, handing over her cash as her toy boy had struggled to keep a straight face.

Amanda wiped her eyes with the sleeves of her Betty Barclay jacket as she remembered how good the lovemaking had been. She'd held off from her announcement until they went for a meal in a restaurant afterwards.

'Someone knows about us,' she'd said, after looking

up from the iPhone tucked on her lap. He hated her tweeting when they were together, but she'd wanted to give her verdict on the restaurant to her online pals. 'They phoned and called to see me. They're threatening to tell your wife.' She didn't tell him she knew who it was. That would only have led to trouble.

He'd swallowed a mouthful of hot toffee pudding as he'd stared at her.

Amanda had slipped her foot under his trouser leg, sliding it up his calf. 'I honestly think it's a blessing in disguise.'

She'd thought that would be the point where they started planning the rest of their lives together, had even fantasized about the wording for the toast. But that dream had come crashing down when he'd replied, 'I need some time out to get my head together. I think it would be good for us if you started dating again. Who knows? I might even come crawling back, begging for forgiveness.'

Bastard, bastard, bastard, she thought now, snivelling. Three years she'd been waiting for him to leave his wife like he'd always said he was going to; three years skulking around behind everybody else's back. He'd made a complete fool out of her. Well, he'd underestimated her if he'd thought she was just going to walk away. She hadn't got to where she was in life by being treated like the shit on someone's shoe.

She squinted as she tried to see the makes of the last

few motors parked in the bays. No wonder she couldn't see straight. She couldn't even tell what colour they were until she was standing right alongside. The strobe lighting overhead was completely inadequate now daylight wasn't flooding in through the wire-mesh walls, and the bulbs were starting to power off, presumably to save on the electricity bill as most of the drivers had gone. How was anyone supposed to find anything with this 'a', 'b', 'c' system going on?

Amanda was trying not to fret, and to breathe deeply; why did it always seem so straightforward on her Pilates ball or a yoga mat? She stopped walking in order to pull herself together.

An automated voice from a car-park speaker announced: 'This car park will close for the night in five minutes. Motorists will not be able to retrieve their vehicles from that point.'

Her breath tightened in her chest. How the hell was she going to find it in five minutes? She wouldn't have time to collect it in the morning, she'd too much on.

Then everything went black.

Amanda froze. All the lights had gone out. She was in the pitch dark. Her heart stalled as she tried to remember which direction the stairs were in. At least in there she could keep one hand on the rough brick wall, which the cheapskate owners couldn't be arsed to plaster, until she got back out on to the street. Maybe there'd be time to catch a staff member before they left for the night.

She'd already established that she couldn't get a signal on her mobile to ring anyone.

She couldn't be the only one here. Could she? she wondered, biting into her lower lip. Things like this didn't happen to her. She was organized, and careful. But she'd been under too much pressure from the banks demanding she repay the loans she'd taken out. Being dumped had been the last straw. She couldn't think or see straight. She started to say a silent prayer – something she hadn't done since she was a kid – when the sound of a set of tyres screeching on the shiny surface made her sigh with relief. Another motorist was close by. Thank God. And then another miracle: in the light from the car's headlights she spotted her own car. Relief washed over her. Amanda hurried towards it, pointing the key fob and smiling as the Beamer's indicators flashed and snicked in response. She stooped down to cup her shoes back on, only ten feet away from it now. The car moving behind her stopped, and Amanda turned to see why, shielding her eyes from the glare of the full headlights with one hand.

She heard a door open, and hoped she wasn't about to be told the car park was closed already.

'Into the boot,' the driver said.

Monday

2

Chief Superintendent Jo Birmingham stood on a gang-plank set in muck, watching a blonde, middle-aged, naked woman being hoisted out of a shallow grave and into a white body bag. According to the iPhone that Jo had just prised from her hand, and which was still working, her name was Amanda Wells. At least, that was the name on the Twitter, Gmail, Yahoo and Hotmail accounts with various numbers on the end set up on the phone.

Jo glanced around in concern at the battering the hexagonal pop-up body tent was taking. It was blowing a gale outside, like a different bloody season in the mountains compared to the one she'd left behind in the city. The tent had needed securing with metal stakes instead of sandbags because just yards beyond the clear-ing – between a sweep of gorse and heather – the ground turned into a sheer drop of sliding shale.

They were at the Sally Gap, pulled in on a side track that had been barely navigable at all by car. The highest pass over the Dublin/Wicklow mountains was a barren, desolate spot, so isolated that walkers were regularly winched to safety by the mountain-rescue helicopter. Most turned back at the sight of burnt-out cars, beds, sofas and electrical equipment discarded along the route up.

'One, two, three . . .' an officer in a white Tyvec forensic suit, kneeling at the head of the body, said to his counterpart at the other end.

There were four of them including Jo, kitted up like spacemen, weaving in and out of the tent.

On cue, the pair lifted either end of a flexible plastic stretcher up and out of the earth. As far as Jo could see, there was no blood on the body, but a black bra was knotted tightly around the neck. Death had turned the whites of the victim's eyes grey, and made the irises cloudy.

The fourth member of the team in the tent was the state pathologist, Professor Michael Hawthorne. He was on his knees alongside the victim, rummaging in his medical bag. He'd been wearing a deerstalker cap and smoking a pipe when he'd arrived. *Like a bloody Sherlock Holmes tribute act*, Jo thought.

Giving a mercury thermometer a shake, Hawthorne instructed the men to put her on her side, so he could take a temperature from the rectum. He'd had to raise his muffled voice to be heard through the white mask over his nose and mouth and the squall battering the PVC tent with shrill screeches.

Jo was trying to glide a finger across the iPhone screen to get into the caller log, but it was virtually impossible with latex gloves on. 'Why didn't she ring for help?' Jo wondered aloud.

'They didn't have them in the nineties, either,' one of the officers joked.

Jo nodded. It was an obvious point, but an important one. An anonymous tipster had contacted a newspaper about the whereabouts of the body, and the information had been passed on. The source had apparently also maintained that the victim was one of Ireland's missing women. Six had disappeared from the Leinster area in a six-year period in the nineties. Their ages ranged from sixteen to twenty-eight. Their backgrounds were as diverse as their professions. None were married, one was pregnant, and one a mother. One was a teacher, the others a waitress, a hairdresser, and a student. One was still in school and living at home, and one was unemployed. A comparison of the presumed killer's modus operandi had yielded no pattern in the times of day or the seasons that they'd been snatched, but all had disappeared from locations in or around the Dublin/ Wicklow mountains, with the result that the area had become known as the 'Vanishing Triangle'.

Although geographic profilers had been brought in to go beyond the dots on the map and predict the killer's employment, place of work, mode of transport and area of residence, none of the bodies had been found. Any new lead on their whereabouts still made front-page news, and their cases were so etched in the public consciousness that all were referred to by their first names. Though there was no hard evidence that a serial killer was responsible, it was widely held to be the only reasonable explanation.

A shoe belonging to one of the victims had been found just a few hundred yards away from where this woman's body had been buried, giving initial credence to the informant's claim. But as the body was still intact and stiff, Jo reckoned it was possible this woman's friends and family hadn't even realized she was missing yet. Rigor mortis took seventy-two hours to relax, which meant she'd been dumped at some stage over the last three days.

The source had been bang on about the location of the body, though, right down to a landmark marking the spot. It was, ironically enough, a headstone situated just outside the tent, and erected in memory of a driver who'd gone off the road a few years back, plunging to his death.

Jo sighed. If this woman had been one of the long-lost women, for the first time they'd have had a crime scene, and a chance of finally giving the families some closure.

Having been approved for promotion to the rank of CS, Jo was all set to swap the city's Store Street Station for this jurisdiction come the end of the week. She'd had to insist that the outgoing Chief Superintendent, Alfie

Taylor, due to retire in a few days, allowed her to attend this dig in anticipation of what could pan out to be a long-running case. The prospect of finding one of the missing women and potentially cracking all six with actual scene-of-crime evidence was the kind of lead that came along once in a lifetime, and they had both known it. As a result, Alfie had begrudgingly kept her in the loop.

Jo resented his condescending attitude. It was true her promotion up the ranks had happened faster than most, but she'd spent the last year acting as a temporary stand-in for her husband and former CS, Dan Mason, who had suffered devastating gunshot injuries in her last big case, when she had been only a DI. Dan was still recuperating, just about walking – with crutches. They were trying to make a go of their marriage again following his brush with mortality. Jo had forgiven him for leaving her for his secretary, in the hope of getting their reunion back on track, but wasn't sure he'd forgiven her yet for what had happened to him. He'd been shot by one of the country's biggest gangland bosses as a direct result of Jo's investigation into the links between organized crime and high-class prostitution. And, though he'd never have admitted it, she suspected he wasn't comfortable with her assuming his role. She hoped the move would make him feel less threatened. Come next week, she'd be swapping drug lords warring over turf for a swathe of suburbs full of neighbours trying to outdo each other with bigger flat screens, Sky boxes and Blu-ray players.

Jo checked her watch – not even half seven yet, but there weren't enough hours in the day for what she'd to get done before she left Store Street. Her existing caseload had to be wound up before Friday, and reports prepared for her successor. On top of that, today was her wedding anniversary, and she'd promised Dan she'd cook a special meal to mark the occasion. There hadn't even been time to make him a cup of tea in the race out the door this morning. She'd also somehow to find the time to squeeze in a half-five appointment with her ophthalmologist for test results linked to a spate of worsening headaches. Jo had had cornea transplants in her teens, and her consultant suspected their deterioration might be responsible.

She took a deep breath. Rule one of making a success of her new job would be learning how to delegate.

Hawthorne, who'd been studying his watch, removed the thermometer and cursed. 'Buggeration.'

'What's the matter?' she asked him, aware the others were smirking at his choice of expletive.

'It's snapped in two,' he went on. 'I'll need to get her back to the morgue. I would have put the time of death as last night, but it's only a guess. Without a temperature I can't be any more accurate than that. A body cools at one and a half to two degrees an hour, but it's much colder up here, so I can't account for the distortion, which may have caused her temperature to drop quicker.'

The sound of the body bag being zipped made Jo turn for a last look.

'What's that?' she asked, spotting something white in the corner of the victim's mouth.

The officers at either end of the body sat back on their hunkers as Jo teased free what turned out to be a scrunched-up plastic bag.

'Just as well I didn't have breakfast,' one said.

Jo knelt down on the carpet of prickly grass to get a closer look. Suffocation and strangulation was a strange combination. Had someone tried to kill the victim twice? Smoothing out each rustling crease, she read a barely legible logo, bleached by time: 'Henry Norton's'.

'Jesus,' Jo said under her breath, remembering that it was the name of a chain of supermarkets that had stopped trading in the nineties.

'What?' one of the officers asked as he shuffled by, carrying the body outside to the waiting van.

He was gone before Jo could answer. But, as she recalled, one of the missing women had been making her way home from a Henry Norton's when she'd vanished into thin air. Her name was Ellen Lamb, and it had been her shoe that had been found up here all those years ago. Jo knew the ins and outs of the case because Dan had been attached to the original investigation. It looked as if there was a link between this body and the

Niamh O'Connor

cold cases after all. The Vanishing Triangle murderer, who'd preyed on women walking alone, had been presumed dead, in prison, or to have emigrated because women had stopped disappearing. Jo prayed he wasn't back.

Tapping the iPhone's caller log with an exposed knuckle, Jo made a quick note in her small black hardback notebook of the last numbers the woman had used. Sometimes the prospect of advancing an investigation had to take precedence over preserving forensic evidence. When her notes were made, she removed the SIM card and dropped it into a clear plastic evidence bag, depositing the handset into another, jotting down the time, date, and location on the white labels on the outside.

Then Jo ducked through the flap and braced herself against the elements. She gasped at the sight of a camera's long lens pointing straight at her from an open window in a jeep parked up opposite. With a sweep, the lens jerked from her to the ambulance, where the body was being strapped on to a trolley.

Jo glared at CS Alfie Taylor. He'd had the nerve to take her aside during a walkabout in his station so as to slip her a list of officers who'd be able to 'compensate' once she replaced him and took charge, as if she was some sort of token female who wouldn't be able to hack it. But he was propped on the bonnet of the jeep, talking to a man with a spiral-bound notebook, who was wearing a puff jacket and CAT boots.

After delivering the evidence bags to her car, Jo hurried over. The photographer gunned the engine, and the reporter glanced in her direction. He leaned in to speak to the photographer as Alfie said something, and then walked to the passenger door, climbing in quickly. Alfie moved out of the way to allow them to head off, and folded his arms as he turned to face Jo.

'What the fuck is going on?' Jo demanded. 'Did you tell the press we were here?'

'Damn right I did,' the whiskey-nosed detective answered. 'Without them, we'd never have found her.'

3

Liz Carpenter was in the kitchen, pouring Rice Krispies into a bowl for her twelve-year-old son, Conor, although 'spilling all over the shop' would have described it better. She'd been half reading one of last week's newspapers, which was propped up on the table in the place where she normally sat. Liz had pored over it every time she'd sat down to eat since, trying to work out why the story of the missing women was being dragged up all over again. She wished the newspapers would just let Ellen rest in peace. It was twenty years since her then sixteen-year-old sister had gone missing, but any mention of her still stopped Liz in her tracks.

She was too preoccupied by all this to ask her husband what was wrong. And anyway, he was in her bad books. Derek was dead late for work, but had just padded into the kitchen in his boxers. He was moving like someone with the hangover from hell, only he hadn't been drinking last night, he'd been working late. He started scanning the inside of the presses, opening the doors and banging them shut.

'We're all out,' Liz said, suspecting he was looking for eggs. She wasn't about to ask. He had some face on him.

She had to hold her tongue so she wouldn't tell him to get a move on. The meat plant where he worked was forty minutes away, and he was due in at nine, whereas she had only a five-minute walk to get to Supersavers, and didn't start till midday. They couldn't afford for him to lose his job.

She snapped back to action, pouring some milk into Conor's bowl, telling him to eat up, and swiping the Krispies on the table into a cupped hand.

Derek moved to the fridge and slugged from a carton of juice, pinching the top closed. 'Any coffee left?' he asked.

His black hair was matted in a clump. Liz picked up Conor's soccer jersey before she answered, folding it against her chest.

'There's a full pot right there,' she snapped, pointing over with her head.

Normally Derek'd have been kissing her cheek and giving her bum a little squeeze at this point. It was practically a ritual after being married for nineteen years, not that she wanted him to touch her today.

She could tell he was really in a mood as well, and sighed as he headed over to the press where they kept the cups. She'd presumed he meant to fill a travel mug so he could take the coffee in the car.

She was still managing to keep schtum as she zipped the strip into Conor's gym bag, and reached for his schoolbag to walk her fingers through the books. They'd been disappearing over the past few weeks, and she still hadn't got to the bottom of it. Conor had an entrance test coming up for a private school that was top of the exam leader boards every year in mathematics. He was really gifted at maths. If he got the marks his teachers were predicting it was going to mean a scholarship. Their days of worrying about paying for the education he needed to develop his talent to its full potential would be over.

She checked to see if he'd finished his breakfast. Conor was sitting at the kitchen table, removing his Rice Krispies from the bowl and lining them up in perfect formation. He was on the autistic spectrum, but so was every second kid in south Dublin these days. It was like an epidemic.

She headed to the sink for a J-cloth, brushing against Derek en route, and hoping he'd take the hint. But he was too busy feeding two slices into the toaster.

Conor bolted from the table, upending the cereal bowl. It rolled off and smashed on the floor. Liz threw her eyes up to heaven. According to the health board course she'd done on managing anxiety in Autistic Spectrum Disorder kids, she should have been presenting him with his card thermometer at this point and asking him how having Rice Krispies for breakfast made him feel. But an accident was just an accident in her book.

Derek blocked Conor's path to the sitting room. He was built like a tank from all the years spent on sites, and lately from hauling animal carcasses. She felt like a slob beside him, having piled on the weight from the stress of the past few years.

Conor stared submissively at the ground.

'It doesn't matter,' she told Derek, keeping the peace.

'You have him ruined. He should clear it up himself.'

He put his spade-sized hands on Conor's tiny shoulders. 'Your mother has enough to do, son. Clean that up.'

'I don't mind doing it,' Liz said.

'I'm not hungry,' Conor said, pushing past and charging into the sitting room.

'You should have backed me up,' Derek said, taking the J-cloth from her, getting down on his hands and knees and clearing up the mess.

'He's got football today,' Liz explained.

'Good,' Derek said, dumping the broken bowl in the bin. 'It might knock the corners off him.'

'Maybe I should keep him home,' she said, under her breath. 'I think Jeff's off sick.'

Jeff was Conor's only friend, and without him around, sport – one of Conor's pet hates – became a million times worse. It was up there with injections as his biggest phobia. The million and one ways the trajectory of the ball could move put it outside his comfort zone. He understood when life was black and white, but couldn't handle shades of grey. Before the recession, he'd had a full-time special-needs assistant to help him communicate in the classroom, too. He couldn't read facial expressions or emotional cues, and it caused all kinds of problems. But the government cuts had hit the weakest. Private schools had much more protection from the ebb and flow of the economy. That was another reason Conor had to get that place . . .

'Over my dead body,' Derek said.

'It's not his fault. Kids on the spectrum . . .'

The television grew steadily louder from the adjoining room.

'They've got labels for everything these days,' Derek grumbled. 'If you start making allowances all the time, he'll be in real trouble. Boys belong on football pitches.'

He pulled the wet clothes he'd been wearing the day before out of the washing machine. Liz stared. There was a full basket of laundry he could have shoved in while he was at it, and saved them the cost of another load. 'Did you put a wash on last night?' she asked.

Derek continued out the back door to hang the clothes on the line. Liz could feel her blood pressure rising. He was still swanning about like he didn't have a care in the world. It was all she could do to stop herself reminding him that his company was looking for redundancies, her seven-year-old Peugeot was sitting on the main road outside their estate with a 'For Sale' sign glued to the windscreen, and it was only two weeks since their neighbours' home had been repossessed.

Jenny and Paul had spent several hours shouting at the sheriff from a barricaded window. They'd been forcibly removed, their belongings scattered in the front garden. It had been heartbreaking. They were just an average tax-paying couple, never in trouble in their lives. Jenny was a hairdresser, but Paul had recently been made redundant. Liz knew if it could happen to them, it could happen to anyone.

Derek arrived back in the kitchen, carrying his shoes caked in muck, and started towards the sink, which was full of dishes.

'My floor,' Liz shrieked, as clods began to fall from the soles.

He placed them back outside, patting the air on his way back in. 'Give me a break,' he said, heading to a press where he kept mealworms to feed the robins.

Liz had to bite her tongue so she wouldn't ask him what planet he was living on. She was sick of being the only one terrified that their mortgage would go into arrears. They'd bought their new house before the country had gone belly up and Derek's building company had gone bust. If he lost his job now, they would lose the roof over their heads. As it was, they were in negative equity.

She got distracted by the sound of the news on the telly blaring that a woman's body had been found in the mountains. Liz headed into the sitting room and told Conor to go and brush his teeth, putting her hand out for him to pass over the remote control.

'She's a goner, right, Mum?'

Catching Conor, she gave him a kiss before he slouched off, and then sat down on the arm of the couch, drawn in by images she recognized.

'Derek!' she shouted, pointing at the screen. The hairs on the back of her neck were standing up. According to the newsreader, there were unconfirmed reports that the victim came from Nuns Cross – where they lived. Theirs was a tiny, five-year-old estate of detached houses in Rathfarnham, a settled suburb on the south side of the city, in the foothills of the Dublin mountains. It was the polar opposite of the ghost estates that had mushroomed up in the boom times, pushing the commuter belt back to the Atlantic. They'd believed themselves lucky.

Liz covered her hand with her mouth as she realized she probably knew the dead woman.

Derek came into the room.

'A woman from Nuns Cross has been murdered,' she told him, horrified.

He sat down stiffly. 'Did they say who?'

'They said her name was being withheld until her

family had been informed,' she answered, realizing Conor was back. She zapped the TV off, and helped him put his coat on. She put his bag on his back, and Derek zipped his coat up. He tousled Conor's hair as Liz gave him a tighter than usual hug goodbye.

'I'll be back in time to help with your homework tonight, son,' Derek promised, kissing his forehead.

'We've got the circus tonight, Dad! Mum got us tickets, remember?'

'Well then, I'll be back in time for the circus, son,' Derek said.

The school bus drew in on the main road opposite and Conor plugged the earphones of his iPod in, sprinting to catch it. A squad car pulled into Nuns Cross, and Liz shivered as she watched it stop in the cul-de-sac next to theirs.

'I'll just see where it goes,' Derek said.

Liz flew into the kitchen, tore off a sheet of kitchen towel and blew her nose, returning to the front door to wait for Derek, keeping the door open only a chink. She knew exactly what the victim's family would be going through, and it was terrible. She scanned the doorsteps opposite for any sign of a casserole, or something left in sympathy, wondering if it was possible the dead woman could live on her road.

Derek arrived back, looking like he'd been hit by a bus. 'It's Amanda Wells,' he said, panting like a sprinter after a race.

'The solicitor?' Liz asked, shocked. She didn't know her very well, although their gardens were literally back to back. Derek had renovated Amanda's office a few years earlier, and it was right around the corner from Supersavers. But Liz had found it so hard to trust anyone since Ellen had died, feeling that most new people just had a creepy interest in knowing the details of what had happened to her sister. And the only way Liz could create some mental space from the claustrophobic feeling of living on top of her neighbours in Nuns Cross was by pretending not to be remotely interested in their business. She'd pulled it off until last Friday . . .

Derek nodded, dropping to his hunkers for air.

Closing the door behind them quickly, she slid the chain lock across, staring at him in disbelief. He still hadn't mentioned what had happened on Friday, the thing he didn't know she knew about, the reason she had barely been able to look at him all weekend. It defied belief he'd think it wasn't worth bringing up, given what he'd just found out.

Liz pushed past him and headed back into the kitchen to look out the window into Amanda's for any sign of activity. She clocked those people you always saw on the telly at a murder scene – the ones in white body suits with elastic hoods and Michael Jackson masks – moving behind the windows, and kinked the blinds quickly.

Starting to fret, she bundled up the newspaper on the

table and dumped it in the bin. Seconds later she pulled it out again and shoved it into the fire grate, still full of ashes from the previous night. Striking a match off the box, she lit the corner of the paper and put it into the grate, holding it down with a poker so it wouldn't fly up the chimney.

'What are you doing?' Derek asked, following and standing over her. 'What's the matter?'

'You can ease off on the devastation,' she said. 'I get it.'

He shifted from one foot to the other. 'What? Don't tell me you're not gutted, too. I know we weren't bosom buddies, but it's so close to home!'

She sighed, shaking her head. Secrets were as bad as lies in her book. What did he take her for? Why didn't he just come out with it and talk about what had happened on Friday? After everything she'd been through with her only sister, he knew as well as she did the way things worked. It was only a matter of time before the gardaí came calling asking questions. If they found out about Friday, the press would follow hot on their heels, chasing a new angle on Ellen's case. Derek had been so bloody stupid. Liz could see the headline now: 'Missing Ellen's Sister in Second Murder Mystery'. And so would the school board deciding whether or not Conor got that place.

4

DS Aishling McConigle tucked her shoulder-length red hair behind her ears as she hurried over to take Jo's coat. Jo was crossing the detective unit, heading for her office and the conference she'd organized. As she passed, Joan McElhinny, the oldest female in the station, handed Jo the mug of black coffee she'd been pouring, and six-foot Sue Grainger strode ahead to open the door for her, closing it once Sergeant John Foxe followed.

Jo transferred a cardboard box from her desk on to the floor. It was full of old files she wanted to take with her when she relocated, as well as a cactus that had no chance of surviving without her. She tapped her ID into the keyboard, not wanting to have to wait for the Pulse 2 – the computer equivalent to Scotland Yard's HOLMES system – to load up if she needed some instant information during the meeting.

Heading for the wipe board to the left of her desk, she ran a cloth over it and then turned back around, pleased everyone was ready. Alfie had not been impressed by her insistence that the incident room be sited here for her convenience, rather than in her new district. But Jo had stuck to her guns, using the excuse that by Friday he'd have retired, and that therefore the right to choose was hers. The truth was that she wanted to cut him out of the inquiry. If he was bringing the press to crime scenes, he might as well be briefing the killer, as far as she was concerned.

And Jo was confident she couldn't do any better than the crew assembled. Rosy-cheeked Joan had worked on the periphery of a serial-killer case Jo had headed up a couple of years back. She was a trooper, not afraid of hard work, with an incredible ability to get through paper-work. Alongside her was freckle-faced Aishling, who had helped Jo find a toddler taken from his mum's car while she was paying for petrol. Six-foot Sue was a new addition to the station, and Jo wanted to give her a break before she left. It would increase Sue's chances of being assigned decent cases in the future. The number of females who'd reached senior rank in the force was minimal.

As for Foxy, it was hard for Jo to imagine how she was ever going to solve a case without him in the future, but as he was planning to retire, she didn't have much choice. Silver-haired Sergeant John Foxe, the station's bookman, was responsible for keeping track of how the lines of inquiry were progressing. He was a clear thinker and a straight talker.

'Where's Sexton?' Jo asked, about her closest colleague in the force.

The females avoided eye contact.

'Not again?' Jo asked Foxy, her tone filled with fatigue.

'He rang in sick,' Foxy replied.

Jo pushed her fingers through her hair. Detective Inspector Gavin Sexton was a friend as well as a colleague, but he was acting the bollocks by not giving a medical reason when he hadn't showed up for work for the second week running. Jo wouldn't be around much longer to cover for him.

'Tell me he sent in a doctor's note,' Jo prompted.

Foxy shook his head.

She sighed. There wasn't time to get into it now. 'Any luck with a photo of Amanda?' she asked, moving on quickly.

Foxy handed over a 'pick-up' of the victim – a photograph from a family member – collected by the officer tasked with the death knock, when news of Amanda's murder had been broken to her elderly parents.

Jo studied the picture, which Foxy had had blown up. In life, Amanda Wells had been a glamorous, if plain, woman who had worn bright red lipstick and had bouncy blonde hair and shiny ivory skin. She was very petite, Jo noted. In the shot, she was sitting at one of those beach-front bars popular in the Caribbean, and looking straight at the camera with a forced smile, holding a cocktail up in a toast. She was on her own, and something about the look she was giving whoever was taking the picture suggested she was worried they were about to run away with her camera. If pictures told a thousand words, this one said Amanda Wells was not going to let the fact that she was alone stop her from enjoying herself.

Heading for the whiteboard, Jo attached the picture to it with a magnet, alongside one taken posthumously in the tent. The contrast couldn't have been starker.

'Amanda Wells,' she began. 'Aged forty-eight ... single ... a solicitor. CS Alfie Taylor got a tip-off from a journalist that one of the missing women's bodies would be found in the mountains. The hack's name is Niall Toland, and he works on the *Daily Record*. The tip was made directly to him and no other newspaper as far as we're aware, and he claims he was specifically told that the body was one of the missing women.'

'I read a story in one of the newspapers about them last week,' Aishling piped up. 'I was only a kid when those girls were disappearing, but I can remember my mum being afraid to let me out to play alone.'

'I was afraid to let my own girls out,' Joan said, closing a button that had come undone on her shirt. 'And they were only little at the time. It creeps me out that that monster might be still out there.'

'I didn't read it,' Jo said. 'What exactly did it say?'

'It showed the three snatch sites where all six were abducted, and joined the locations up with a dotted line to make a perfect triangle around the Sally Gap,' Aishling said.

Jo pointed to the photograph. 'Amanda had a meal with a man in Temple Bar on Friday night. We need to establish who he was ASAP. How long's the battery life on those iPhones?'

'Depends on how often it was used,' Sue said.

'It was last used on Friday night,' Jo said. 'I saw it on the caller log.'

'Then it could have stayed powered on from Friday night to Monday morning.'

'How do you know about Amanda's last movements already?' Joan asked. 'You only found her a few hours ago.'

'She was tweeting from it and the last landline number she dialled was to a restaurant,' Jo explained. 'I phoned it. The manager remembered Amanda. He said the man she was with had dark hair and was younger. They came in together at around ten, but ended up arguing, and she stormed out at half past. She paid for the meal. The CCTV over the restaurant door was down, so we've no idea who the man is or if he took the row to heart and decided to follow her and have the last word. Identifying him is our first line of inquiry.'

Jo turned to Foxy. 'Job one, I want Aishling to arrange the collection of any CCTV available from Eustace Street, where the restaurant is located. The manager's agreed to help with a photofit. And we need to organize searches in the vicinity of the restaurant to see if we can find Amanda's car.'

Moving to her coat on the stand, Jo rummaged her notebook out of a pocket, snapping the elastic off. 'It's a navy convertible BMW.' She wrote the registration on the wipe board. 'I contacted the officer on duty at Amanda's home, and her car is not there. You need to have the streets in and around the restaurant checked, Aishling, and also the multi-storeys. If there's still no sign, go to the pounds.'

'Got it,' Aishling replied.

Foxy noted it down.

'We're going to need a team with questionnaires doing door-to-door inquiries in Amanda's estate,' Jo continued. 'And show me the questions for approval when they're ready,' she added wearily.

The sentence got a laugh. There'd been an infamous mix-up in a recent inquiry, and the police social club's pub-quiz questions had been circulated in error.

Jo turned to Sue. 'Can you check the databases here and in the UK to see if we can find a match for the killer's modus operandi? He stuffed a plastic bag in her mouth, and he strangled her with her bra. It could be potentially as good as a signature.'

Sue wrote the details down in her notebook. 'Daphne asked me to sort through Dan's filing cabinet, so this way I won't die of boredom while pretending to be totally focused.'

Daphne was the Human Resources administrator. 'Why's she got you sorting Dan's files?' Jo asked, annoyed. As acting CS, she should have been consulted.

Sue shrugged. 'She just asked me to pull everything out, and to do a quick list of the status of his investigations before the changeover. Convictions, acquittals, that kind of thing.'

'What?' Jo pushed, wringing her hands together. They'd have to contact him to sign something like that off, but Dan had endured enough, in her book. He'd been put through the mill last year on a disciplinary hearing. She didn't want him getting paranoid.

Jo pressed her fingers between her eyes.

'You OK?' Joan asked.

'I'm fine, it's just the early start. We headed up at first light. Do you mind if I turn the lights off in here?'

After getting the nod, Jo flicked the switch off, and the blue hue from the fluorescent bulb overhead flickered out. Headaches were something she lived with on a daily basis. The room dimmed, but was still brightly lit from the glow in the detective unit outside.

Jo turned to Joan. 'Will you get in touch with Niall Toland, who got the tip-off? I know reporters famously never reveal their sources, but it'd help if you can establish if Toland knew who called in the information and is protecting them out of some misguided sense of confidentiality, or if the source really was anonymous. Also, I want to know what time he got the information, and how. Did the call come through the office switchboard? If so we'll need to speak to the *Daily Record* receptionist, too. What can they tell us about the voice? What exactly was said?'

'Newspapers use automated answering systems these days, to save on staff costs,' Sue said. 'It's a curse for anyone trying to give them a story.'

'You know a lot about it,' Jo pounced.

Sue reddened, but was upfront about it as she worked her black hair into a scrunchie that had been around her wrist. 'I used to go out with a hack.'

'In which case, Joan, it might be better if Sue took this one,' Jo decided, addressing Sue directly. 'I want to know if the killer has been in touch with Toland before or since. We may need to organize a tap on his phone. And that reminds me . . .' She headed back over to the coat stand, and pulled out the plastic bag containing Amanda's SIM, handing it to Foxy. 'Can you get this into an iPhone ASAP? I've sent the handset it was in to the lab for analysis in the hope of fingerprints, and maybe even a DNA profile from a saliva cell, or a blood group from sweat. But you can use this to give me a list of any incoming or outgoing texts, starting from her last day and working back, and including any social-networking messages – with a separate list of what's in her emails. I also need her contacts listed alongside the stats of who she was ringing, and who was ringing her. I'm not holding out much hope, mind—'

'Why's that?' Foxy asked. 'I thought a phone was like a personal microchip these days.'

'The killer took Amanda's clothes,' Jo replied. 'Why would he leave her phone unless there's something on it he wants us to find? And if she was holding it before she died, why didn't she use it? I didn't even need a PIN to get into it.'

'Right,' Foxy said.

Jo folded her arms. 'Which brings me to one last thing you need to know. There may be a link to the missing-women case after all.'

Foxy shot her a quizzical look. 'Solely because she was found in the Vanishing Triangle?'

Jo explained the significance of the Henry Norton's plastic bag recovered from Amanda's body, and the fact that they had found it so close to the spot where Ellen Lamb's shoe had been left.

She walked back to her chair and sat down behind her desk. 'That said, I don't want this angle overplayed. The last thing we want is the press whipping up public hysteria and everyone running around like headless chickens. I think it's much more likely the journalist's source is the killer, or at the very least someone close to the killer, so let's not feed his ego. How else could he have known about the body's whereabouts? If we're in luck, the source will turn out to be Amanda's date from Friday night, but it's a big if . . . That's it.'

Getting straight to work, Jo reached for the keyboard

as the officers began to exit, only Foxy remaining to finish his notes. Typing Ellen Lamb's name into the system, Jo scanned the file for any new information. In the details about the prime suspect, a name she knew only too well practically jumped off the screen. In more recent times the individual in question had been quizzed about a road-rage incident, so his new address was also tagged to his name.

Slumping back, Jo stared in disbelief. It turned out that Derek Carpenter lived in Nuns Cross in Rathfarnham, where Amanda Wells had lived. Jo studied the dark-haired man in the photograph on the file and realized that he looked a lot like the description of Amanda's mystery man, which she'd got from the restaurant manager.

'What is it?' Foxy asked, walking over.

When Jo didn't answer, he looked over her shoulder at the screen.

'Looks like you found your link to the past,' he said.

'It can't be that simple,' Jo said. Derek Carpenter had been the prime suspect in the missing-women's case all those years ago.

'I thought you didn't believe in coincidences.'

Jo tabbed through the details until she got to Derek Carpenter's name, clicking 'enter' to run a search for his record. Even if a suspect had never been convicted of a crime, cases they'd been suspected of were kept on the system. That's how the road-rage incident had been recorded. Derek had eight convictions, all for joyriding as a juvenile, she observed. He'd been let off with a caution on an assault charge.

Foxy was still reading alongside, and he pointed his pen at a code on the top right of the screen, showing someone else had logged in and was looking at the same page. Jo moved the mouse to the sequence and CS Alfie Taylor's name came up.

'Brilliant,' she said.

'What's the matter?' Foxy asked.

Jo folded her arms. 'Dan was part of the team that looked into Ellen Lamb's disappearance.' She went on to explain how he had interviewed Derek Carpenter all those years ago, and had ruled him out.

'Alfie's decided he wants to go out with a bang, and this case is perfect for that,' she said, getting up, grabbing her mac, and pulling it on.

'It doesn't matter who finds the killer, only that someone does,' Foxy said.

'Think about it,' Jo said, crossly. 'If Carpenter did bump off those women and get away with it for all these years, why would he leave something with Amanda's body that would lead us straight back to him?'

Foxy shrugged.

'I need a wingman,' Jo said, buttoning her raincoat up to the neck. 'Sexton had better be on his deathbed when I find him.'

5

2000: Wapping, London

The copyboy was doing his best not to stare. It was his first day in the job and he didn't want people to think he was some kind of pervert. But he'd never in his life seen a woman like her. She was giving orders to a room full of men: he hadn't known that kind of woman existed. The type he knew would have smacked the back of his head, or read him the riot act for so much as reaching for the Sun – they all wanted to mother him, because he didn't have a mam. It was just him and his old man, who worked in the paper's printing works. That's how he'd got the job.

He ran a set of chewed fingernails along the tips of his spiked and bleached fringe – the only part of his head not to have been shaved. It was still gelled up; that was good. He rearranged the elastic of his Calvin Kleins over his tracksuit bottom's waist. They'd called him Slim Shady when he'd arrived in the newsroom a few hours earlier, and that was good, too, made him feel like someone.

Wiping his dripping nose on his sleeve, he went back to the sandwich order. He needed a hit of Lynx badly, but he had to sort this lot out first – he didn't want to lose this job, not now he had seen for himself how good some men had it. He'd already spent the wages he'd yet to earn on a stash of cocaine he'd washed down with ammonia his da had got in a hardware shop. No amount of sniffing would ever give him a high that came close to crack, but it would get him through the day without unravelling.

He started tearing little holes in the greaseproof wrappings to find which filling was where. He'd made a list, but the letters he'd scrawled for names alongside the requests kept dancing in front of his eyes; the words were all jumbled up. If he could have made the sounds out loud, he'd have got somewhere by now, but he didn't want them to hear him trying to read. He'd dropped out of school a year before his father had noticed. He'd have got away with it, too, if the women in his block of flats hadn't reported him to social services. Bitches. With a job of his own, nobody would be able to touch him again. He'd be his own man. One who could look at tits in public as much as he wanted.

Beads of sweat pricked to life and dribbled down his temples. The hot chicken one had gone cold. A voice inside his head told him he could walk out right now, and nobody would give a toss, but he wanted to watch her for a bit more, so he kept at it, even if there was still their bastarding change to sort out. He wasn't even going to let himself think about that bit yet. He was going to deck his father tonight when he came back from the pub. He'd promised there'd be no reading or writing involved in the job. He'd said the editor started out as a secretary, and that all the copyboy needed to be able to do was blag his way around. Fucking liar.

A man in a striped shirt, braces and gold cufflinks on his white cuffs came marching over, grumbling. He rummaged through the contents of the sandwich box until he found the label he wanted and then he pulled it clear. He stank of some poncy aftershave, and messed up the small bit of ground made. The sarnie the editor had wanted had gone AWOL now; the copyboy was going to have to start all over again.

'I want it for lunch, not tea,' the man said, stalking off.

The boy flipped him one.

The editor glanced over her shoulder to see what the fuss was about and spotted him giving Mr Dickhead the bird. The copyboy's cheeks reddened. But she just grinned, like she agreed, and turned back to what she was doing. She was ten yards to his right, leaning over a desk, her chin resting on her hand, studying a computer screen.

The copyboy was in love. He wondered what the

man sitting at the desk, his face just inches from her's, was thinking. He had an Australian accent, had combed the smig under his chin into a plait, and wore a chunky silver ring on his thumb. He looked like a faggot. The copyboy hated him.

'Make it bigger, Nick,' the editor was telling the gaylord.

The words 'Sarah's Law' increased on the screen over a picture of a little girl with brown eyes whose hair was in a ponytail. She looked a bit like the sister the copy-boy used to have before his mam took off. It was so long ago he could barely remember.

'Even bigger, Nick,' the editor said, putting one hand on the back of his computer chair and standing up.

She wasn't beautiful, or pretty. The girls in his complex spent every minute of every day getting their look exactly right. He didn't know what it was about the editor. Maybe it was the confidence she oozed that made him feel like he was going to do anything for her from here on in.

Gaylord said, 'We're at 124 points as it is.' The piercing in his tongue gave him a slight lisp.

The copyboy wanted to punch his lights in. He hated queers, blacks, Pakis, Poles and pikeys – in that order. His mother was Irish, otherwise the pikeys would have been a lot higher on the list. They ate their dead.

'Just do it,' the editor told Nick. She rubbed the grey circles under her eyes.

Nick started with an N, the boy thought, running his finger down the list till he found the name. He'd drawn an egg beside it, and from the stink in the box, it took only a couple of seconds to locate the only egg salad. He made sure nobody was watching, then peeled back the wrap and let a gob drop on to it. After wrapping it up again, he headed over and put it on the nonce's desk.

'Thanks,' she said, leaning across and grabbing it even though it wasn't hers, peeling open the paper and taking one half in her hand. 'He's got spirit, that one,' she said to Nick, giving him a wink.

Nobody had ever said anything like that to the copyboy before. His chin went up a notch. She was licking the egg filling starting to drip on to her hand. The copyboy smiled back. For the first time in his life, he felt like he belonged.

6

Liz set the house alarm, deadlocked the front door, criss-crossed her handbag across her shoulder and set off for Grange Road. What had happened to Amanda was tragic, but she had to think about how it could affect Conor, and the potential impact on his future. It was only a couple of weeks since she and Derek had sat in front of the stuffy school board in a wood-panelled room and been grilled about their application for the scholarship programme.

'Personal circumstances will not be an issue if Conor passes the entrance exam,' the principal had said, running a finger down the parting of his neat grey moustache.

Liz had felt Derek, sitting beside her, bristle.

'We've taken boys from all walks of life over the years,' a woman with Margaret Thatcher hair, who'd been introduced as the parents' representative, had agreed.

'Our only concern is anything that might bring the alma mater into disrepute,' a priest on the principal's left had added. 'Conor will be up against the best and the brightest, and the choice for scholarship might mean looking beyond the grades to the most suitable family.' He'd paused to clear his throat. 'So, if there's anything in your history you feel might be relevant, now is the time to bring it up.'

Liz had blinked and smiled wanly. She had taken Derek's hand and squeezed tightly to stop him from getting defensive and asking exactly what they meant. They'd both known exactly what the school board were driving at. After twenty years living with the mystery surrounding Ellen, Liz and Derek could pick up a morbid curiosity vibe from a mile away.

For Conor's sake, Liz had swallowed her fury and assured the board of governors that her family had nothing to hide. She'd quoted the school's Latin motto, '*Fides et Robur*', and had assured them that trust-worthiness and steadfastness were the cornerstones of her own humble home. 'All we want is the best for our son,' she'd said.

That's why she was getting out of the house. She couldn't stick another second waiting for her phone or doorbell to ring. It was only a matter of time before the press or police called, demanding to speak to her. She knew exactly the way it worked. She'd been going out with Derek about six months when she'd first been door-stepped. Ellen had been missing for three of them. Liz was about to turn nineteen, and had moved out and into a flat with Derek. Up until then, the press had only ever approached her parents, asking them for another public appeal, 'To keep Ellen's memory alive in the public's consciousness.'

'How many times can you say, "We can't move on?"' Liz's father used to rant after he'd politely given them whatever sound bite they wanted. He'd been diagnosed with cancer, and after each call used to fade away another little bit. He wouldn't change the home phone number, though, just in case. He'd died within two years of Ellen vanishing.

'We have to keep the media onside, and Ellen's face in the paper,' her mother would try to cajole. 'You never know . . .'

Liz had been caught off guard when she'd been approached. It was a Saturday night and she and Derek were walking home from the pub, half-cut, when a reporter had literally appeared at their door, like he'd been sitting in wait. He had stepped up, pointing a Dictaphone at her mouth. He was young, with a big moon face and a bush of curly brown hair. The linseed smell of his bottle-green wax jacket still filled up her nostrils all these years later.

'I'm sorry to drag things up,' he'd said in a Northern accent, giving her a sad smile, 'but my boss is going to kill me if you don't give me some kind of a line about how your family is coping, and if you're planning to commemorate Ellen tomorrow.'

It would have been Ellen's seventeenth birthday the following day. That's why Derek had taken Liz out, to try and get her mind off it.

'She doesn't want to talk,' Derek had said, putting his arm around her and trying to give the reporter the brush-off.

'With the greatest of respect, that's for her to say,' the journalist had replied. 'What if Ellen reads the story and decides to get in touch?'

'They found Ellen's shoe in the mountains,' Derek had snapped, stepping closer to him. 'Do you really think she left it there and walked back down barefoot? Use your loaf.'

'I'm just saying it might appeal to the killer's conscience,' the reporter answered, pushing his chest out.

'It's OK,' Liz had told Derek, drawing to a halt. 'You never know . . .'

'That's right,' the reporter had jumped in. 'A few words might just make the difference, jog someone's memory.'

'As long as you don't make out like she's dead again, or write anything about trying to appeal to a killer's conscience, I'll do it,' Liz had said. 'That would upset my mam and dad too much. They believe she's still alive.'

He'd written it down. 'So will there be a birthday cake in your house tomorrow?'

Liz had looked at him like he'd lost it.

'I mean, something like this happens, people can't bring themselves to change the covers on the missing person's bed, so I just thought maybe . . .'

'We won't be having a cake, or a party,' Liz had said, filling up. 'That's too creepy.'

'Are you happy now?' Derek had asked the reporter.

The man had kept his eyes trained on Liz. 'Do you think it was someone she knew?'

'I don't know,' Liz had answered, feeling confused.

'I mean it was a busy street, it was daylight, she must have been offered a lift by someone she'd recognized. That's why the cops always persuade the family members to do a public appeal. They need to get their faces out there to see if anyone witnessed them up to anything suspicious on the date in question.'

'Are you saying you think someone she knows had something to do with it?' Derek had asked, full of aggression.

The reporter had tried to backtrack. 'Not necessarily. I was just talking generally.' He'd turned back to Liz. 'So how are you going to mark the day, then? You can't go to the graveyard like most people, so what will you do?'

'We don't have anything planned,' Liz had said. 'We'll just get up in the morning and try to keep going.'

'What about a vigil outside Henry Norton's, maybe?' the reporter had pressed. 'We can get a photographer there tomorrow if you agree. It will help keep her memory alive. Like you said, "You never know."'

Derek had given him a shove. 'Cop on.'

'Touch me again and I'll have you done for assault, mate. This has nothing to do with you.'

'I've nothing more to say,' Liz remembered saying, before she'd pulled Derek's arm to tell him to leave it.

But the reporter wouldn't take no for an answer. 'What's your problem?' he'd needled Derek. 'Why are you so afraid of me trying to help catch the killer? Have you got something to hide? You've been in trouble with the law before. What's the matter?'

Derek had turned and decked him. Afterwards he'd said, 'She asked you not to mention that word.'

Liz could still see the way the reporter had staggered back clutching a bloody nose. As Derek had led her away, she'd spotted a car on the far side of the street with the driver's window open. She remembered seeing the reporter turn his thumb up and then down at it with a puzzled expression, like he was waiting for a verdict. An arm had appeared out the window of the car opposite with the thumb pointing up, and the reporter had smiled.

The cops had called for Derek later that night, following up the reporter's complaint, and had asked him questions about Ellen. That was bad. But it got worse the next day when the newspaper ran the picture of Derek throwing the punch under the headline, 'Fiery

Temper of Boyfriend of Missing Ellen's Sister Revealed'. The story was full of quotes from unnamed 'close friends' of Liz who'd said she'd completely changed since she'd started going out with Derek. Liz could still remember them word for word. One had said: 'Liz used to be a bubbly, happy-go-lucky girl who was full of fun, but it's like she's got something on her mind that's weighing her down now. She's completely withdrawn into herself.'

Another had claimed: 'Liz and Ellen weren't like sisters at all, they weren't close, they moved in completely different circles. Liz was always jealous of Ellen because she had the looks and the brains.'

The details of Derek's convictions were printed in a panel, reversed out of black ink to make it stand out more, with no mention of how he'd grown up in a house with eight kids and a violent drunk for a father, or that he hadn't once gone off the rails since he'd started going out with Liz. Nowhere had it said that maybe Liz had changed because her baby sister had disappeared off the face of the earth, or that her parents were in denial that Ellen might have been killed because the alternative was too horrific for them to contemplate.

'For fuck's sake, why don't they just come out and say that I buried Ellen up in the mountains?' Derek had asked Liz. 'They may as well have. That's what everyone is going to think.'

He was right. Most hurtful of all, Liz's parents

seemed to believe it. Derek and Liz had tried to undo the damage. They'd gone to a solicitor, who'd sent the newspaper a letter warning them that if there was any further insinuation in the future that Derek had had anything to do with Ellen's disappearance, they would sue.

In every story from then on, Derek was 'the prime suspect who cannot be named for legal reasons . . . a Svengali-type figure who has put a close relative of the missing girl under his spell'.

Snapping back to the present, Liz spotted a garda walking towards her, and hurried towards her car, which was parked on the pavement outside the estate in the hope of attracting a buyer. The keys were still on her house ring.

She didn't want to face the police yet. She hadn't even begun to think about what she'd say when they asked if Derek had been home last night. If she told the truth – that he'd been working late – they would ring Derek's workplace looking for confirmation, and that kind of smoke, even without fire, could lead to him being fast-tracked towards redundancy. She was going to drive around the block now rather than risk the garda knocking on the window. Liz pulled the 'For Sale' sign off the windscreen of her car, and rolled her neck, which felt like it was about to snap.

She put the keys in the ignition, and stared in surprise

at the red petrol light as it came on. She'd filled the car up before leaving it out so she'd be able to bring any prospective buyer for a spin. Something else was niggling her. It was the bonnet, she realized, staring at it through the windscreen. The car had been clean when she'd left it out, but now it was spattered with mud splashes.

The car juddered as it moved off the kerb and landed on the road. Liz strained her neck the other way so she wouldn't have to acknowledge the garda as she passed. As she did so, out of the corner of her eye she spotted a pale-blue chiffon scarf on the passenger seat. She reached for it, and held it to her nose. The perfume smelt distinctive, expensive, and familiar. It brought her right back to her short time in Amanda's office on Friday. A hollow feeling struck up in the pit of her stomach. Stuffing it into her pocket, she put the car in gear and took off.

That was another reason Liz didn't want to have to be interrogated, the one she'd been putting out of her mind since hearing the news this morning. She'd witnessed a terrible row between Derek and Amanda on Friday. Derek still had no idea she'd seen it, and she hadn't mentioned it to him either, so she wouldn't have to tell him why she'd gone to see the murdered solicitor in the first place.

Why hadn't Derek mentioned taking her car somewhere off the beaten track? Had he given Amanda a lift somewhere on Friday after their row? Was that where Amanda had gone? If so, why had he taken Liz's car instead of his own?

Whatever happened, it would have to wait. If the gardaí found anything to link her murdered neighbour to Derek, it would lead to no end of suspicion. And that would mean Conor's life would change irrevocably.

She drove towards the nearest garage. The detour would mean she'd end up being late for work, but Liz had to prioritize now, and the only thing that was going to stop Ellen from dominating the future just as she had the past was to get this car cleaned inside and out.

7

In all, Liz reckoned she'd spent less than five minutes in Amanda's company on Friday. Enough time to realize that Amanda Wells was a control freak, and that was putting it nicely purely because of the terrible end she'd met. There were a few other choice words Liz could think of that would have more accurately described her . . .

Liz had been up to the solicitor's office because she'd already waited several weeks for Amanda to return a form she needed verified by a peace commissioner in order to complete an application for a home-tuition grant for Conor. Liz wanted to get him some extra grinds before his entrance exam in the subjects he was average at, but Friday had been the deadline for receipt of the annual batch of applications. Those extra hours might mean the difference between Conor getting the scholarship or not.

'It will go in the post today,' Amanda's secretary had reiterated every time Liz had rung.

When the form still hadn't arrived by D-Day, Liz had waited until Amanda's secretary had walked by Supersavers at lunchtime, and then nipped around the corner to the solicitor's office, hoping to light a fire under Amanda herself. Liz knew Amanda's office was sometimes left on the latch at lunchtime while her secretary popped out for a sandwich, so she'd seized her opportunity and slipped in through the main entrance, walking down the corridor and right up to Amanda's office door. She'd knocked and put her head around the door without waiting for an answer. Maybe that was why they'd got off on such a bad footing. Maybe Amanda had thought Liz was being presumptuous. Maybe the fact that Liz was used to seeing Amanda every morning with a towel wrapped around her hair in an upstairs window, and every night drinking a bottle of wine in front of the TV, had given Amanda the hump. Maybe Liz had thought it OK to go straight in because Amanda lived so close. She couldn't have been more wrong . . .

She tried to remember what she'd said to make Amanda, sitting in a black leather presidential chair behind her leather-embossed desk, act like Liz had just done something really inappropriate. To make matters even more intense, the stamp that Liz wanted so badly was literally sitting on a pad of ink between the two of them, closer to Liz than Amanda, ironically enough.

It wasn't supposed to have been a favour; Amanda

had made it one. Having rummaged through her in-tray, and taken one look at the voluminous form, she had stated: 'Not if your life depended on it, and I have good reason.'

Liz had reached up to her hairnet self-consciously. She hadn't understood, but she hadn't had time to get into it, not if she was to get the form back that day. 'Please, it won't take a minute, it has to be returned by close of business.' Ordinarily, she'd never have left something so important to the last minute. If Amanda's secretary had-n't given her the runaround, she'd have organized some other peace commissioner to stamp it, but she'd made the mistake of holding out, believing Amanda – a neighbour at home and work – would come through. Liz didn't have time to try and find anyone else on Friday without risk-ing missing the deadline. As it was, she was going to have to hand-deliver the form.

She'd tried to explain to Amanda the difference it could make to Conor.

'I told you: no,' Amanda had answered, stonily. 'And like I said, I have good reason.'

'Please . . .'

'What part of no don't you understand?' With that, she had moved to the door, and had held it open for Liz to leave.

Liz had tried again, for Conor's sake, but Amanda had given the door a bang once she was on the other side of it.

But Liz, who had pins and needles in her hands from fidgeting with her fingers, hadn't left Amanda's building straight away. Not when there was so much riding on that form. She'd wanted time to think, so she'd detoured to the toilet on the way out. She hadn't needed to go, or wash her hands, brush her hair, or reapply her lip gloss. It was just a split-second decision to have a think about what had just happened, and it had been made so quickly that it hadn't even required a change of pace. She'd simply ducked into the door on the left, bolting it behind her, and lowered the toilet seat. Because the WC for Amanda's office was situated in the hallway, on a corridor leading to the street door, Amanda was none the wiser. It wasn't like she had stood in the doorway waiting or watching for Liz to exit the building.

The fact that around ten seconds later, when Liz was mentally rewording her request for Amanda in the john, the door to the street had banged – in or around the time Liz would have been expected to exit – probably confirmed the misconception in Amanda's mind.

At first, Liz hadn't paid much attention. She'd been too wrapped up in her own worries, trying to come up with a new approach to make Amanda understand that this was Liz's son's life. On the toilet seat, she'd practised various ways of grovelling and pleading with Amanda to reconsider. She'd been determined not to leave without at least giving it one more shot. What she'd really wanted to do was to burst back in and ask Amanda what she knew about Liz's life, or Conor's daily struggles, that enabled her to dismiss them so out of hand, but that wouldn't have served her purpose. Things would have been different if Amanda had had kids of her own, if she'd understood what it meant to be a mother, but that was another thing that couldn't be said. Since all she'd wanted was the form signed off, she'd decided to be a pest and to go back and beg Amanda to reconsider, or, at the very least, get the form off her to try and get it signed by someone else.

Liz had stared at the ceiling tearfully. Who did Amanda Wells, in her tailored suit, think she was? What kind of neighbour didn't help another out in a time of need?

She'd just taken a step towards the door to head back in for another try, when the sound of muffled shouting from Amanda's office had made her freeze. She'd pressed her ear to the wall.

'Now it's your turn, is that it?' Amanda had shouted. Liz could hear her as clear as day. 'Get out.' There'd been a pause. Liz had strained but been unable to hear the other voice, only the resonance – it was a man's – and then Amanda had said again, louder than before, 'I don't owe you a red cent.'

It had sounded like the man was trying to reason with Amanda, Liz had guessed, based on her own earlier experience.

'How dare you? This is extortion! I said out,' – this time Amanda had given a screech that made Liz put a hand to her chest – 'and if you ever come near me again, I'm going to tell your wife all about what kind of man you really are.'

That must have pressed the man's button, because his muffled voice had risen. He'd shouted back, 'I told you before. I'll tell your boyfriend's wife about you myself!'

It had made Liz wince to hear it. Not that, in the circumstances, she didn't agree with the sentiment.

'Get off,' Amanda's voice had said again. 'Let go. Don't touch me. I'll have you done for this. I'm going to have you charged with assault. You think things are bad for you now . . . by the time I'm finished your wife will have left you, and you'll be facing a prison sentence.'

Something had slammed against the wall with such force that the toilet-roll holder shook.

Liz's stomach had clenched. She had to go back in there. But what if Amanda got angry that she was still around, and refused to sign the form? Then again, Amanda might be grateful that she'd come to her rescue. Liz had still been mulling it over when the sound of a heavy bang had made her heart stall. Something had dropped, or been thrown. The row was getting more vicious. Liz had tried to think what in the office could have landed with that weight, but there was nothing, bar Amanda herself. Indecision had made her jittery. What should she do? The seriousness of it all had demanded action. She'd reached for the handle. Something was better than nothing. Liz's hand had frozen at the sound of Amanda's office door opening and footsteps marching down the corridor. Steel-tipped ones, she'd realized from the clinking.

Liz had opened the toilet door slightly and peered towards the exit just in time to see the back of her husband's pick-up jeep driving away from Amanda's glass window. Just remembering this now brought back the same feeling of dread. She'd filled in the gaps. She'd thought he was in work, but obviously he'd come back to chase up some of the money he was owed. Amanda hadn't paid Derek for the job he'd done a few years back, like so many of his other clients just before the bubble burst. His business had gone bust a year later. Liz had had no idea he'd used brutal, savage tactics like the one she'd overheard to try and keep himself afloat. She'd felt sick.

And then she'd remembered Conor. She would apologize profusely, backtrack, explain the pressure they'd been under – that Derek was only trying to do the best for his son, just as she was – and then she would once again ask Amanda to sign off Conor's form. Walking tentatively back up to the office door, she'd given it a light rap. When there was no answer, she'd swallowed her mortification and opened it anyway, only to find the place empty. Amanda had completely vanished, but only Derek had exited the building.

Where had she gone? Had he taken Amanda with him? Liz hadn't been able to see if he was alone or if she was with him, but she was sure she'd only heard one set of footsteps.

A moment later she'd spotted the stamp still sitting in the middle of Amanda's desk. A stride, a glance over her shoulder, a double-check that the stamp's date was correct – it wasn't, a tweak of the dial fixed that – and then she'd pressed it into the spongy pad and transferred it to the box on her form.

Amanda's signature she'd forged later.

The tension in the house since Friday had been all one-sided. Liz wasn't talking to Derek, could barely look at him, and he'd no idea why. He'd have freaked if he'd thought Liz had forged an official form, because after what he'd been through with Ellen he was obsessed with doing things by the book, paranoid he'd be pulled up and charged at the first slip-up.

8

Jo pressed the doorbell of Gavin Sexton's flat on Dorset Street for the seventh time, her phone sandwiched between her shoulder and ear, as she stepped back on the pavement for a better view of the flat above a bookie shop, five minutes from the station.

It was half ten and she was waiting for Dan to pick up while watching for any sign of Sexton. She needed to ask her husband about Ellen Lamb, but without upsetting him. He was highly sensitive at the moment, and she was worried he was slipping into a depression. He was a proud man, and her being the breadwinner while he was off on sick leave had put further strain on their relationship. It had been a ropey start to their reunion after their separation. They'd split after Jo conceived their youngest son, Harry, some sixteen years after getting pregnant at Templemore training college with their eldest, Rory. Jo had assumed Dan wasn't coping with the prospect of becoming a father again when their careers were so demanding. But when he'd moved in with his secretary of ten years, Jeanie Price, who'd also since had a baby, she'd had to wonder. The dogs on the street knew the baby wasn't his, because their blood types would have made it impossible for Jeanie to need rhesus positive injections during the pregnancy if Dan had been the father. But Dan was still paying maintenance and hadn't asked for a DNA test yet. Jo didn't want to force the issue, but it was going to have to be broached at some stage.

'Hi, love,' she said, as the call connected.

'All right?'

'I need to talk to you about something,' Jo said. 'Can you mute that for a sec?'

'Two seconds,' Dan said.

Jo could have sworn he'd actually turned *The Jeremy Vile Show* bloody well up. After waiting for the result of a DNA test, Dan finally killed the sound, declaring, 'Poor bastard.'

Jo bit her lip so she wouldn't say something she'd regret.

'Do you remember Derek Carpenter?'

'I was shot in the back, not the head,' Dan snapped. 'Sorry. Yeah, course I remember the man also suspected of being the country's biggest serial killer.'

'It's about that girl we found in the mountains this morning,' she explained.

'Why? What have you got on Derek?'

'The victim lived on the same estate as him, and the

place where we found her body was within yards of where Ellen's shoe was found.'

'Is that it?' Dan scoffed. 'I wouldn't mind being a fly on the wall when they try and persuade the DPP that that one will stick. Derek Carpenter's harmless.'

Jo wished it didn't feel like she was pulling teeth. She was on his side, just worried her own involvement would cloud Alfie's judgement when it came to Dan's role. She'd enough guilt when it came to Dan without needing Alfie adding unnecessarily to it.

'Hang on, it's not your jurisdiction yet, is it?' Dan said, defensively. 'Why are you taking such an interest?'

'Why do you think?'

'I don't need you going to bat for me,' he snapped. 'Carpenter had nothing to do with what happened to Ellen Lamb, or the other missing women for that matter.'

'How can you be so sure, Dan? What's your take on what happened?'

He sighed. 'The Ellen you've read about in the papers wasn't the real Ellen. They beatified her after she disappeared. The real Ellen was an angry young woman. She hadn't been coming home at night, and was refusing to tell her parents where she'd been. She didn't get on with her sister. The more her father tried to discipline her, the more she rebelled. And there'd been an admission to Tallaght Hospital that the parents didn't want to talk about, either. She'd tried to overdose.'

'Can you remember what Derek's alibi was?' Jo asked. 'I don't doubt your judgement, but—'

'It was watertight. He was with Liz, Ellen's sister. The one he married since. She corroborated it.'

Jo felt herself tense up. 'Was she reliable? Wouldn't she have been conflicted?'

'It was her sister that had gone missing,' Dan said.

The sound of the TV started to creep up again in the background. Spotting a curtain twitch on the upper floor where Gavin's flat was, Jo wound up the call.

'OK, thanks. I'll see you later.' After hanging up, and shoving her phone in her pocket, Jo cupped her hands over her mouth and looked up.

'Open up, Gav! I know you're in there.'

She put her finger on the bell and kept it there.

After a pause, and again no response, Jo put on an oriental accent and roared, 'Sexy massage clock ticking, mister. You want me to start knocking at doors to find new customer?'

This time she heard the thud of someone taking the stairs two at a time, and seconds later, the door opened on to a stairwell that led to the first floor.

Sexton was holding a towel around his waist and using one end of another, dangling from his neck, to scrub his dripping wet hair dry. 'What do you want?'

Jo clipped up the stairs and headed into the living area, where she started gathering up empty pizza boxes and Coke cans, depositing them in the bin. The place was a mess but not grotty yet, she noted. *Pot . . . kettle . . . black . . .* Jo thought about the state of her own home. Keeping house always ended up slipping to last on her daily list of priorities.

Pulling open the fridge, she removed out-of-date eggs, mouldy cheese not wrapped properly and a bowl of – she wasn't quite sure what. Jo made a face as she moved to the bin and looked around for a disinfectant spray and a roll of kitchen towel.

'What are you doing?' Sexton asked. He headed over to the bedroom door and closed it, then plonked himself in a blokey leather armchair, jerked the footrest up and pointed the remote control at the telly, before reaching for a box of cigarettes and lighting up. Jo bent to retrieve the empty biscuit tin full of filter stubs doubling as an ashtray, and took the cigarette from his mouth and stubbed that out, too.

'Can't you leave it? I'm in the middle of something.'

Jo ignored him. Her patience was wearing thin. She knew Sexton had been through the mill with his wife Maura's suicide, but he wasn't even trying to move on. If anything, he was getting worse. She spotted at least two cigarette burns on the arms of his chair, where the foam filling was clearly on view. If he was falling asleep pissed with a fag in his hand, he was headed for disaster.

Sexton seemed to be making a conscious effort not to put up any more resistance. He was settling down for a snooze, leaning back on the headrest and crossing his stretched legs at the ankle.

Jo crinkled her nose, and moved to the window, which she shunted open. 'It smells like somebody died in here.'

'Yes, my great-aunt did, last week. She came over to visit, and keeled over.'

Jo wanted to believe he was joking, but couldn't be sure. 'I'm sorry. Why haven't you been turning up for work?'

Sexton reached for the small of his back. 'I've put a disc out. The painkillers are playing havoc with my stomach. That's why the place is in a state. I can't bend.'

'Ah, back pain, of course,' Jo answered. 'No doctor's cert?'

'I can't get out and about to get it,' he said.

'But you managed it for the medication.'

He held her stare. 'My great-aunt stockpiled. Her nickname among her friends was "the mule". She was bringing me a consignment.'

'Is that right? Have you got any Solpadol by any chance? My head's splitting.'

'I'm all out, sorry.' He paused. 'I thought you'd have taken a holiday before you started in the new gig.'

'I wish. We found a woman's body in the mountains.'

'Yeah, I heard about it on the news.' Sexton looked around for the packet of fags, pulled out another, then, after shaking the empty matchbox, loped over to the kitchen, where he leaned over an oven ring with the cigarette perched between his lips, puffing to get it going and turning the plate off once he'd managed it.

Jo filled him in on the incidentals. 'I think the killer wants us to start looking into the case of Ellen Lamb, back in the nineties. She was—'

'I remember,' Sexton said, reaching for the kettle. 'Only a teenager, that one. Walking back from the shop, wasn't she? Bastard. I always reckoned it was someone she knew. Derek Carpenter probably. She would have trusted him and taken a lift off him. How else could she just have vanished into thin air? Cuppa?'

'Sure,' Jo said, moving a pile of old newspapers aside and clearing some room on the couch. 'The thing is, as it turns out, the prime suspect for murdering the woman we found this morning in the mountains is Derek Carpenter. He's married to Ellen's sister now. They live on the same estate as the dead woman.'

Sexton's eyes widened. 'He was a nasty piece of work, that one,' he said, spooning some coffee into the cafetière, and reaching for the boiling kettle.

Jo leaned forwards. 'What makes you say that?'

'He attacked a reporter. Milk? Sugar?'

'Black, thanks. Maybe the reporter provoked him.'

'Nah, Carpenter had a lot of previous. They just couldn't pin it on him.'

'He was just a kid. I checked, and all he ever did was steal cars. It happens.'

'Why are you defending him?'

'I'm not,' Jo said. She paused. 'Dan interviewed him years ago when he was first nominated, and ruled him out. He confirmed Carpenter's alibi stood up.'

Sexton stopped what he was doing and turned, giving her a look as if he didn't believe she was serious. 'Dan's fucked,' he said out of the side of his mouth, the fag dangling from under his top lip. He carried the mugs over, and passed one to Jo, taking a slurp from his own, and then headed over to the window to tap his cigarette ash out, leaning over to check nobody was standing directly underneath in the car park below.

'You don't know that,' Jo argued. 'Dan would never make a mistake like that. For all we know—'

Sexton cut her off with a glance.

'See, that's exactly what I'm scared of . . . everyone jumping to the easy option and it clouding everything.'

'So you've abandoned the obvious solution and gone for an obscure one, that the killer is framing Derek?'

'Exactly.'

Sexton nodded in little increments. 'The shoe will tell a lot,' he said. 'Science has moved on since that was found. They can test for mitochondrial DNA now from the tiniest sample. If Carpenter's is on it . . .'

'Did I ever tell you you're brilliant?' Jo said. She aimed her phone and pressed a button. It made the noise of a camera shutter.

'Have you just photographed me?'

Jo curled her lip as she admired the shot. 'I need your help on this case. I've got Alfie Taylor yapping at my heels. Besides, nobody's going to believe your back is still out in this position.'

Something banged behind the closed door. Jo stared in its direction. 'Old, was she, your aunt?'

Sexton stood up and positioned himself between Jo and the door. 'I'm not well enough to come back to work yet. How's Dan holding up?'

'He'll be a lot better when he comes to terms with what's happened. He needs to get on with his life.'

'I don't need a lecture, Jo.'

'Come back to work, then, and I'll spare you one.'

'I'm not fit to work.'

'What are you going to do if you're fired?'

'I'll be all right. This great-aunt who died never married and had no kids. She left me a nice house. It means I won't have to worry about cash for a while. Jo, this job may be a vocation for you, but it's not for me. As a matter of fact, I don't think anyone should do it for life. I've seen too many sick things nobody should have to – movies of men and women interfering with little kids. You see enough of what people can do to each other, you start seeing only the worst in them. I need to get away for a while.'

'Don't you want to help put those kinds of people away?'

'I told you it wasn't Maura's name at the end of that suicide note. Do you even remember?'

Jo looked at the ground. How could she forget? It had taken Sexton two years to open Maura's suicide note, but instead of finding closure, he'd fixated on the fact that Maura had signed it with her middle name. The reason Jo hadn't brought this up again was because she thought he was seeing only what he wanted to see – that Maura might have been murdered, and her suicide staged by the killer.

'You never once offered to help me get to the bottom of it. Do you know how much it would have meant to me if you had? You're the best I ever worked with. Don't you get it? If someone else did this to her, I get my life back. Maura didn't choose death over life with me if someone killed her.'

Jo put her hands together like she was praying and raised them to her mouth. She wanted to choose her words carefully. 'Gav, I don't believe anyone else was involved. I'm sorry. I don't want to pour salt on an open wound, but I wouldn't be serving your interests if I only told you what you wanted to hear.'

'Go back to work, Jo. I'm not coming with you. If I was heading up that case, I'd be arresting Derek.'

Jo rubbed the back of her neck uncomfortably. 'You and Maura used to live in my new district, right? What if I promised that I'd set up a cold-case incident room to look into the circumstances surrounding her case? Would you help me then?'

Sexton smiled. He stretched both arms up to the ceiling, and then leaned over and tried to touch his toes, stopping midway when his belly got in the way.

'Fuck, I think I really might have done my back in now,' he said. 'When do we start, chief?'

'Now. We're going to the meat plant where Derek works. I need to talk to him. Don't look at me like that; I said "talk to him", not "arrest him". If I'm right, he's got nothing to hide and will cooperate fully.'

'And if you're wrong?' Sexton asked.

Jo pretended she hadn't heard, so she wouldn't have to answer. It would only have led to a row.

9

After filling up her car in the forecourt just a mile from Nuns Cross, Liz selected the credit card least likely to be declined from her bag, telling the cashier to put a car wash on the bill while he was at it. She tapped her foot, waiting the nerve-racking couple of minutes for it to go through. There was a shopping centre in Nutgrove nearby that did valeting. She planned to take it there next. She wouldn't be able to relax until she'd had the car cleaned to within an inch of its life, even if it was midday and she was running late for work.

Breathing a sigh of relief as the teller handed over her receipt, card and car-wash chit, she went back to worrying about her son as she headed out to the pumps. Liz had given up work when Conor was first diagnosed, packing in her job as a secretary so she'd have the time to source and prepare the right kind of mood food, drop and collect him from occupational and speech therapy, and bring him for one evaluation after another. He hadn't been able to string a coherent sentence together until he was eight, but he was making incredible progress now, and if he got a place in that school it would all have been worth it.

A school like that could set him up for life, and not just with an education. He'd have contacts in all the right places when it came to getting a good job, the kind of qualifications that meant the difference between being an eccentric and an oddball. Dyspraxia went hand in hand with his condition, making him unable to organize his thoughts and really bad at simple things like cleaning up. He was going to need a good income to be able to afford a cleaner and the kind of help that would make him independent of his parents. She and Derek wouldn't be around for ever, and with no siblings Conor would always have to fend for himself. Liz was determined to give him the best start in life, and right now that meant keeping the finger of suspicion away from Derek.

Pulling the handle of the driver's door, she got back into the car, glancing at herself in the mirror. Liz put her hands on either side of her face and pulled away the worry lines and the bags under her brown eyes. She tried to frizz a bit of life into her red hair. It looked so lank and lifeless these days. Not like Ellen's. Hers had been strawberry blonde, and so full. Liz closed her eyes and made a conscious effort to stop her emotions from going downhill. This was not about Ellen any more, it was about Conor. It felt like she was worrying all the time, and she knew if she carried on like this she was headed for an early grave. But after twenty years, she had a good idea how people's minds worked. If Derek was pulled in for questioning over Amanda's murder, they'd say the chance of Liz having a sister and a neighbour murdered in a lifetime was one in a million, unless she was married to someone like Fred West. Conor would go from being a special-needs kid to a murderer's son. 'Like father like son,' they'd say. He'd be treated like a weirdo.

Checking the code on the chit she'd just purchased, she stretched her right arm out the window to enter the numbers on the car-wash keypad. The green car-shaped light started flashing. Liz pressed the clutch, put the car in first, and guided it in over the grid draining the excess water, which faced a set of multicoloured rollers. They started to whirr, the noise building.

What all the people who'd felt sorry for her over the years didn't realize was that she'd become a fighter. What had happened to Ellen had made her as tough as nails. She carried a can of Mace permanently in her bag, and she'd signed up to enough self-defence courses to learn exactly how to jab her elbow into an attacker's balls, whack her fist into his chin, and stamp on his instep while screaming 'No', should he grab her from behind. She'd read all of Stephen King's books, and still watched every crime drama going on telly, wanting to bring it on, to prove to herself nothing could ever hurt her that much again. She was acutely aware that there was one exception. If anything happened to Conor, it would kill her.

The red came on and she lowered her right foot on the brake, put the gearstick into neutral and pulled up the handbrake. She reached into her handbag on the passenger seat for her tube of foundation. Then, with a start, she realized that she hadn't screwed off the bloody aerial. She'd lost one before; they cost a fortune to replace. She glanced at the rollers; they were spinning faster now, but still not moving towards the car, meaning there was still time. Dropping the make-up back in her bag, she pulled the door handle and hopped out. The driver of a beat-up Honda Civic queuing up behind her started to flash its headlights on and off and hoot the horn to warn her that what she was doing was lunacy. Liz didn't have time to get into it with him.

Standing at the back of the car, she turned the aerial anti-clockwise as fast as she could, managing to jump back into the car before the rollers hit. She leaned forwards to the dash to try and root out a CD she liked. A bit of music might help relax her a bit. Something upbeat. Selecting *Kylie's Greatest Hits*, she turned the volume up to high just as the sprinklers swept great sheets of water and suds over the windows. She shook droplets from her hair and watched the windscreen turn white like someone had draped a sheet over it. The noise outside and in was deafening. *It's a good thing I'm not claustrophobic*, she thought, as a solid horizontal bar came straight for the windscreen, blowing away the soapy water and climbing up towards the roof.

The rollers began to spin so fast the multicolours blurred into one as they swept towards the car. Something in the rear view caught her eye and Liz turned, horrified to see a great hulk of a man sitting in the back. Her breath caught in the bottom of her throat. Her hand moved to the handle, but the rollers were on either side of the door now, there was no going anywhere . . .

'It's OK,' he said, putting an arm forward through the gap between the seats and resting a hand on her shoulder. 'We haven't met, but I live in Nuns Cross. My name's George . . .'

Liz gasped, put her hand on her chest and took a big gulp of air. Her heart felt actual physical pain. Her eyes blinked rapidly and when her hand stopped shaking she stuttered, 'How did you get there . . . ?'

He took his hand back.

'I was parked right behind you. I tried to get your attention because I need to have a word. I called to your house earlier, but you weren't home. I couldn't believe my luck when I saw you getting out of the car. I had to hop in quickly or I'd have been drowned.'

Liz was still frozen in shock. She needed to use a loo badly, had almost wet herself in the horror of the moment. Slowly, she twisted around to study him properly. She recognized him all right. He had a round, ruddy face and a goatee. He normally didn't drive that car. She'd often passed him in a clamper's van. She'd never heard him speak before. His accent was inner-city Dublin. It reminded her that Derek had mentioned having a run-in with him a couple of years back.

'That guy is either brain-dead or seriously fucked up,' Derek had said, after he'd had to fork out eighty euro for parking illegally outside a hospital to get Conor in as quickly as possible after some scrape he'd long since recovered from.

'You scared the life out of me,' Liz said.

'Yep, if you wanted to do away with someone, I guess this would be the perfect way, right?' The man moved his hands either side of her neck, and pretended to choke her.

Liz leaned forward, as far away from those hands as she could. 'Sorry, what did you say your name was?' Her heart was still racing.

He offered his hand between the seats. 'George Byrne.'

She'd sooner have run her hands over a snake, and she hated snakes. 'What's so important it couldn't wait, George?'

'I need to talk to Derek. Where is he?'

'He's at work, George.'

George hesitated, like he had something on his mind. 'He's not answering his mobile.'

'He's working! He's not supposed to. I have to turn mine off in work, too. What's this about? Why did Derek give you his number, anyway?'

'I want to take this car off your hands. I saw the "For Sale" sign on it. My girlfriend's learning to drive, and I could do with an old banger.'

Liz blinked. 'And this was so urgent, you had to jump in my car and nearly give me a heart attack?' George nodded, completely missing the irony. Liz sighed. 'I'll think about it.'

'I'll pay you in cash now – five hundred euro. That's good money at today's prices.'

Liz tucked her hair behind her ears. Her skin was crawling and her mouth was dry. But she wanted rid of this car even more badly than she wanted George out of it. 'You've got a deal, George,' she answered, 'on one condition.'

'What's that?'

'I want the change of ownership details backdated to last week.'

George screwed up his face.

'Derek's got a supplier pursuing him for a job he can't pay,' Liz lied, babbling as she watched George's eyes narrow. 'This supplier has a court order entitling him to an evaluation of our assets . . . On paper the car is worth a lot more than even Derek wants, though you and I both know nobody's buying anything for its true value these days.' She forced a smile.

'Deal,' George said, looking pissed off. 'I'll drop around tonight for the keys.'

10

Sexton sat reading a newspaper on a fake-leather couch alongside a half-dead Swiss cheese plant in the reception of Mervyn's Meats while Jo quarrelled with the receptionist.

'Would Mervyn Van Dyke come to reception?' the blonde with dark roots had just asked in a Dundalk accent. Her red lipstick, which matched her fingernails, smeared the wire mesh covering the microphone.

Jo leaned over her counter. 'I asked for Derek Carpenter. Is he here or not?'

'I'm not at liberty to say. Mervyn's the gaffer. He'll be here any second.'

Sexton transferred his feet to a pine-effect coffee table, crossing them at the ankles.

'Either page Derek Carpenter immediately, or I'll have you charged with obstructing a police inquiry,' Jo warned.

A set of swing doors to their right opened, followed by a waft of fried food. 'You're interrupting my lunch,

Tiffany,' a portly man in a butcher's white overcoat and cap said.

Jo held up her ID. He glanced at it, and then took a bite of the sausage sandwich in his hand, and spoke through a mouthful of food. 'You can either join me, or wait ten minutes.'

'We're investigating a murder, Mr Van Dyke,' Jo said, not hiding her annoyance.

'This is about Derek and that girl murdered in the mountains, right? I've already had a call from your lot this morning . . .'

Jo glanced at Sexton in surprise. He put the paper down, and stood up.

'. . . and like I already said, he doesn't work here any more,' Mervyn continued. 'He was sacked two weeks ago. If you want the details you'll have to join me in the canteen.'

He was gone again before Jo could argue.

Jo shot Sexton a look as they headed past a pokey cabin on a scaffolding balcony that had a bird's-eye view of the factory floor, where eviscerated halves of pig carcasses were being chopped into joints by men in white coats. Jo headed into a stainless-steel kitchen with red quarry tiles that Mervyn's runners squeaked on. 'I ran Carpenter's social security number on the system before coming out,' she told Sexton out of the side of her mouth. 'He can't be gone long, because he hasn't claimed unemployment benefit yet.'

Mervyn pulled out one of two free chairs at a long white Formica table, and sat down. The rest of the places were filled by male workers all dressed in the same white coats and caps. Jo sat in the last remaining chair, opposite him. Sexton dragged a chair over from a different table and straddled it.

'This is Tom, our security man,' Mervyn said, pointing to the man sitting beside Jo.

A man in his seventies, with thinning hair, wearing a navy jumper and trousers, looked down quickly after a brief nod and then continued to slurp soup from a stainless-steel bowl. His spoon clinked every time it hit the metal.

'We're under pressure,' Jo told Mervyn, glancing at her watch.

He pulled one flap of bread off the half of his sandwich still on a plate, and squirted ketchup all over it before reaching for the brown sauce and doing the same.

'Tell the chief superintendent here why we got rid of Derek, will you, Tom? I would, but as it is, I get sued if I don't have the right number of toilets, if my fire plan isn't satisfactory, or if I'm too touchy-feely with the female members of staff. The last thing I need is a cop accusing me of making inappropriate comments. You never know these days what a judge will decide is worth compo. I should never have given Derek the benefit of the doubt for bumping off all those missing women from years back. If he's to blame for this one vanishing, for all I know her family could come after me.'

Tom covered his mouth with a rolled fist as he began to cough. A flush spread up his neck.

'I don't know if Tom's going to be able to rise to the occasion,' Mervyn scoffed, laughing at his own private joke.

Jo put an arm out to stop Sexton from standing up and grabbing him by the scruff of the neck. She leaned across the table on her elbows. 'Get on with it, sunshine,' she told Mervyn, nonplussed. 'We don't have all day.'

A matronly waitress arrived with a tray and began to transfer some of the empty dishes on to it. 'Derek was caught downloading dodgy stuff on the gaffer's computer,' she said in a tired voice.

'Is that it?' Jo turned to Mervyn for confirmation.

He nodded, grinning and picking food from between his teeth.

'You live a sheltered life if you think that's going to shock me, sunshine. I thought from your name and accent you came from one of those liberal countries, like Holland.'

Mervyn's face became grave. 'I'm from Copenhagen, actually. I grew up on a pig farm. I'm more Irish than the Irish themselves.'

Jo eyeballed him. 'What brought you here?'

'The green pastures,' he said, deadpan. 'If you want

to ask me any more questions, I want my solicitor with me.'

'It's Derek I need to know about,' Jo said. 'What exactly did he do here?'

Mervyn sneered, and drew a finger across his throat. 'He worked in the abbatoir.'

'According to our records, Derek worked as a builder before he joined your firm,' Jo said, unfazed. 'So what I'm wondering is why you employed someone with no experience in the meat trade, who'd been in and out of the papers after his wife's sister disappeared?' She looked around the room, and let her gaze settle on a man opposite whose face had been tattooed to look like a skull. 'He doesn't look like he's got an agricultural background, either. There's a distinct lack of female staff on your factory floor, and, no offence to you, Tom, but you're no Arnie Schwarzenegger, suggesting to me that you don't have to worry about security at all, Mervyn. Why would that be?'

Mervyn didn't blink.

Jo pulled out a pad and pen. 'I want the name of your recruitment company.'

Mervyn threw his half-eaten sandwich back on the plate. 'I believe everyone's got the right to be presumed innocent until proven guilty. We all make mistakes. As far as I'm concerned, when you do the time you've paid your debt to society. So, yes, most of the people who work here have criminal records. I source them from

PACE, you see, a halfway house that rehabilitates prisoners back into the community. Call me altruistic, I don't mind. I like to do my bit. I'm like one of those secret millionaires on the telly, without the million.'

Jo held his stare. 'Like I said, it's Derek I'm interested in. I want his mobile number, Mervyn. He's not on a contract with any of the mobile-phone companies, I've already checked. That means it's a pay-as-you-go number. You give me that and I'll be on my way.'

Mervyn reached into his pocket and started to scroll through his contacts.

Jo made a note of it as he called it out. With a number, she could have Derek's whereabouts pinged to within a few yards, triangulated between the nearest masts. Whatever dodgy operation Mervyn had on the go would have to wait until she'd found Derek. Jo was starting to come around to the possibility that Derek might be up to his neck in what had happened to Amanda.

11

'Is this the only organic onion you have?' the customer asked.

Liz reached back for the vegetable she'd just swiped, switching hands to shrug her arms out of her coat. She'd just arrived in Supersavers, and hadn't had a chance to catch a breath after taking a seat behind her till. She might as well have been a million miles elsewhere, though, with everything else going on in her head. *Why had Amanda's scarf been in her car? Had Derek really been working late last night? Why was the car so dirty? Why had he been so dead set on washing his clothes? Had George followed her to the garage?*

'She's not paying a blind bit of notice,' the woman told her son. Liz knew Nigel and Maud to see from Nuns Cross. Maud was in her sixties, with a severe bob and one of those big-headed, little-bodied dogs lodged under her arm. Nigel was late thirties, with sideburns, thinning hair, and a bright-yellow golf jumper knotted over her shoulders. They'd called to Liz's door once, looking for a contribution to pooper-scooper bins for the estate. Liz had sent them packing. 'The only thing that would be worse than stepping in dog poo would be having to pick it up and hermetically seal it,' she'd told them.

Lifting her foot off the pedal that operated the conveyor belt, she entered the numbers of the barcode on the label stuck to the onion to delete the purchase.

'She didn't say she didn't want it,' Nigel said.

Behind them, Frieda, a banker's wife who lived across the road from Liz, snorted and folded her arms impatiently. Liz glanced from her to Dolores, sitting at the till alongside, reading her horoscope in a magazine. She wished Dolores would get her finger out. She was in her late forties and permanently single, big into angels and country music. She came into work every day looking like Dolly Parton. Her hair had got even higher since a cringe-worthy audition on *The X Factor*, but in true Dolores style she'd taped photos to her till like a shrine to the highlight of her life.

With a sigh, Liz beeped the onion through again.

'Mum didn't say she wanted it either,' Nigel piped up. 'She wants to know if you have any others we could change it for in the back.' He was enunciating his words as if he was talking to a foreigner, or someone who worked a till because they didn't have the brains to do anything more taxing.

Liz bit her tongue because she needed the job.

Everything in her life had changed since Derek's business had gone bust. His building company had specialized in extensions and renovations at a time when the banks were writing to home-owners pleading with them to borrow money. Those years had enabled them to buy her dream house. He'd worried she'd find it humiliating to have to serve their yummy-mummy neighbours wearing a shiny blue pinafore with her hair scraped up under a cap, but Liz wasn't like that. A job was a job. She wasn't going to let anyone take her home without a fight.

'I heard on the radio that a woman on your estate was strangled with her bra,' Dolores said. 'But there's not a mention of it in the papers.'

The old lady at Liz's till clicked her tongue. 'We drove up the mountains this morning for a look just before coming here. We couldn't get near it, though.' She sounded disappointed.

Liz was appalled. Bloody rubberneckers. She held up the onion belligerently.

'It'll be all right in a stew,' Maud grumbled.

Liz put the onion to one side, ready to be packed. Then she wiped her eyes on the back of her sleeve. There was a George Michael song playing on the store's radio that had been Ellen's favourite. 'RIP,' she said.

Frieda stared. Liz hardly knew her. She was always flying in and out of her house, packing her three sons into a people carrier and carrying TK Maxx bags. She ran a personal shopper and styling business from home. She'd put a flyer in Liz's letterbox once, offering to 'detox her wardrobe'. Usually, she appeared on the other side of her griselinia hedge when Derek was cutting the grass or washing the cars, joking – with come-to-bed eyes – that she'd have to bribe her own husband to do the same.

'Your Derek renovated her offices, didn't he?' she asked Liz.

Liz looked up, conscious it sounded loaded. 'That was a few years ago—' she muttered.

'Was the onion kept out the back?' Maud interrupted. 'I wouldn't want anything a rat might have peed on.' Her bulgy-eyed dog started to yap.

Liz pressed yet another button to summon David, her spotty manager, in his twenties, with more self-importance than brain cells. He was on the phone at the customer-service counter, beside a poster-sized photograph of himself on the wall. He caught her eye and turned his back, continuing the conversation.

Liz rubbed the back of her neck, unnerved because Nigel was standing right behind her waiting to pack. He was always in the shop, reading the magazines and newspapers from cover to cover because he was too cheap to pay for them, or holding his arm out by his mother's side. Usually, he didn't utter a word; he just packed, and reacted to his mother's directions not to put anything soapy in with anything edible with the patience of Job. There was a whole generation of men just like him who would never leave the nest now that the banks didn't give mortgages to anyone any more.

Dolores looked back over her shoulder again. 'I heard that she had some very dodgy clients,' she whispered, with a twitch of the mouth.

'Oh, give over,' Liz snapped. 'Whatever happened to not speaking ill of the dead?'

Liz scanned the customer-service desk. David was off the phone now, but still showing no sign of paying her a blind bit of notice. She put her finger on the buzzer, and this time kept it on. When that didn't light a fire under him, she re-entered the onion's barcode to cancel the sale, ripped its sticker off, and stuffed it in Maud and Nigel's shopping bag with the other items, saying, 'Tell you what, I won't say anything if you don't.'

David sauntered over. His shirt collar was so tight it looked like it was going to shear his Adam's apple off.

'This aisle is free, madam,' he told Frieda.

Dolores put the paper down.

'No, I want to talk to Liz,' Frieda said.

Liz glanced at her in surprise.

David put his hand on Liz's shoulder to cut in. 'When you finish up here, you can take your break early,' he said.

'Why?' Liz asked him, looking at her watch. It was only half twelve, and she had barely been there five minutes. 'I took a phone call for you just now.

Your Derek's had some kind of accident in the car.'

Liz jumped to her feet.

'No need to panic,' David said. 'His was the only car involved. He went off the road and straight into a wall. He's in St Vincent's.'

'Are you OK to drive?' Dolores said as Liz grabbed her coat.

'Let us know . . .?' Frieda called after her.

Liz didn't answer them. The words just wouldn't come out. She hadn't felt this scared since Ellen had vanished.

12

2000: Wapping, London

The copyboy stepped into the elevator – arms bent at the elbow, bales of morning newspapers stacked up to his chin. Neither of the two suits standing side by side asked him what floor he needed, and his elbow was too big for the buttons. The suits were going to the top floor, the one that made the hacks move like condemned prisoners when they got summoned up – accounts.

'What if that mob had killed her?' the bald one was asking.

He was wearing Right Guard Sport. The copyboy was an expert when it came to aerosol brands, from years spent searching for the perfect high.

'We'd have to do a giveaway of free dictionaries,' Nivea Cool Kick joked back.

Right Guard wasn't amused.

Nivea put his fist up to his mouth and tried to turn a laugh into a cough.

'I know the circulation is up, but if you ask me it's a step too far,' Right Guard blustered. 'I realize naming and shaming is giving readers what they want, but we're dealing with ignorami here.'

'Ignoramuses,' Nivea corrected. He looked like he'd just remembered his place, and tried to make light of it. 'Paedophile . . . paediatrician. You have to give the peasants some credit for getting the "pae" bit right.'

'Yes, because paedophiles put brass plaques on their gateposts declaring their predilection so anyone who didn't get their copy of the News of the World *will know exactly where they live.' Right Guard argued. 'We can't condone vigilantism . . .'*

They passed the second floor. The copyboy was still trying to find a way of pressing '5'.

'Blair was asked about it during Prime Minister's Question Time,' Right Guard blustered.

'I'll organize a dinner,' Nivea suggested. 'Reassure Westminster we're on top of it.'

They were at the fourth. If the copyboy didn't hurry, he was going to be in the shit. With a shunt, the elevator stopped, and the doors slid open. The editor stepped in. The copyboy's load started to slide; he just about saved it with the tip of his chin. Her arm stretched out. Her finger pressed '5'.

'Congratulations, darling,' Right Guard said, kissing her on both cheeks. 'You're a genius. You should see the figures for advertising.'

'*Absolutely inspired,*' Nivea said. '*Where did you get the idea?*'

She turned on them. '*A little girl was snatched from a cornfield, raped – and murdered because an animal like Roy Whiting thought that way he wouldn't have to go back to prison. People have a right to know who their neighbours are. That's what Sarah's Law is all about.*'

They were at the fifth.

'*Shocking,*' Right Guard said. '*I've got an eight-year-old. I wouldn't be responsible for what I'd do if I got my hands on him. Hanging and quartering is too good for them.*'

The doors opened. She stepped out. The copyboy followed, hiding his smile behind the pile of newsprint.

13

At the nurses' station, Liz was refusing to accept what the nurse with the sorry smile was trying to imply.

'If you like, we can have a counsellor come and have a word with him,' the nurse had just said.

Liz simply wanted to know where Derek was, and could have done without the pseudo-psychological assessment thrown in, thank you very much. Ellen used to specialize in that, too.

'Dump him,' she used to say all the time, 'he's a mentaller.'

Liz hadn't stood for it back then, either.

'Why would Derek need to talk to a counsellor?' she asked.

The nurse raised an eyebrow, like Liz was missing something. 'It's a clear stretch of road.'

Liz shook her head, muttering, 'No way,' under her breath. Derek was under a lot of pressure, and she was prepared to take her fair share of the blame for that, but he would never do that to her – take his own life – not when he knew what she'd been through after losing Ellen. He'd seen first-hand what it meant for someone he loved to have to shoulder even one tragedy in a lifetime.

'He doesn't need a counsellor,' she told the nurse.

'Well, if you do change your mind, you know where I am. And if you can convince him to stay overnight that would help, too. We've a room available in private, but he's refusing to stay.'

'Private?' Liz presumed Derek's Voluntary Health Insurance subscription had lapsed with the family policy when they'd stopped meeting the repayments. Foreign holidays, gym membership and even health insurance all belonged to the good times – before Irish taxpayers were held liable for fat-cat bank managers' bad debts, and the word 'lifestyle' got supplanted by 'existence'.

The nurse sensed Liz bristling. 'He's got to stay under observation because although he hasn't broken any-thing, he's concussed. Why don't you sit down, my love? You've had a nasty shock.'

Liz swallowed the lump in her throat. A small show of kindness, and she was all set to dissolve. She felt a pang of guilt. Maybe Derek had picked up on how she'd been willing him to hurry up this morning, maybe he'd been speeding and that was the reason for the crash.

She made her way down the corridor, scanning each room in the ward, too upset to wait for directions. It only took a minute to find Derek, anyway. He was sitting on a bed just inside one of the doors, pulling his jeans on under one of those skimpy hospital robes that tied at the back. The sight of his face – covered in cuts and bruises – made her breath catch in her throat.

'I thought you fancied pulling a sickie this morning, but this might be taking it to an extreme,' she said, attempting a joke.

Derek looked up from under his dark, bushy eyebrows, but not at her. He buttoned his jeans, and flopped back against the pillows. The whites of his eyes were yellowish against the starched white covers.

'Sorry. I'm so sorry, love.'

'What are you sorry for, you big galoot?' She kissed his face, and then sat on the edge of the bed, reaching for one of his callused hands. She loved him, and had to give him the benefit of the doubt. She wasn't about to give up on her marriage even if, worst-case scenario, she found out he'd had a fling with Amanda. It made sense if that was the reason why their argument had become so heated. She and Derek would get through this. Life had thrown a lot worse shit at them. Kill himself? Derek? Not in a million years.

'The pick-up's a write-off,' he replied, wincing.

'Cars can be replaced.' She tried to rub the back of his hand, but her watch snagged on a cannula. 'Why's this thingy here? Are they giving you antibiotics?'

Before Ellen had disappeared, when things like

117

wanting to be something had mattered, Liz had dreamed of becoming a nurse. She'd been like a sponge when it came to soaking up medical information. If they were pumping him with intravenous antibiotics, he might have an infection as a result of an internal bleed.

'What happened?' she asked.

He shook his head and shrugged.

'Where?'

'Near Buglers.'

She pictured the spot. It didn't make sense. Derek was a brilliant driver. They'd grown up on the same council estate in Tallaght; he'd lived just a few doors down. He'd spent his childhood taking cars apart, putting them back together and being unable to resist taking them for spins when he shouldn't. That was another big reason she wanted to give Conor the best start in life.

'Maybe you fell asleep at the wheel. You've been working too hard. You looked wrecked this morning. I'll head home and pack you an overnight bag in a bit. You'll be getting your own room. Pyjamas, toothbrush, that kind of thing . . .'

'Don't bother,' he said quickly. 'I'm not staying. I've got to get back to work.'

'You can't work. They'll just have to manage without you until you're well.'

His tone changed. 'If we lose the house, it won't matter if Conor gets the scholarship. He's only eligible for the place if we live in their catchment area.'

Liz could have recited the wording of the small print on the form, but she wasn't going to rub Derek's nose in it. Not here, and definitely not now. 'They're talking about debt forgiveness for people who can't make their mortgage repayments.'

'It'll never happen,' Derek said. 'What about the people who've already lost homes – would the banks give them back? Or the ones who are still paying – would they be allowed to stop?'

'I'll ring the bank, see if I can't get them to postpone a few payments till you're back on your feet. I'll tell them you were almost . . .' She stopped short again.

'Don't ring the bank under any circumstances,' Derek blurted, sounding rankled. He sighed straight away, like he regretted saying it.

Liz couldn't put a comment like that down to concussion. 'What do you mean?'

'Nothing.'

A nurse came over before Liz could pursue it. 'We've got other patients we have to consider,' the nurse said. 'Technically, visiting hours are not until this evening.'

'I'll only be another minute,' Liz promised.

The nurse looked unconvinced, but left them to it.

After waiting for her to go, Liz reached into her pocket and drew out the blue scarf. 'It was in my car.'

He stared.

'It's Amanda's. How did it get there?' she asked.

'I . . .'

'If people put two and two together . . .'

'Love . . .'

Liz cast a nod in the direction of the nurse. 'Something like this puts everything in perspective,' she said through a gritted jaw. 'We have to put Conor's needs first.'

'Yes,' he answered. 'That's exactly what I tried to tell Amanda. The stupid cow wouldn't listen.'

14

'What?' Liz asked icily.

Derek scanned the ward, throwing dagger looks at an old man in a dressing gown who was shuffling towards an empty bed, wheeling a drip as he moved. Liz barely breathed while she waited for Derek to get on with it. The nurse passed by again and tapped her watch pointedly, catching Liz's eye.

'Is Conor OK?' Derek asked, shooting a swift glance at the nurse to remind Liz that they had to be careful.

Liz went along with the change of subject, nodding. 'Conor's good.'

Derek looked worried, and tried to hide it.

'Why?' Liz asked.

'I just thought he was acting a bit weird this morning.'

She wanted to get back to the other conversation but she couldn't help being drawn into this one. 'What do you mean?'

'He just seemed a bit funny.'

'What kind of funny?'

'You know, like he'd something on his mind funny, as against his usual odd-as-two-left-boots funny?'

Liz folded her arms. 'He's not odd, he's—'

'Yeah,' Derek cut her off. He never liked her talking about Conor's condition.

'It's probably the thing with his books,' Liz said, monitoring the nurse. Two patients away now, still too close. 'I was thinking that maybe one of the other students in the class might be trying to sabotage his results.'

'No,' Derek said. 'That would be evil.'

'It exists,' Liz said. After a pause she added, 'There are people who would kill for a place in that school. Remember Tonya Harding, the ice-skater whose husband had Nancy Kerrigan whacked in the leg so she could win?'

'Vaguely,' Derek answered, craning his neck to make sure the nurse had moved out of earshot.

'You were saying?' Liz hissed, getting him back on track.

He breathed heavily through his nostrils. 'I have to get everything out in the open. There are things I haven't told you about Ellen, because I love you so much, Liz, and I was too scared of losing you before. But now I'm all out of options. At the start I thought I was doing the right thing not telling you what happened to her . . . why I . . .' He stopped, closed his eyes, and took a deep breath. 'But because of what happened to Amanda, there's no way around it. Before I tell you any more, you have to believe that everything I did back then, I did for you, and the only reason I'm digging the past up now and coming clean about what I did is for Conor's sake.'

Liz was completely floored. Her chest felt like it was about to cave in. She'd been trying to keep the past buried for the same reason. A throb struck up at the back of her head. 'What did you do?'

His eyes filled. 'I went to Amanda to ask for her help. I wanted some legal advice. I needed to find out what would happen if the gardaí got new information that helped them to find Ellen ... where someone would stand in relation to a prosecution after so much time had passed. I thought I could trust her because ... remember that job I did for her that she never paid for?'

Liz nodded and shook her head. She was so confused. 'What new information? How would you know where to find Ellen's body?'

'Yes ... no ... just listen for a sec. Because Amanda never paid me for the job, I felt that I wasn't asking for much. That's why I felt it was OK to confide in her, to tell her what happened all those years ago, to ask her for advice. But she was a complete bitch, Liz. She wouldn't give me the time of day, stopped taking my calls. I dropped in to talk to her and told her if she was going to be like that she could pay me what she owed me, and she went berserk. She started threatening to tell you, and I said some things back because I knew she was having an affair with a plumber I'd worked with. She started whacking me. It was everything I could do to restrain her. I know it's wrong to speak ill of the dead, but she had it coming . . .'

Liz's hands were so tightly clenched that her fingernails were drawing blood. She felt confused, tired in her bones. Her throat started to close; she could feel her entire life disintegrating.

Derek became sheepish. 'I'm so sorry about everything, love. All I ever wanted was to protect you . . .'

'What new information about Ellen? Protect me and Conor from what?' she asked louder.

A squeaking sound over her shoulder made her almost jump out of her skin. The nurse was back with a medicine trolley, asking Derek if he needed more painkillers.

'I promise only another minute,' Liz said, making a quick cross on her heart.

The nurse shook her head. 'No. It's not fair on the others. You'll have to leave now.'

Liz stood slowly. The nurse moved to the next patient.

'You've had a bad accident,' Liz told Derek.

'I'm not losing it. Is that what you think?'

'I think if you say any of this to anyone else it's going to hurt our son. I need time to think.' Liz turned and didn't look back. Once in the corridor she rushed to the nearest loo and vomited. After flushing the toilet she went outside to splash her face with water, and tried to slow her thoughts down. All these years she had believed everything Derek had told her, when everyone else – her own mother and father, the public and the police – considered him the prime suspect for what had happened to Ellen. By backing him, she'd helped him to keep up the pretence that he was a regular guy. Now she'd discovered she had no idea who her husband really was.

Think, think, think, she told herself. *What was there to think about?* a little voice inside her head answered. *At the very least, Derek was a liar. At worst, the man she'd slept alongside for twenty years, the man she'd thought she knew better than anyone, the man who'd fathered her child, was a monster.*

It felt like her mind was playing tricks. She wondered if it was possible that any minute now she'd hear her name called and would open her eyes to find someone in a white coat with a bright light shining behind them telling her she'd just had the mother of all nervous breakdowns.

But as impossible as it was to fathom, to believe, she had to accept the facts. Derek had wanted to confess. She couldn't take it in – that the same hands that had comforted her could have taken her only sister's life, and disposed of her body. That the lips she'd kissed every day for the last twenty years had told lies that had ruined her entire family's life. Liz took a deep breath. She was going to have to go back. She had to hear him say it, not hint it. She wanted to watch his face when he said he'd murdered Ellen, and then and only then would she believe it.

But by the time she'd established that the coast was clear and the nurse had moved off the ward, Liz returned to find Derek's bed empty. The only sign he'd been there at all was his mobile phone, which was still on his bedside locker. Liz grabbed it and stared. Derek never went anywhere without his mobile. He never forgot it, he never lost it, it was always charged, and if he couldn't answer, he always got back to her as soon as he could. Derek knew exactly how much Liz panicked when she couldn't contact him. Keeping in touch was a must after what she'd been through with Ellen. By leaving his phone, he might as well have left her a note saying that she was on her own from now on.

15

Liz felt queasy the entire bus journey from the hospital to the meat-packing plant on the Naas Road where Derek worked. As if things weren't bad enough, having had the nurses trawl the hospital for any sign of her husband to no avail, her car had refused to start in the hospital car park. She'd had to knock all the extras off her insurance policy a couple of years back, so dialling the AA to bail her out hadn't been an option. Covered in a lather of stress-induced sweat, Liz had continued on foot, hurrying out to leafy Nutley Road. At the T-junction with embassy-belt Merrion Road five minutes later, she'd caught the 47 bus.

Fifteen minutes after abandoning her car, she'd steadied herself using the bars on the back of the head rests and walked to the front of the bus, pressing the red bell with her thumb so the driver would pull in on Pearse Street. It had taken her another ten minutes to walk to George's Quay, via the Docklands. By 1.45 p.m., she'd stepped on to the 141, leaving the new

Samuel Beckett Bridge over the Liffey – the one in the Lotto ads that looked like a harp on its side – and the tilting-pint-glass conference centre behind her on the final leg of her journey to the Naas Road.

Liz didn't know if Derek had gone to Mervyn's Meats, but it was the only place she could think of through her pounding head to start looking for him. She was all over the shop: her hands clammy, her stomach in a knot. The shock to her system had left her completely drained, and she swung from disbelief to horror. It was like her head and heart had gone to war. Her head told her it all made sense now. She was having flashbacks to her parents' warnings. They'd never trusted Derek, had taken an instant dislike to him, to the point where he wasn't allowed to cross the threshold of their house. Even Ellen had had the jitters around him, and had never approved. *Had something happened, even back then, that Ellen hadn't wanted to mention?* she wondered.

Guilt lodged itself as a block in the bottom of Liz's throat. *Had she really helped her sister's killer get away with the crime for all these years?* When she thought of how the police, and the press, had also taken a stand, and how she had arrogantly written off their judgements, along with everybody else's, so she could maintain the egotistical lie to herself – that Derek loved her and that Derek couldn't harm a fly – she couldn't breathe.

A voice inside her head kept playing devil's advocate. *How could her husband have had a whole other life she'd known nothing about? How could she have been living with a complete stranger? Maybe Derek had had such a bad knock to the head he'd been raving. Maybe paranoia was a side effect of concussion. Maybe he was the one having a nervous breakdown.*

Or maybe she was in denial, she decided. She took his phone out of her pocket and started to do something she would previously have thought beneath her – scrolling through his texts – hacking into her husband's phone like some kind of bunny-boiling female. But she had to find out what was going on. There were only two texts, both unopened. The first one said, 'The game's up, dickhead. Amanda said you tried to blackmail her and that you assaulted her. Now she's dead. Convenient that. We know who you are. Where are you?'

Liz gasped. She clicked down to the details but didn't recognize the number. She dialled it without hesitation.

It answered after one ring, 'About time,' a man's voice growled.

Liz didn't answer. She barely breathed. She wanted to say, 'Who are you?' and 'What the hell is going on?' But the words wouldn't come out. And something else was making her heart stall. The voice was familiar.

'Derek, stop mucking about, where are you?' the man raged. 'I want to negotiate terms.'

Liz's hand moved to cover her mouth as the raspy

Dublin accent had the exact same effect on her as in the car wash earlier. It was George the clamper on the other end of the line. *Maybe by 'negotiate terms' he meant the sale of her car, but why hadn't Derek told her they'd discussed it? And what had George meant when he'd told Derek the game was up in the text? Why all the aggro, calling Derek a horrible name?* She hung up quickly, and clicked open the second text sent by 'Mervyn' – the name of Derek's boss – scanning it: 'You're a dead man walking.'

Liz stared, horrified. She held the phone away from herself like it was a bomb about to go off. *What the hell was going on? What had Derek got involved in? Who had he brought into their lives?*

She gave a start as the phone rang. George was trying to ring back. She didn't answer and waited a minute after it had rung out before dialling 171 to get into Derek's voicemail, to see if he'd left a message

Derek had three messages, the robotic voice announced. Liz listened aghast as the first began to replay. 'You don't know who you're dealing with,' George snarled.

The next message was her own: she'd rung on the way to the hospital to say she coming, asking if he was all right and explaining that she'd heard he'd been hurt. Her eyes filled as she heard herself promise him that everything would be OK.

The final one had been left on Friday at 10.35 p.m.,

and Liz listened to a woman's voice: 'Fuck you. You're just like all the rest. No man is going to bully me any more. I'm going to spill the beans.' Liz was in no doubt who that was, either. Even if she hadn't scrolled through Derek's contacts and managed to match the number listed there for Amanda Wells to the missed call in Derek's caller log on Friday night, she'd have known. The sound of Amanda's plummy vowels were also etched deep in her recent memory, making her feel about one inch high.

Liz shivered. She thought about Friday, and what she had seen and heard in Amanda's office, and how bad it all looked from where she was standing for Derek, whom just this morning she'd still loved. She thought about what could happen if people who didn't care about her husband started putting two and two together and deciding Amanda's killer was in their midst. She thought about her son, and how his life would change irrevocably if his father became the prime suspect for a woman's murder all over again.

Swallowing, she dialled back into Derek's voicemail and pressed '5' to erase the messages one by one. Next, she went through the texts, deleting them quickly. What option did she have? She'd been gullible, naïve, and stupid. But if he was found out, she'd be hounded, like Maxine Carr, the girlfriend of Ian Huntley who'd killed those two girls in England, and been presumed guilty by association. She'd have to go into hiding for Conor's sake.

She took a few deep breaths, but the airless over-heated stink of carburettor fumes being pumped back into the bus through the air con only made her feel worse. Her head was racing. What if the gardaí started that slow drip of information to the press, the way they had last time, so the pressure to get Derek before the courts resulted in his arrest? If that happened, their lives as they knew them would be over. She could forget about setting Conor's adult life up for good. She hated herself for thinking it, but she couldn't stop: if he'd died in the crash that morning, it would have been a solution of sorts . . .

A nudge to her ribs made her turn and glare at the man sitting too close to her on the seat. He was elderly, but dressed in a smart suit, with a razor-sharp crew cut of snow-white hair, and a set of false teeth too big and too white for his mouth. Liz had tried to inch sideways a couple of times, but the friction of her shiny Supersavers pinafore against his suit had made such a loud squeak that she'd stopped. She wouldn't have minded, but he was as skinny as a rake. There was plenty of room on his side.

Catching her eye, he indicated the inspector standing beside them.

'Ticket,' the inspector barked, in a way that meant he'd asked at least once already. Liz fumbled through all her pockets, then all over again, before spotting her ticket on the floor beside the man's feet. She tried to lean down to pick it up, but couldn't reach at the angle. He retrieved it for her and handed it over. The inspector punched a hole in it and gave it back.

'You ask me, it's a disgrace they keep putting the cost of fares up when nobody has a shilling,' the man said as the inspector moved off. He had a Limerick accent and a briefcase on his lap.

Liz turned her head to stare out the window. They were at the Bewley's clock at Newland's Cross. It was 2 p.m., and the traffic was heavy – HGVs were tail-gating across two lanes, the air outside was thick with exhaust fumes. She wasn't in the mood to talk to any-one. She had enough problems of her own. She wanted to be left alone so she could think.

'Do you agree?' he asked out of the blue.

Liz glanced sideways. The man had a deep tan and cold eyes.

'That the cost of living has gone through the roof. You got children?'

'Just the one,' Liz mumbled. She checked her own phone. Still no calls, texts or emails from Derek.

'Let me guess – a boy, right?' the man said.

Liz pretended not to have heard, straining to look out the window. Why did she always have to end up beside the nut jobs when she took public transport?

'What age? Let me guess – twelve, right? Conor, isn't it?'

Liz turned slowly. 'Who are you? What do you want?'

'Drink, drugs, unprotected sex, it's a jungle out there when you're young and innocent and have no father-figure to protect you. Anyone can get to you anytime.' He pulled a couple of schoolbooks from his bag.

Liz gasped. She recognized Conor's handwriting on the front. She snatched them off him, and then stood and tried to get past. The bus was crowded, but the word 'Help' wouldn't come out. The man's legs didn't move an inch to let her by. His bony hand did, though. It reached out and gripped her wrist.

'Then there's the worry that a kid will take it all too seriously, do themselves an injury. Tell Derek to stick to the agreement if he knows what's good for him. Got that?'

She nodded rapidly, felt faint and sat down. He stood and made his way to the front of the bus – which was pulling up outside Derek's factory – before stepping off. Liz's head was spinning. She stood and frantically pressed the red bell button to stop the driver moving. Gripping the seats and bars to steady herself, she hurried out the folding bus doors.

16

Liz tailed the man at a distance, never letting him out of her sight. She watched in disbelief as he walked into Mervyn's Meats. He worked with Derek! How had he got his hands on Conor's books? What had Derek done? What had the man in mind for their son? Who was Derek messing with? What agreement? If it turned out Derek had put their son at risk, Liz would kill him herself with her own two hands. Nobody was going to hurt Conor as long as she still had a breath left in her body.

Hooking her fingers in the wire fencing, she took in the dreary, windowless plant, built in the shape of a chimney stack. The patchy, uneven grass verges were in need of tending. The sign above reception was in the same orange italic bubble font as on the wage slips and company newsletters that came home every month.

Spotting a familiar face on duty in the security hut, she hurried over. Tom was a former plasterer who'd worked for Derek's building company before it had folded. His pension had been wiped out in the global meltdown. Derek had managed to secure this job for him operating the lever that let the jeeps pulling animal carriers in and out.

Tom tipped the peak of his cap back at a tilt when he saw her, walking out to meet her. He didn't look pleased, or surprised, Liz noted. He looked worried.

'What can I do for you, Liz?' he asked, checking the entrance to the building over his shoulder.

'Who was that man who just went in, Tom? The oldish one in a suit, with white hair and the over-sized false teeth?'

'I didn't see anyone go in,' he answered.

'You couldn't have missed him. It's not five minutes ago. He's skinny as a rake and has horrible, mean eyes.'

Tom shook his head like he hadn't a clue.

'Is Derek in there?' Liz asked, not trying to hide her impatience. She'd lost count of the number of times she'd invited Tom over for dinner, feeling sorry for him at home on his own. And after everything Derek had done for Tom, he could have been a little bit more helpful.

'Derek? No. Why?' Tom asked.

It was clear from his rigid expression that he was trying to decide politely how to tell her to move off.

Liz tried to explain about Derek's crash.

Tom didn't seem in the least bit surprised or bothered. He was starting to really piss her off. She looked beyond him into the hut at the wall-to-wall posters of bare-breasted women – their arms stretched behind their heads – tacked to the slatted wooden walls. Liz shivered. Her stomach lurched. An open-bar electric heater was drying up the air. Tom's sandwiches wrapped in tinfoil were on a corner of a desk in there, beside a flask, and smelled of bacon. She felt sick again. She'd thought he was a sweet little old man. She'd invited him into her home. *How well did anyone know anyone?* she wondered. She took a deep breath of fresh air.

'I got to get back to work, Liz. I really got to get back to it now, you know.'

'I'm going, but if Derek stops by, maybe you could give me a ring.' Liz scribbled her number on the top sheet of his clipboard.

'Why would he stop by here?' Tom asked. There was a real edge to his tone. 'He was fired two weeks ago. If he shows up here again, he's a dead man.'

There was that horrible phrase again. What the hell had Derek done?

17

The mobile-phone analysis on Amanda Wells's number was back by the time Jo and Sexton got to Store Street, and Foxy took her through it in her office as Sexton kept Alfie Taylor at bay in the bustling incident room outside. It was clear from the heated conversation she'd picked up walking across the unit that as far as Alfie was concerned he was the only chief superintendent heading up the case, and he was furious Derek Carpenter hadn't been arrested yet. She could tell by the way Alfie was gesticulating on the far side of the glass that he was also now hopping mad that she'd set up the incident room in the city centre, rather than in the burbs where he was based.

Foxy pointed at a line of type on a sheet of green and white striped computer paper. 'The mobile number you got for Derek was bouncing off the same masts as Amanda's late on Friday night. It looks like Derek was the mystery man with her in the restaurant.'

Jo leaned on her palms to scan the information on the

printout. She pointed to Amanda's last call at 10.35 p.m. to Derek's number. 'If they were together, why would she need to ring him?'

'Well, the restaurant manager said Amanda stormed out after a row. Maybe Derek rang to apologize, or to find out where she'd gone.'

Jo wasn't convinced. 'Nobody calms down in five minutes. Is Derek's number listed in Amanda's phone as a contact?'

Foxy nodded. 'Yes, but not by his name, Amanda had saved his details under a number – twenty-nine.'

'That's the number of his house,' Jo said. 'Any other contact between them?'

'Lots from him to her on the Friday, in which he demanded she pay him what he was owed. There's only one message from her to him, left at 10.35 p.m. that night. In it, she said she was going to "spill the beans".'

'Shit,' Jo said, holding her hair off her face and looking out into the detective unit.

Sexton was sidestepping Alfie in both directions to block his path, and looked set to rugby tackle him.

'Alfie also found out Derek recently took out a hefty life-insurance policy on his wife,' Foxy explained.

'His wife, or the whole family?' Jo asked.

'The whole family,' Foxy admitted.

'So maybe he was being sensible, or maybe he was feeling under threat,' Jo said crossly.

'He also came into an unexplained six-figure sum.

Perhaps he was blackmailing Amanda over something.'

Jo bent down and took the cactus out of the cardboard box and placed it back on her desk. 'What about Amanda's account? Did the equivalent amount go missing?'

Foxy shook his head. 'No. If anything she was broke, and lonely.'

'Lonely?'

'Why else would she do so much online networking? She actually tweeted when she arrived at, and was leaving, the restaurant . . .' He rustled through the folding sheets to find the one he wanted, '"Men are all pigs. I can confirm." I asked Sue to contact the people she communicated that to, and they didn't know her at all, other than online.'

'Social networking is an oxymoron,' Jo remarked.

Aishling stuck her head around the door. 'We've found the Beamer.'

Jo gave a victory clench, and waved her in quickly.

Aishling entered, and Jo shut the door behind her as she handed over a brown cardboard document. 'We also found this.'

Jo shot her a quizzical look and then studied it.

'Amanda's car was in a multi-storey in Temple Bar,' Aishling explained. 'These were inside it: deeds, for a couple in Nuns Cross. I know that Amanda was the local solicitor, so it's not unusual that she'd have them, but it's mad that they're just in her car and not in a bank safety-deposit box. Without them, those homeowners have nothing to show for their mortgages.'

'What were their names?' Jo asked.

'Frieda and Charles McLoughlin. I checked, and Amanda did handle the sale of their house for them, so it's not unusual that she'd have the deeds, it's just weird where she left them.'

Jo turned to Foxy. 'Were the McLoughlins listed in her contacts?'

He rummaged out a sheet of paper and ran his finger down a list. He shook his head.

'Does she have a contact listed as "thirty-one"?' Jo asked, glancing at the deeds.

He looked up, surprised. 'Yes.'

'Ring it later from the landline and see if it's them. Any other numbers there?' Jo asked.

Foxy nodded and counted under his breath. 'Lots.'

'Get me a list of them and find out if they correspond to owners in Nuns Cross, too.'

'OK,' he replied.

'Aishling,' Jo said, 'can you see if you can track down the shoe that belonged to Ellen Lamb years back? It'll be in storage somewhere. When you locate it, we need it tested for mitochondrial DNA. I'll organize a sample from Derek Carpenter when I call to his house.'

Aishling nodded, and ducked back out, holding the door for Joan to slip in. As a result, Jo managed to over-hear part of Alfie's animated argument with Sexton. He was saying, 'What she needs to do is park her career and go home and look after her children.'

Alfie reacted to Sexton looking over his shoulder, appalled, to check if Jo had heard that one, by turning and trying to get Jo's attention himself, but Jo ignored him. Alfie went back to jabbing a finger at Sexton.

Jo skimmed through the questionnaire Joan was handing her for approval, which she'd wanted to see before dispatching anyone to knock the doors in Nuns Cross. She said, 'Yep, yep, yep, and scratch that one.'

'What's wrong with that one?' Joan said, over her shoulder.

'It's enough to ask the neighbours if they saw anyone acting suspiciously,' Jo explained. 'You don't have to ask if they've seen anyone they recognize acting that way. It's going to make them think they don't have to mention seeing strangers, and it's pointing the finger at Derek.'

She turned to Foxy. 'I want to hear that Friday-night phone message Amanda left for Derek about "spilling the beans". Her tone will tell a lot. Maybe it was a private joke.'

Foxy made a face. 'Not with the opening words, "Fuck you." There's no way it was a joke.' He moved to her landline, glanced from the printout, where he'd circled Derek's number, to the phone, and put Jo's phone on speakerphone. He entered Derek's number, placing a five before the service provider's code. He pressed hash and the factory default PIN of four zeros to get into Derek's messages.

'You have no messages,' a voice said.

'He's wiped it,' Foxy reacted.

'Did you transcribe it?'

'Yeah. Alfie's got it. He thought that it might have been a reference to their affair.'

'Now they're having an affair? We haven't established it was definitely him in the restaurant yet.'

'He fits the description. Oh, and he was in a single-vehicle crash today,' Foxy pointed out. 'A matron called Sheila Franklin in St Vincent's Hospital assessed him, and thought he seemed depressed.'

'What about his car?' Jo asked.

'It was a write-off, has gone to the scrapyard. Come to think of it, that's one way to get rid of a car, isn't it? I'll organize having it collected, and get forensics to comb it.'

Jo went back to the printout. 'What time exactly did Derek's phone ping in Temple Bar?'

'At nine in the evening. It was back in Nuns Cross by ten.'

Jo walked a biro through her fingers. 'But Amanda stormed out of the restaurant at half ten. This should be enough to let Derek off the hook.

'Alfie thinks it's possible he dropped the phone to cover his tracks.'

Jo sighed. 'He would. So why leave Amanda's with

her? Come on! I take it Derek's didn't ping in the Dublin mountains?'

'I'm not sure what the mast situation is like up there.'

Jo flicked the sheet with a finger. 'But this says he went home after town.'

'Maybe he left his phone back?'

'You think he drove home to drop his phone back, and then carried on up the mountains – where there may or may not be a signal – with her body in the car?'

'It's possible. It's called the CSI effect. The way offenders are up to speed on the technology from all the crime drama on TV.'

'Did Hawthorne get back with Amanda's time of death yet, so we can cross-reference exactly what time she must have died and then try and work everything else out from that?'

Foxy shook his head. 'Hawthorne's phone's off. His secretary says the PM's done, but he hasn't had time to do up the report. He's tied up in court for the rest of the day.'

'Fuck's sake, we need to know now. If she died after Derek returned home, it's going to change everything. He's off the hook.' She glanced at her watch. It was almost three. 'I'll catch Hawthorne on the way out of court.'

Foxy lifted the phone on Jo's desk, which had started to ring.

'And put the restaurant manager on standby,' she

144

went on, opening her door. 'When I get back I'm going to bring Derek in for a line-up, to establish if he's the mystery man in the restaurant.'

Foxy started talking into the phone before she'd finished. After listening for a few seconds, he covered it with his hand and called after her, 'Derek's phone is back in Nuns Cross.'

Jo nodded and reached for her own mobile, which had started to ring. It was one of the crime-scene officers at Amanda's house, informing her that Liz Carpenter had just arrived back at her home. 'Any sign of Derek?' she asked the officer, frowning when she heard his reply, and thanking him before hanging up.

'Right, I need to find out Amanda's time of death,' she said, turning back to Foxy.

'I don't have time,' she told Alfie, who had started trotting after her. 'I've got to get to the central criminal court before four o'clock to catch the prof.'

'You'd better make the time,' Alfie told her. 'And you can call off your Rottweiler,' he said, motioning at Sexton. 'I've just come from a meeting with the assistant commissioner. Until I officially retire on Friday, and you are technically promoted on Monday, I'm the head of this investigation. You should have moved on Carpenter this morning, like I would have. If the press find out that the killer of six, and possibly seven, women is still out there because of your relationship with your nearest and dearest, someone's head is going to roll.'

'Is that a threat?' Jo asked, sounding tired.

'It's a reality check. As is the fact that it looks like you're protecting Dan.'

'And why would I do that?' Jo asked, turning to face him.

'Maybe he covered up something for Derek Carpenter all those years ago that could come back to haunt you both.'

'What are you talking about?'

'You've given Derek Carpenter a head start to get away.'

What annoyed Jo most was that Alfie clearly knew something she didn't, but she wasn't about to give him the satisfaction of being asked what that was. After a pregnant pause he said, 'Derek Carpenter's phone is pinging in Nuns Cross.'

'I heard.'

'You heard?'

'It doesn't mean he's there!' Jo said. 'Liz could be carrying it, for all we know. Derek would have been seen arriving back.'

'I'm sending a team to check,' Alfie said. 'You can join them if you want. It's up to you.'

18

Unlike Professor Michael Hawthorne, who was currently sitting in the witness box of the Central Criminal Court giving evidence, Jo would never have acknowledged the accused's lawyer during cross-examination by making eye contact. Having passed on Alfie's offer to go directly to Nuns Cross to bring Derek in, she'd come to court to try to pin the pathologist down on Amanda Wells's time of death once and for all. She watched through spread fingers as Hawthorne shook his head earnestly while his theory about the cause of death was ripped to shreds. She could tell by the way Sexton was jiggling his leg on the bench beside her that he was thinking the same thing, too. If either of them had been in Hawthorne's seat, they'd have been straining their faces towards the judge – to send a signal to the jury that the senior counsel representing the accused was not worth giving the time of day to.

She and Sexton knew the innocent-until-proven-guilty concept would have been rigorously tested by the

Chief State Solicitor's Office and the Director of Public Prosecutions before a suspect ever came to court. The public had no idea how hard it was just to get a case tried these days, or how much crucial evidence was ruled inadmissible. There were a million and one ways that body language could be used to talk to a jury without anyone needing to utter a word. Not that Jo had the arrogance ever to try and predict what a jury might do. Their verdicts never ceased to surprise her, which was ironic considering that one jury always looked interchangeable with the next. That was the way she liked it. There was something about a collection of tracksuits, Christmas jumpers and old T-shirts wielding the real power in court that always managed to subvert the pomp of those entitled to wear wigs and gowns and look down their noses. Barristers were actors first and foremost, in her opinion. They cared about their delivery, their performance and winning – not about the truth, not about justice.

The barrister – thumbs tucked into the sleeveless pits of the black waistcoat under his cloak – had just cut Hawthorne off. 'No further questions.'

Hawthorne took a moment to bang his notes together on the bench before stepping down from the stand.

Jo made a beeline for him as he pushed through the crowd at the back of the court, Sexton following close behind. 'Any chance of a word?' she whispered to Hawthorne.

'Not now, I've got a garda driver outside waiting to bring me to Galway for a slash-hook killing,' he complained. A set of handwritten sheets on yellow foolscap, contained in a manila folder under his tweed jacket, started to spill out. Jo caught them before they fell, and then used them to lure him outside.

'Won't take a sec,' she assured Hawthorne, flicking a speck of fluff from his shirt.

Sexton held the door for them as they headed out on to the circular mezzanine floor of the new courts complex. Jo leaned over the marble balcony, notes dangling from her hands. 'That girl you PM'd – what was the story? I need the time of death urgently.'

'Which one?' he asked, snatching back his paperwork. He only had two assistants, but between them they handled more than six hundred unnatural deaths a year.

'The girl in the mountains, Amanda Wells.'

'Alfie Taylor's girl?'

'I found her,' Jo said.

'Striking-looking woman,' Hawthorne remarked. 'Well proportioned.'

Jo folded her arms. 'Sometimes I worry about you.'

Hawthorne didn't bat an eyelid. 'There were no defence wounds . . . either she knew him, or he took her completely unawares.'

'Fuck's sake, that narrows it down, then!'

'Language!'

'What about the plastic bag?'

'We found fibres inside it, navy gingham. My assistant will ring you once we have the rest.'

'Did you get any DNA?' Jo asked. 'Was she raped?'

Sexton stood listening with his hands in his pockets.

Hawthorne shook his head. 'Nothing came up under the UV light.'

'Not raped, and nothing robbed as far as we can tell. Even her iPhone was left in her hand,' Sexton said, trying to work it out.

'Look, I really have to go,' Hawthorne said. 'I'll have the report for you tomorrow.'

'I need her time of death,' Jo said. 'It's our only hope of ruling a suspect in or out. I know you're busy, but—'

Sexton threw his eyes to heaven and turned away.

'It's got nothing to do with my workload, for once,' Hawthorne said. 'I have an assistant taking her temperature on the hour every hour to establish the precise drop, it's the only way to be certain—'

'Temperature?' Jo exclaimed. 'How's there still any temperature? I saw the rigor had set in for myself. She must have died at least—'

'If it *was* rigor mortis,' Hawthorne cut in. 'I can't rule out cadaveric spasm . . .'

Jo stared.

'. . . when death occurs due to intense emotion such as fright, Birmingham. If she was scared to death, she might have died much, much later than we originally thought. Rigor, on the other hand, takes three to four hours to set in after death, reaches its peak after twelve hours, and lasts for up to three days. Depending on which it was, she could have been dumped very close to the time we found her. We may even have passed her killers on the way up.'

Jo tapped her foot. 'Prof, we know she was in a restaurant at half ten on Friday night. We found her at half seven on Monday morning. It's imperative we establish if we should be appealing for anyone who may have seen her alive on Saturday and Sunday, or if she was already dead by then.'

'Tomorrow,' Hawthorne said, starting towards the lift.

Jo trotted after him. 'But what about the bag in the mouth and the bra around her neck?' she said. 'If the cause of death was suffocation or strangulation, wouldn't that rule out the cadaveric spasm theory?'

He stopped and turned to face her, breathing through his nostrils slowly. 'It's to do with the grip. Drowning victims often grab on to reeds in an effort to save themselves, but if death is brought on by cadaveric spasm, the reeds will stay in their grip – as opposed to being washed away. So, yes, the victim's hyoid bone was broken, indicating that choking pressure was indeed applied to her neck, but you saw for yourself how tightly that phone was gripped in her hand. I wouldn't be surprised if her neck was strangled after the event. It's entirely possible the bag and the bra were added, the clothes removed, and even the phone put in the victim's hand in the staging of the scene.'

He stepped into the lift.

'That doesn't sound like our supposed serial killer, does it?' Jo asked Sexton as the elevator doors slid shut.

19

2001: The Dorchester, London

After flicking a piece of fluff from his smart wine-coloured waistcoat, the waiter transferred four drinks to the silver-plated tray, glancing over at the table he was about to serve. The blonde-haired woman, who looked a lot like Princess Diana, was sitting at a table with four chairs. Opposite her was a Dubai prince in flowing robes, and beside her a black-haired geezer in a bright tie and sharp suit. The Arab's suitcase was propped up on the empty seat facing her.

The waiter found it hard not to stare. The likeness was scary. Her hair was cut the exact same way as Princess Di's, and when she glanced up to see if anyone was looking at her, it was with the very same set of too-good-for-this-earth eyes. The waiter reckoned she was milking it.

Propping the tray up on his fingers, he carried the drinks over at shoulder-level, ice cubes tinkling and pretzels standing to attention. The part-time job he'd applied for and had got some months back, as a waiter in the Dorchester, was just for this moment in time. All he had to do was bear witness, report back, and above all be sure not to bump into the suitcase, or make eye contact with the fake sheikh sitting opposite the princess, legend that he was – the King of Sting!

'He's ignorant of the countryside,' the Duchess was telling the men. 'His wife is even worse, she hates the countryside. She hates it!'

The waiter knew how whoever they were talking about felt. He'd gone fishing once on a community policing project, and been eaten alive by insects. But he'd come a long way from his childhood, and it wasn't as if he was about to get into it with them anyway. Time and place and all that, or 'Ho hum', as they all said around here. He placed the silk- and lace-embroidered coasters down first and the G&Ts on top.

Close up, she was better looking than the dead princess; she'd better features – a smaller nose, and stronger bone structure. His mam used to drink her tea out of a mug with a picture of Di on her wedding day. It was still at home; he never used it, but he liked looking at it. It felt like she was looking back.

But this princess seemed far too preoccupied by what was going on to notice him. She had just said something and was pulling a face. The waiter glanced at the sheikh, who had thrown his head back and was laughing. He could feel the 'fuck off' vibe loud and clear in the way the sheikh didn't so much as glance back. If the other two at the table even suspected a previous acquaintance, he'd have blown it, and could forget about ever going back to his real job in the newspaper. He almost spilled a drink trying to get on with it, then; attempting not to be noticed. It looked like he'd got away with it—

'He sounds like a puppet, unfortunately,' the countess, or duchess, or princess was telling the sheikh.

There were reporters in the palace and Downing Street, too, the waiter knew. It was said that an investment of that calibre usually took a few years to come good.

He couldn't think of any job he might get along the way that would ever tempt him to walk away from the newspaper. Working in the Dorchester would only have been good if he'd wanted to see how the other half lived and enjoyed being constantly treated like the shit half. There was no class system in a newspaper, that was the best bit. Inside the newsroom, it didn't matter where you came from, or what you had, all that mattered was the story.

Take the sheikh, aka the investigations editor. He'd got his first story exposing family friends who sold pirate videos. It had earned him two weeks' work on the News of the Screws *when he'd been just sixteen. Since then he'd been blazing a trail, living it up like a lord. He earned over a hundred thousand pounds a year, but could live off his expenses – sleeping in hotels, being driven around in limousines, and moving about with an entourage to keep up the pretence of his alter ego. His technical team – aka bodyguards – were standing behind him now, paying close attention to the suitcase, making sure it was recording everything. The closest he'd come to being rumbled on a story was when a soldier who'd served in the Middle East approached him speaking Arabic. The sheikh might have grown up in Birmingham, but he'd turned that situation around by refusing to speak in Arabic to a white man, and had managed to keep his cover. For a Paki, that was impressive.*

The waiter had heard enough. He carried on, and put the tray under the bar. After telling the manager he needed a leak, he found a quiet place where he could ring the newsroom to tell them what he'd heard, to give them an early heads up on the exclusive so they could come up with a headline.

20

By 4.30 p.m. Liz was standing in her hallway, the phone pressed tightly to her ear with a trembling hand. She'd phoned a taxi from her mobile outside Mervyn's Meats after being frogmarched out like a common criminal by Tom – who'd got the bloody job through Derek in the first place! It had cost an arm and a leg, but there was no way she was getting back on a bus. She was exhausted, and was still reeling from what she'd found out today – that Derek had not only been fired, but that whatever he'd done had so pissed off his employers that they wanted to kill him, and had sent someone to intimidate her precious son. Then there was her neighbour George, whose messages on her husband's phone were, to her mind, virtually death threats, too. *Was that the real reason he'd had the car crash? Had someone been following him? Had his brakes been tampered with?*

She'd never thought there'd be a worse day in her life than the one when Ellen disappeared, but today had been it. And just when she'd thought it couldn't deteriorate further, she hadn't even had the chance to put the kettle on before the cops had landed on her doorstep, demanding to know where Derek was.

They'd only just left the house, after producing an arrest warrant for him and barging in – criss-crossing each other in the hall and going through every room – checking under beds and even in wardrobes, as if they'd expected to find him hiding there. She felt sick, exposed, like her own home was no longer safe. Her life was unravelling. She was so traumatized she was numb, and had switched into automatic mode, trying to plan what to do next.

On the other end of the phone a man in the bank was about to tell her how much deeper in the shit than usual they were, now that Derek had no job. She needed to start making plans to shore up Conor's future. The news that Derek had been lying through his teeth to her should not have come as a body blow, given everything else she'd discovered today, but her stomach literally felt as if it had been punched, and she kept one hand holding it while she waited. Where had he been going every morning when he'd said he was off to work? And how had she not noticed that his wages had stopped coming in? Where had he fled to when he'd left the hospital, and why had he still not been in touch? These were the questions making her doubt not just who her husband was, but who she was, too. What planet had she been living on? If she was the kind of person who hadn't noticed what was going on right under her nose, was it any wonder that she hadn't realized Derek might have been involved in Ellen's death?

Chewing a nail, she listened to the teller tap her personal details into the system.

'Here we are,' the voice on the other end of the phone said. 'You have one hundred thousand, four hundred and thirty-three euro and seventy-nine cents in your account.'

'Sorry, I said my name was Liz Carpenter, of twenty-nine Nuns Cross, Rathfarnham; maiden name, Lamb; date of birth, the twenty-sixth of September—'

'Yes, I heard you,' the man answered. 'You have one hundred thousand, four hundred and thirty-three euro and seventy-nine cents in your account. Is there anything else I can help you with?'

Liz felt her centre of gravity shift, as if she was standing on a ship and the ground was moving beneath her. Her head felt so light and fuzzy her hands didn't feel connected to her body. She was aware she'd just tried to bang the phone down, but her palms were so clammy, the handset slipped from her grasp and fell on the floor. The man on the other end was asking if she was still there, but time had started moving differently. Even though everything was now in slow motion, she didn't feel there was time enough even to bend to retrieve and replace the receiver. She took the stairs two at a time.

'What's wrong, Mum?' Conor called from his room.

'About a hundred thousand euro,' Liz said under her breath. She'd collected Conor from school on the way home from Mervyn's Meats in a taxi, shaken to the core by the incident on the bus, and not taking any chances with his safety now her husband had turned into some kind of predator. She'd told Conor she was collecting him early because of their trip to the circus. She'd been expecting a barrage of questions, but when they hadn't come she'd suspected it was because he was glad to get out of football training. She'd have cancelled the circus trip in the blink of an eye if Conor hadn't been Conor. But a promise was a promise and, trivial as it might seem to an outsider who didn't understand his condition, she wouldn't let him down.

Pulling open her wardrobe, Liz started to root through Derek's pockets. How was she going to explain all of this to her son? She'd never lied to him, and wouldn't, but how could she tell him the truth? That by some incredible coincidence, at a time when they shouldn't have been able to meet their basic bills, they'd come into an unexpected windfall; that his father, the man she thought she knew better than anyone, was a stranger to her.

Finding nothing in Derek's clothing, she moved to the dresser and rifled through the socks and underpants. The bedside locker was next: she upended each of the three drawers on to the bed. The only thing worthy of further inspection was a box of Durex, which turned out to be unopened; a book of chequebook stubs, which showed no unusual payments in or out; and Derek's passport, which she noted was out of date.

Liz moved to the window and pulled the cord of the blind. She could see right down the side of Amanda's house to the garda crime-scene tape still fluttering out the front.

Her gaze veered to Derek's home office, a Portakabin bordering both their gardens. It still bore the sign 'Derek's Building Services – Extensions, Renovations, Attic Conversions' from the days when he'd needed somewhere to run the administrative side of his business. It was still his bolthole. Realizing that he probably spent more time in the home office than he did in the house, she rushed downstairs, not needing to grab the key by the back door, because the gardaí had been out there too, less than half an hour ago. Hurrying across the flagstones set in the grass, she fumbled with the Chubb lock to open it, and let herself in. Inside, she started to tear apart the room, which contained a desk, fan, filing cabinet, phone and Derek's tools. She didn't even know what she was looking for, just that when she saw it, she'd know.

Ten minutes later, Liz sat back on her hunkers and covered her face. The place looked like a bomb had hit it, but there was absolutely no clue here, either, as to what was going on. The hem of her trouser leg snagged on a loose floorboard, and as she tugged it free, it lifted a little. Liz looked around for a screwdriver, then sat back and pried the board loose, pulling up another and then another. Underneath she found an incised square in the black plastic sheeting. The screwdriver dropped from her hand when she peeled it back and saw what was underneath.

It took a second to realize that the wailing sound was coming from her. Leaning forwards, she pulled out the items hidden in there: a crumpled, pleated navy skirt covered in a blue mildew, a V-neck jumper, a navy gingham blouse and a single brown shoe with a distinctive ankle strap. It was Ellen's uniform, and one of the shoes she'd been wearing the day she'd vanished. The other had been found twenty years earlier in the mountains.

She tried to stand, but her knees felt as if they were going to buckle. Her hands shook. *That was it then*, she told herself, *the end of any niggling doubts. There wasn't going to be a rational explanation. Derek was someone who hurt women.* It was all true, her worst fear: he'd murdered her only sister in cold blood, and in so doing, he might just as well have killed her parents. Her mother had died three months after her father, of a broken heart as far as Liz was concerned. Liz didn't think anything could be worse than Ellen disappearing, but that was before the man that Conor called Dad became the country's most notorious killer.

21

Liz was trying to stop hyperventilating by fanning air at herself with her hand when Conor pressed his face up to the fogged Portakabin window, and then opened the door. Ignoring the trashed interior and the hair stuck to his mother's face with snot and tears, he calmly said, 'Mum, there's someone at the door for you.'

Liz went into a blind panic. She bundled Ellen's uniform into a drawer in Derek's desk, and then dived towards his array of tools to arm herself.

'Stay here,' she warned Conor, holding a nail gun and a lump hammer.

Pacing down the hall, she thanked her lucky stars for the first time in her life that Conor had closed the front door after answering it, which was the logical thing to do, if not the socially acceptable one. Peering through the spy-hole, Liz realized it was only her neighbour, Frieda, standing there, holding a bottle of white wine in one hand and a lasagne dish in the other. Pulling open a drawer in the hall table, Liz transferred the tools into it and shoved it closed.

She opened the door slowly, leaving enough of a chink to allow her to stand sideways in the gap. Based on the smell, she presumed a stick of garlic bread was what was wrapped in foil under her neighbour's arm.

'I was thinking you could probably do with a glass of this after the day you've had,' Frieda said, holding the bottle up.

She was dressed in a North Face fleece-lined windbreaker, and Rock & Republic jeans, with a pair of Dubarry deck shoes. Her hair always looked like it had been blow-dried in a salon.

'I appreciate the gesture, but it's a really bad time right now,' Liz said, scanning the street over her shoulder.

Frieda put a hand up. 'Look, insensitive as this may sound, I'm going to say it anyway. We need to make sure something like this doesn't stick. You know . . . put people off buying here, I mean. I don't want to sound mercenary, but Charles has been offered a job in Berlin. We're going to try and put our house on the market soon. No offence, but nobody's going to want to live in the kind of place where women get murdered, let alone next to someone with any kind of question mark hanging over them. Charles said we should get our stories straight—' Frieda pulled a face for Liz to fill in the gaps. When Liz didn't react she said, 'Charles was talking to Amanda on Friday. She told him that Derek had assaulted her. The gardaí called earlier asking if I'd seen anything. I didn't say a word. Yet.'

Liz opened the door wide. 'Come in.'

She followed as Frieda headed for the kitchen.

'How's Derek, anyway?' Frieda chirped, not waiting for an answer. 'I presume he's OK because, and I hope you don't mind, I rang the hospital and they said he'd gone home. Is he here? I didn't see him come in.'

She didn't seem to be expecting an answer as she pulled open the oven door and slid the dish in, studying the knobs before turning up the heat. Frieda had ripped out an identical kitchen in her own house, to fit in a mock-Aga and one of those American stainless-steel double-fronted fridge/freezers that dispensed freezing water and ice cubes. Liz knew, because she'd called once when her post was delivered to the wrong house. Frieda had said she'd have made coffee, but she didn't know how to operate the 'mother ship' – a state-of-the-art cappuccino and espresso maker her husband, Charles, had got her for her birthday.

Liz went to the tap and turned it on, running her hands under it, but resisting the urge to splash her face.

Frieda was busy clattering in the cutlery drawer. 'Anyway, I thought you needed this more than I did.'

'Why?' Liz asked, sorry it sounded so defensive.

'You seemed to take what happened to Amanda really hard in the shop today, and then to have to deal with Derek's crash on top of everything . . .' She stopped talking to stare. 'Are you OK?'

'I don't know what I'm going to do,' Liz said, walking over and pulling out a corkscrew.

'Why? What's the matter? You look a bit funny. Have you been crying? Your face has gone all red.'

Liz nodded and used the pointy tip to rip the plastic seal on the bottle, unfurling it and twisting the corkscrew in the top.

'It's just such a shock,' she said, attempting to pull herself together, and looking out into the garden through the set of French doors at Amanda's house opposite. She sighed. Conor was still in the Portakabin. He'd wait there indefinitely if she didn't tell him it was OK to come out.

'Tell me about it,' Frieda said, her eyes narrowing. 'I mean, she was one of my clients.'

'Just hang on a second,' Liz said, opening the back door and running down to the Portakabin to tell Conor it was OK, he could leave. He bolted out and back into the house, and was thundering up the stairs when Liz got back inside. Frieda looked like she expected an explanation, but Liz didn't give her one. 'You were saying that Amanda was one of your clients...' she prompted.

'Right, I did her colours. She was autumnal.' She walked in front of Liz and made a frame of her fingers and thumbs while studying her face. 'I'm thinking you're spring, but it's only a guess. I'd need to do a proper consultation. Amanda asked me to organize a couple of those bags the charities leave on the doorsteps for her, too. She wanted to go through what I'd picked to throw out before signing it off. It's part of the service. A client gets their wardrobe cleared out by me, and feels good about it because they've donated to charity. I only take what I can tell hasn't been worn for years, or is out of fashion. People are such hoarders. You wouldn't believe how hard some people find it to part with ancient clothes. Nobody's giving away anything at the moment, but that's a different story.' She paused. 'I still have her stuff,' she said, raising her eyebrows.

Liz broke down.

Frieda put her hands on her shoulders. 'I didn't realize you and she were close.'

Liz pressed her hands against her face, which was bathed in sweat. She felt so overwhelmed, like she had nobody to turn to any more. The only person she had ever really opened up to was Derek, but after everything that had happened she desperately needed to talk to someone. 'I barely knew her. It's Derek. I don't know what I'm going to do.'

Frieda stepped back. 'Why?'

Liz hesitated. She didn't know or trust Frieda, but the words just blurted out, 'He's gone.'

'Gone . . .' Frieda exclaimed.

Liz slumped into a chair, thinking, '*God forgive me, that might be better*.' She was starting to feel as much a stranger to herself as Derek had become to her.

'What do you mean? The hospital said he was fine when I rang,' Frieda followed Liz's gaze to Amanda's house and back. 'Oh. You mean that gone.'

Liz shifted her weight to the other foot and then back. 'I need to talk to him. We've come into all this money. I don't know where it's come from.'

Frieda turned away, sloshed out the wine into a pair of hastily organized mugs, and handed Liz one, knocking hers back. She drained it, then topped up her glass and drank that, too, keeping her eyes trained on Liz, who barely sipped hers.

'There's something . . .' Frieda said, looking uncertainly at Liz. 'You'd have to keep it between us . . . Charles would kill me if he knew I was talking about it.' After a pause she blurted, 'Only, we were being blackmailed by someone about some bother Charles had in the bank over some dodgy mortgages. We paid the blackmailer the money in the end. It was small change compared to what we could have lost. It's just, I found a letter in Amanda's clothes that she'd forgotten to send, you see. She was having an affair. She'd written to her boyfriend's wife telling her everything. Why would she do that unless she was being blackmailed, too? So then today I started wondering, if, because of Derek's past—'

The doorbell rang before Frieda had a chance to finish.

22

Jo held up her ID as Sexton put the flat of his hand on Derek Carpenter's door to make sure that it wasn't closed in their faces. They hadn't been able to access Nuns Cross by car as it was one of those gated communities, and Sexton was fit to be tied. A council worker, sitting in the back of a waterworks van parked beside the Nuns Cross landscaped green, had ignored his calls for advice and help over access. The man had kept sipping slowly from a flask, and gone back to his newspaper. After three minutes Jo had thrown in the towel and told Sexton to park up, telling him to arrange for the gates to be decommissioned for the duration of the investigation.

'I'm Chief Superintendent Jo Birmingham and this is Detective Inspector Gavin Sexton,' she told the frightened-looking woman who answered the door of Number 29, whom Jo recognized from old newspaper photographs as Liz Carpenter, though she'd aged more rapidly than Jo had expected. 'We're investigating the murder of your neighbour, and we'd like to have a word.'

'Derek's not here,' Liz said breathlessly.

Her eyes looked puffy, and her skin blotchy. The tip of her nose was red, and she was talking high in her throat.

'Your colleagues have turned my house over already, looking for him today,' she went on. 'They're not long gone. I told them I didn't know where he was. He had a bang to the head. He's not himself. I haven't been able to get in touch with him myself.'

Jo had a nose for lies, and believed her, or wanted to. 'Do you want to report him as a missing person?'

'No.'

Jo's eyes widened. She'd answered too quickly and too emphatically. On second thoughts, she was hiding something.

'Not yet,' Liz added quickly.

Jo tilted her head. 'Can we come in?'

'Why?'

And now Liz Carpenter was overly defensive, which suggested to Jo she was afraid of something. She needed to establish what Liz was scared of, or who. 'To talk more comfortably, that's all.'

A slack-jawed woman with an expensive haircut appeared over Liz's shoulder. 'I'll see you later, Liz,' the woman said, attempting to sidestep past Jo, muttering, 'I'm just a neighbour.'

Sexton blocked her path as Jo pulled out her note-book. Liz's neighbour's eyes bulged.

Snapping the elastic off, Jo licked a finger to flick through the pages. 'What's your name and address?'

'Me?' the woman objected. 'Why? I saw nothing.'

Jo studied her face. Belligerence was weird from a neighbour in the circumstances – a woman on the next road had been murdered! 'What's your name?'

'McLoughlin . . . Frieda. I live across the street, in number thirty-one,' she blurted. 'But I barely knew Amanda.'

Jo caught the way she glanced at Liz when she said the last line. Jo had found the page she was looking for, but Sexton nudged her to indicate Darth Vader leaning over the banister at the top of the stairs. A thin boy with a close-cropped haircut took the mask off.

'Mum, when are we going to the circus? Dad said he'd be back. So where is he? He never breaks his promises. Is he dead?'

Liz looked horrified, and moved towards Conor, leaving the door ajar.

Jo stepped in, pretending to be more interested in Frieda, but keeping an ear cocked for Liz's answer to her son.

'I need you to come down to the station later,' Jo told Frieda, scribbling Foxy's name on one of the cards she'd had printed with her new title. 'Ring this sergeant to set up a time.'

'But . . .' Frieda blurted, one hand attaching itself to her chest. 'What about? Why? I've done nothing. This is harassment.'

Jo wanted to see Liz's reaction to this statement, but she'd gone from motioning the kid to go back to his room to clipping up to the top of the stairs, where she rubbed the palms of his hands roughly. Rory wouldn't have let Jo touch him when he was that age. Any contact with Mum would have been 'icky'. The boy looked pre-pubescent, but Jo would have expected him to be younger because of the fact that he was still dressing up. The kid's fingers looked double-jointed, and he was bending his hands at the wrists at a peculiar angle. He was grimacing. *Special needs*, Jo thought, feeling a wave of sympathy for Liz. *She'd had more than her fair share of crosses to carry.*

'Something belonging to you has been found in Amanda Wells's car,' Jo told Frieda, who lurched towards the notebook, craning her neck to read Jo's notes.

'What? What's my name doing in there? Am I a suspect? This is unbelievable.'

Liz came back down the stairs as the boy headed off towards a bedroom.

Jo sighed. 'If you don't mind me saying, neither of you seems particularly concerned with the fact that a woman was murdered so close to home. Neither of you has asked me how the investigation is going. Anyone would think, from the way the pair of you are acting, that you'd simply been greatly inconvenienced by Amanda Wells's death.'

Frieda snapped the card from her and headed out.

Liz shook both hands in frustration. 'I knew Amanda to see. Our conversations consisted of, "Nice day, isn't it? . . . Garden's looking nice . . . Pity about the rain." I'm not going to pretend I'm cut up over it when I'm not. I've enough on my plate.'

'Dealing with Derek?' Jo asked.

Liz sighed heavily and turned for her kitchen. Jo raised her eyebrows at Sexton and followed as he closed the front door gently. Dialling Derek's as she walked, Jo held her own phone away from her ear to listen. A phone trilled to life. Liz snatched it off the kitchen table and glanced from it to Jo, who disconnected the call.

'No prizes for guessing who's the apple of your eye,' Jo said cheerily, motioning towards the photos of the boy upstairs stuck to the fridge with bright magnets. He'd been snapped on a horse . . . playing the piano . . . aiming a crossbow.

Liz moved to a press and, without saying a word, pulled out a clanging pot. She turned a tap on full force and held the pot under it. 'I've to get his dinner on.'

Jo raised her voice over the water. 'I need to find out where Derek was on Friday, Saturday and Sunday.'

'With me.'

'The whole time?' Jo asked.

Liz nodded vigorously, banging the pot down on the work surface. She reached for a potato and started peeling it into a bin. Sexton arrived in the room, grabbed an apple from a bowl, and started munching.

Jo moved to the window and looked across the gardens. 'Let's start with Friday evening, shall we? What time did Derek get home?' Liz blurted, 'He didn't do it.'

'Do what?' Jo asked.

'Oh, give over.' Liz threw the potato and knife into the sink. 'I've been through this all before. I know the way your lot work. You're all the same. Be all nice one minute, so as to walk me up the garden path the next, trying to get me to say something that I didn't mean. Derek had nothing to do with what happened to Amanda. He was here with me all weekend. We've got a Sky box and we plonked ourselves down in front of all the stuff we missed during the week because we were too busy working.'

'Derek's not working, though, is he?' Jo remarked. 'Nice place this,' she added.

'You want to know how we afforded it, is that it? We bought our first house for half nothing, and sold it for a small fortune when times were good, that's how.'

'For someone with nothing to worry about, you're wound up like a spring,' Jo said.

No answer.

'As bad as things may look where you are, lying is

going to make them a hell of a lot worse,' Jo said. 'You could be charged as an accessory. Who's going to take care of your son then?'

Liz walked over to the kitchen table and sank into a chair. She studied her fingers.

'I need you to give a statement,' Jo said more gently. 'Will you come down to the station tonight?'

'I've got to organize a minder for Conor. I don't want him involved.'

'That's no problem,' Jo said.

Sexton thumped his chest and started to cough hard.

'I'm scared,' Liz said to Jo.

'All you have to do is tell the truth,' Jo said, giving her one of the new contact cards too.

Walking out the front door, Jo turned to Sexton, who was staring at her. 'What?' she asked.

'I can't believe you just did that. You walked away, just when you'd got her eating out of your hand. You should be taking her statement now, before she has time to change her mind or her pervert husband changes it for her. She was about to shop Derek.'

'I don't have an arrest warrant for her, and she doesn't have a solicitor. If I take it now, some clever barrister will argue it's not admissible in court and in all likelihood a judge will agree.'

'You sure that's the reason?' Sexton said.

'I'm going to pretend I didn't hear that. I want her to believe we're on her side. She's the key to this case, and

175

I get the impression she's a decent skin. Anyway,' she said, nodding her head at the waterworks van. 'We've got friends who'll tip us off if she heads out.'

Sexton glanced over at the council workman, his expression changing as the penny dropped. 'You're joking! He's one of ours?'

'You should have clocked it from his office shoes, or the fact that this place is off council limits, like all new developments. It's maintained by a management company. The residents pay fees like in an apartment block. It's a surveillance van. We're monitoring computers and phones. If Liz tries to contact Derek, we might just find out exactly where he is'

23

2002: London

The old dear had gone to make some tea. The cub reporter was on his first doorstep, and he was not leaving empty-handed. He stretched both arms up over her fireplace, taking regular checks over his shoulder to make sure she hadn't come back as he removed a framed photo from her wall. His nails were non-existent, so trying to prise back those metal bits keeping the backboard in place was a nightmare. The sound of footsteps made him freeze; he tried to hang it back up, but the string wouldn't catch the nail. He sat down quickly, letting the photograph slide to the far side of the couch. There was a lighter patch on the wall where it had been.

'I never asked you if you wanted milk in your tea,' she said, all croaky.

'Yes, please,' the cub said, like butter wouldn't melt. He smoothed the creases from the suit he'd picked

up for a pound in the charity shop in Notting Hill.

He got back at the picture as soon as she was gone again, managed to dig the snaps free with his flesh, bleeding all over it in the process, but flicking the photo free of the glass. He was here after work, on his own initiative, something his boss was always banging on about. He'd seen enough of the way it worked in the newsroom if you wanted to get on. It didn't matter whether you were a university graduate on an intern programme from a fancy journalism college. It didn't matter whether your name was Jasper or Cosmo, or where you lived, or what you drove, or even if you drove. It didn't even matter whether you could write, or whether you could talk about how much you'd read. The only thing that mattered was your last story. And if you phoned a copy taker, you never even had to write a word.

The irony was he'd passed a couple of hacks on the doorstep, even one from his own paper who hadn't recognized him.

The old lady was back. Without a tray. The cub stood; it was all over anyway.

'My daughter-in-law rang and said I should have asked you for ID.'

'Course,' the cub said, reaching into his suit jacket for the laminated card he'd organized just in case.

She squinted down her nose at it. She still hadn't noticed the wall yet. Good thing too, or he'd have had some explaining to do.

'What did you say your name was?'

'Maurice,' the cub said.

'And I won a competition?'

'That's right, I was just sent to find out which prize you fancied most. The holiday, the car or the cash. It's up to you, sweetheart.'

'My daughter-in-law is going to help me choose, she lives just around the corner.' The doorbell went. 'That's her now.'

She tottered out to open it. The cub jumped up and paced into the kitchen, slipping out the back door, and then vaulting the garden hedge and taking off.

He admired the pick-up hidden under his jacket once he was in the clear. A notorious killer as a boy – classic. So what if he'd stolen the picture from a little old lady? The killer was an evil bastard, deserved whatever he had coming to him.

A reporter's job was to get the story, and that was the beginning and end of it. If people didn't notice what was going on under their noses, it was their problem. He didn't need to apply for a job in Downing Street, or the Defence Forces, or Buckingham Palace to get a story. Just like the fake sheikh, he was already someone else.

24

Jo pushed the door of the detective unit open and stared in disbelief. Alfie had started a bloody conference – without her! He was standing at the top of the room, shirt sleeves rolled up, nodding like a bloody donkey as members of her team answered his questions. The room was chock-a-block with a new set of faces – detectives from his station, she presumed. Instead of Alfie setting the pace, time was being wasted briefing him, from what she could see. She walked her shoulder blades against the tension, rolling her neck. The nagging pulse in her head had turned to a steady throb.

'Breathe,' Sexton said quietly, gripping her elbow lightly and leaning in to her ear. 'He only wants what you do, to catch the killer.'

'No, he wants it to be open and shut. It's not.'

'For who, Jo? Even Liz Carpenter thinks her fucking husband did it.'

Jo shrugged him off, and walked in.

Alfie looked up as she entered. 'You're late, Birmingham.'

'My office,' she demanded.

Alfie shot her a look. A nervous ripple of laughter stopped as quickly as it had started.

Jo kept going. Alfie stayed put.

'Still no sign of Derek?' Alfie called after her.

After opening her office door, she turned around. 'Liz Carpenter is prepared to cooperate. This way, we won't have to use up the number of hours we can detain him unless, and until, we need to.'

'She's been protecting him for twenty years,' Alfie said. 'So, forgive me for saying so, but I'll believe it when I see it.'

Jo slammed the door, aware her every move was being scrutinized by the team outside. She held her hair off her face as she studied the notes still on the wipe board, turning as Foxy followed her in. Sexton was hanging back, she noted.

'Look at it positively, Jo,' Foxy said 'All those extra resources out there can be put to good use.'

'Alfie brought a hack to a crime scene,' Jo fumed. 'If he feels he owes it to the press to tell them the latest developments, we might as well invite the public into the incident room to watch.'

'So what are you going to do?'

'I'll tell you what I'm not going to do. I'm not going to stand out there and pretend I've got respect for

181

someone who wants the easy solution to be the answer, and to have this case sewn up because he's retiring on Friday. Can you brief me on any updates? How did the inquiries go? Any other offenders come up with the same MO?'

Foxy shook his head. 'There are lots of incidences of killers who stuffed gags in the mouth, and lots of killers who strangle with bras on the database here and in the UK, but not one with both in combination. It seems to be someone who hasn't come up on the radar for this kind of offence before.'

'Go on, say it,' Jo prompted. 'You think it was Derek, too.'

'That's not what I said.'

'That's what you think, though.'

He didn't answer.

Jo sighed. 'What about Ellen Lamb's shoe? Any luck finding it?'

'It's gone to the lab for analysis.'

'Great.'

Out of the side of her eye she could see Alfie pointedly glaring in her direction. Jo continued to stare at the wipe board. 'What about the CCTV from the surrounding area? Did it throw any light on who was with Amanda in the restaurant?'

'They're still trawling through it. They've narrowed it down in terms of time, but it was a busy night and they're trying to enhance the couples who came into shot passing the restaurant door at the relevant times. But there are hundreds, it's time-consuming.'

'What about colleagues? They might know something about her love life.'

'There's only a secretary.'

'Slot her in for an interview with me, this evening, along with Liz and her neighbour.'

'She's a "he",' Foxy said. 'Jo, you're taking on too much. Your ophthalmologist rang to see where you were.'

'Shit,' Jo said. She'd forgotten about her appointment. 'Any news from the dragnet on the ground? Did the questionnaires yield any new information on the door to doors?'

'Alfie stopped them,' Foxy said.

'Why?' Jo said, outraged.

'He was afraid any visible presence would scare Derek off.'

'What about the covert team? Did the waterworks team in Nuns Cross tap any unusual phone conversations, or spot any emails that we could use?'

'They've been told to report directly to Alfie. He's playing that one very close to his chest. You'll have to ask him yourself.'

Jo gave a humph of exasperation and put her hands on her hips. 'And Sue? How did she get on with Alfie's reporter pal, Niall Toland?'

'Sue tried to interview him in the *Daily Record*

offices, but said she couldn't get a straight answer from him. Sue said her ex recorded every phone call with his sources, though, and that a lot of them were paid.'

'For fuck's sake, am I going to have to do everything myself?' Jo headed for the door.

'Where are you going?'

'The paper's only around the block. With any luck, I'll catch that Niall Toland before he clears off for the evening.'

'What will I tell Alfie?'

'I'll tell him myself,' Jo answered, pressing the door handle. 'As long as there's a chance Liz Carpenter is coming in here later, he can't stop me.'

25

Down the close at Number 31 Nuns Cross, Frieda McLoughlin had just guided Liz into her kitchen, and Liz was settling Conor down at the table with what remained of his homework. Through the window, Liz could see Frieda's husband, Charles, tossing some burgers at a barbecue in the back garden. A few feet away, a group of neighbours were talking at a patio heater. Frieda had contacted them to see if anyone else was in the same boat, blackmail-wise. Four sets of neighbours had admitted they'd been under the same pressure. Suggesting that if they suddenly started assembling it might arouse suspicion among the gardaí, who'd been in and out of Nuns Cross all day, Frieda had come up with the barbecue plan. 'Neighbours gathering for something like that looks normal,' she'd said. Liz craned her neck trying to see who was there, but pulled back quickly when she spotted George the clamper. *Not him*, she thought. He terrified her. She glanced at the clock. It was 6.30 p.m.

'How much longer to the circus, Mum?' Conor asked.

'Not long,' Liz said, rubbing his back. 'We'll have to head down to the garda station for a bit after, but it won't take much time.'

'Aw, Mum. I don't want to go there. Why can't I stay home? When's Dad coming back?'

Liz swallowed. She combed his short hair with her fingers. The love she felt for Conor made her heart ache. She'd do anything for him – whatever it took to keep him safe. Her heart and her head were at war over the things she'd found out today. The past had come back to haunt her, and she kept reliving the last time she'd spoken to her sister, something she dreaded thinking about.

Liz closed her eyes as the memory swept over her again.

'Hurry up, big hole,' Ellen was shouting through the locked bathroom door again. That day, Friday, 1 November 1992, was a date that would matter a hell of a lot more than any Christmas or birthday in the Lamb house from then on.

Liz had guessed from the pitch of Ellen's voice that she was peering through the keyhole. She'd reached for a towel to drape it over the handle quickly, just in case, wondering if Ellen was always going to be the bane of her life. She'd been trying to pad her boobs evenly in the bathroom for the previous fifteen minutes. It had seemed so important at the time, because Derek Carpenter, her first love, was due to pick her up after school, and she'd wanted to look right. He'd said he was taking her somewhere special.

Ellen had been bitchy ever since Liz and Derek had got together. Liz had never had a boyfriend before. Ellen had been trying to break them up. She'd also followed Liz and Derek from school with a gang of her mates, taunting them from behind. Ellen just wasn't used to Liz, who was ten stone, and carried her puppy fat in all the wrong places, getting any male attention, and especially not from someone cool and streetwise like Derek. Ellen, who had an hour-glass figure and weighed eight stone, had always acted as if she was in direct competition with Liz over everything. Clothes were not an issue because of their different sizes, but shoes were a never-ending source of dispute.

When Liz had decided she wanted to study nursing after school, Ellen had announced she wanted to become a midwife.

And since Ellen was the baby of the family, she'd also got away with a lot more stuff. Take the night Ellen had said she was having a sleepover with a girlfriend, but it turned out she'd pitched a tent in the grounds of the Hellfire Club with a group of guys and girls from her year, in order to get pissed as a fart on a six-pack of Amstel and shots of Jägermeister. Their parents had found out after Tallaght Hospital had phoned to say Ellen's stomach was being pumped. If it had been Liz, she'd have been given the third degree, but Ellen had been mollycoddled like she'd had her appendix out.

And just the previous week, Ellen had stayed out all night on two occasions, worrying their parents sick. They'd almost called the gardaí, convinced she'd been murdered or abducted. Looking back, it had been like some kind of freaky prophecy.

But Ellen had turned up for school on both days, claiming she didn't know what the fuss had been about, she'd just lost track of time and stayed over with friends. Her friends had been cagey about the details.

From the far side of the bathroom door on that last day, Liz had turned on a tap to drown out the sound of Ellen demanding she get a move on. She'd wanted more time to go through their mother's make-up bag. She'd rummaged around for the foundation and black kohl eyeliner. Applying it had taken a lot longer than she'd thought it would, as she normally didn't wear any, and her eye kept closing and watering whenever she'd so much as tipped the nib off her skin. Ellen, on the other hand, had become adept at applying upper-lid liquid liner with Christine Keeler-style precision. Several smudges later, Liz had grown more and more frustrated as Ellen had got more and more bolshie on the far side of the door.

'I swear to God, I'm going to tell Mum and

Dad exactly how big a slut you are,' Ellen had called.

After backcombing her hair, Liz had flushed the toilet to keep up the pretence, and emerged from the bathroom, all set to head downstairs for her breakfast.

'The state of you,' Ellen had said, bunching her long hair in a scrunchie. 'You're meeting him again, aren't you? When are you going to finish with that loser? Everyone's going to think we're both skangers if you keep going out with that swamp life. He's a toerag. He's been in a juvenile-detention centre, and it's only a matter of time before he ends up in Mountjoy. He's going to beat the shit out of you, and he'll be one of those blokes who burns their other half in the back garden, or buries them under a patio.'

'Mind your own business,' Liz had said, brushing by.

'I'm going to make him my business. If you won't dump him, I'll have a chat with him myself and give him a few home truths about how our family will never accept him, and how you'll be dead to us if you stay with him.'

Liz still felt the hairs on the back of her neck stand on end the exact way they had all those years ago. She'd turned and lunged at Ellen, grabbing a clump of her hair.

'Stay the fuck out of my life or I'll kill you,' Liz had said.

It made Liz sick now to remember it. If she'd known she was never going to see her sister again, she'd have told her how much she loved her; she'd have put her arms around her and refused to let go. Instead, she'd spent more than half her life having to cope with a last conversation that was horrible and hateful. It wasn't like she could even talk to anyone else about it. After Ellen had vanished, all the bad stuff about her had disappeared, too. Anyone who'd reminisced had only ever talked about the perfect daughter, pupil and friend. Ellen had become the perfect sister, and Liz had discovered what it really meant to live in her shadow.

Liz had only released her grip on Ellen's scalp that last day at the sound of their father's voice calling up the stairs, 'Which one of you two can call to the shops after school for a few bits for the dinner?'

Liz had kept her eyes locked on Ellen's and had shouted down, 'I've got study club after school today.'

For a split second, she'd thought Ellen was going to give the game away. There was a defiant glint in her stare. But Ellen had just stormed into the bathroom, slamming the door behind her.

Derek hadn't turned up outside the school that day to collect Liz, like they'd planned. He'd turned up at her house later, apologizing for being late, not explaining why. He'd made no mention of seeing Ellen, and Liz hadn't asked him if she'd stopped by. When things had heated up after the reporter had put him in the frame, he'd asked Liz to cover for him, claiming he'd lost track of the time – and she'd agreed.

But today, after everything she'd found out, Liz knew in her heart that Ellen had gone to see Derek just like she'd threatened. Maybe that's why Derek had . . .

Snapping back to the present was easier than letting her head go there. 'I'll have all the answers for you soon, darling,' she told Conor.

Through the window she watched Charles shooting the breeze with George, who was slugging from the neck of a bottle of Bulmer's. George slapped Charles's shoulder and whispered something when he clocked Liz looking out, and Charles turned to look, giving her a quick salute.

Liz pretended not to have seen. George scared her, and she could barely look at Charles now she knew his sideline was ripping people off. He was wearing a pair of knee-length combat shorts, flip-flops and a shiny plastic apron that turned his torso into a buxom French maid, and acting like he hadn't a care in the world. It made her sick to the stomach to think of all the Jennys and Pauls of this world, who'd signed up to a lifetime of debt for a home they would never be able to live in, thanks to him. Bile rose in her throat, reminding her that since her own husband probably had more to hide than anyone, she wasn't exactly in a position to judge.

Liz looked over Conor's shoulder at his meticulous handwriting. 'I always said you were a bit of a genius,' she said, sniffing. 'Want a snack?'

Even though he'd had some of Frieda's lasagne, he was too literal for the kind of food that got served at a barbecue. If you told Conor he was good as gold, he went looking for the gold. One time, he'd been asked to take part in a school table quiz, but had declined because he didn't know enough about tables. If you used a phrase like, 'Hold your horses,' he'd answer, 'I don't have any horses.' Hot dogs were, therefore, non-runners . . .

He shook his head. 'Not now, Mum, thanks anyway. Maybe later.'

Frieda took her by the elbow to lead her outside to the others, whispering that she suspected some of the neighbours were lying, and that it would turn out even more were affected than just this bunch.

The sky may have been the colour of granite and dusk falling but Frieda had slipped right into character, just like her husband, and was tottering around in a shirt knotted at the front, denim shorts and red espadrilles. She'd even lit an insect stick, though it was too cold for the midges. Even her legs had broken out in goosebumps, Liz noticed.

'So I heard Derek totalled his car,' Charles said over his shoulder as they arrived out. 'Are you going to go for a jeep again? Stay away from those Mitsubishi Pajeros, will you? Only cream crackers and drug dealers drive them, it would bring the tone of the whole place down.'

He chortled, only Liz was pretty sure he wasn't joking. Once, when she, Derek and Conor had gone on holiday a few years back, they'd come home to find the shrubs she'd planted in the front garden had been trimmed to within an inch of their lives. A note in the letterbox from Charles had said they'd started to make the street look shabby.

'So, Charles,' she piped up, rubbing warmth into the tops of her arms. If she had to make idle conversation, she'd a few questions of her own. 'Were you able to do anything for Jenny and Paul?'

On the day of their neighbours' eviction, when all hell had been breaking loose next door, Charles had offered to put a call in to the bank to help broker a new arrangement for them to get their house back. But having got everybody's hopes up, he hadn't bothered to come out of his house again to tell them what the result of his conversation with 'senior bank executives' had been.

Charles drained the last of his beer, and dangled the bottle upside down so Frieda could see he needed another. 'Nope, Jen and Paul let their situation go too far. It was their fault, essentially. Nothing the bank could do. That house could turn out to be a bloody nightmare because of where it is.'

Jenny and Paul's house bordered what remained of an old convent which had given the estate its name. An unresolved right-of-way issue meant it could potentially be used as a cut-through by anyone who wanted to get from one side of Rathfarnham to another.

'It's only a matter of time before squatters move in,' Charles continued. 'An empty house like that is just asking for trouble. Jenny and Paul should be fined for being so irresponsible, if you ask me.'

Liz saw red. 'I suppose if they'd been able to gamble other people's money, lose it all, and get a government bailout on their debts and a fat-cat bonus for their trouble, maybe they wouldn't have been so screwed,' she said.

Charles jerked his head back from an angry tongue of flame that had just shot up with a loud sizzle of burning fat.

'Whoa,' he said, reaching up to check if his hair was singed.

'Can I have a word about your car?' George asked.

Liz hadn't had a chance to get it towed from the hospital yet. She wasn't about to put George off the sale by telling him it wouldn't start. The sooner she got rid of it and any forensic evidence it might potentially yield, the better.

'Can I collect it tonight?' he asked, stepping closer.

'Tomorrow suits better, George. I've something on tonight.' She moved off before he'd a chance to object.

The garden was a bog-standard suburban rectangle, about fifty feet long and the width of the house. A granite rockery planted with Alpine shrubs, dwarf grass, and bright, wild mountain flowers – purple bunches of tumbling aubrietia, delicate yellow helianthemum and bursts of pink soapwort – ran along the border fenced with woven hazel. There was a bottle-green mini-marquee taking up most of the striped lawn, and white plastic fold-up chairs had been lined up inside it in front of a long buffet table where bowls of cling-film-covered salad, stacks of plates and bundles of cutlery sat waiting for the guests.

Liz headed for some decking just outside the French doors because there was nobody there, and sat down on the edge of a sunlounger, keeping her back to George, who had walked over to a small feature pond to throw chunks of bread roll to big, dishwater-coloured whiskered fish that kept coming to the surface to feed.

Liz wondered what the Madigans, a pair of retired dentists who lived in a corner house, could want to keep hidden. They had no children, spent winters in an apartment in Marbella, and were more often seen heading in or out in their tennis whites than their civvies.

She gave a quick wave to Kim and Kate, a lesbian couple who looked like pop stars with their sharp hair styles, face piercings and tattoos. They ran a hygiene business, collecting and dropping off sanitary-towel bins to and from public places, and drove top-of-the-range sports cars.

Nigel and Maud were there, too, and Liz pondered what the mother and son, who'd given her such a hard time in the shop this morning, could have done that was dodgy.

Frieda clanked a couple of bottles together and gave a little wave to indicate everyone should move into the mini-marquee. 'Liz has to leave early, so we'd better get started.'

'Where are you off to?' George asked, sidling up to Liz.

'I'm taking Conor to the circus, and then I've to go to the garda station,' Liz said quickly, looking away.

He put a hand in his pocket and took out a bunch of fifties, offering them to her. 'I've got cash here for the car. I want to take my girlfriend out for a lesson tonight. Where is it?'

Liz pointed to Charles and Frieda at the top of the tent, clapping their hands for attention.

'Let's get started,' Charles said. 'We all know why we're here, best not to rake over it, given what happened to Amanda. It goes without saying that it's tragic, but we wondered if what's going on with us might be connected. I'm going to be the first to lay my cards on the table to get this thing started.'

He gave a little cough. 'So I'm going to be completely upfront, but only if you're all willing to do the same, otherwise what's to stop everyone else here from getting in on the blackmail act?'

After a show of nods he cleared his throat. 'Someone's been blackmailing me over my bank's involvement in the sale of three hundred and fifty mortgages for a property developer whom my bank had also funded. The paperwork would suggest that the bank was aware the developer had already gone bust when it sold the mortgages to the homeowners – who never got their homes. On paper it all looks clear-cut. The reality, of course, is that it was a complete over-sight. I just didn't put two and two together. My commission is long spent, so it's not as if I could even pay it back.'

He doesn't sound very convincing, Liz thought.

'Obviously, if I'd known, I wouldn't have allowed people to put good money after bad. Right, that's my guilty secret out in the open,' he went on. He clapped his hands together and rubbed them. 'So, now you know what they've got on me, who'd like to go next so as to even the playing field?'

After a prolonged pause, George stood up. 'Someone is accusing my staff of breaking into cars to replace valid tickets with old ones, so as to clamp them. They want the same amount as you, Charles, a hundred thousand euro. I don't have it, but shit sticks. If they start mouthing off, I'll lose my tender with the council. That will cost me a lot more in the long run.'

He sat back down. Frieda gave a little clap.

Liz looked away in disgust. She believed every word of what George had been accused of. He was a gutter-snipe.

'The person wants a hundred thousand euro from us, too,' Kate said, standing.

'Why?' Frieda asked.

Kate hesitated until Kim touched her hand. 'Our first big job in business was with the women's prison. We got to know a lot of the girls. If we could help them get things in and out, we did.' She paused so the neighbours could put it together. 'Now we've got contracts with all the hospitals. We're like George. We couldn't afford to lose that business. It would finish us.'

Liz clicked her tongue. If they'd been smuggling drugs and phones into a prison, they were no better than the prisoners in there, as far as she was concerned. The papers were always going on about murders that had been ordered by prisoners. That young Latvian mother killed on the doorstep of her Swords home was one. The gardaí had had to carry her little boys over her body so the forensic people could do their job. It had been horrible.

Mr Madigan stood up. 'I had a practice in Dubai that I didn't declare to the Revenue. The blackmailer wants the same amount from us as everyone else. A hundred thousand euro. It's our nest egg.' He sat down again, and his wife put her arm around him.

'Tax evasion is the lowest of the low,' Liz muttered under her breath.

Nigel flicked his hand up.

'A pyramid scheme,' his mother explained, snivelling.

'We had to change our names. If they find us, we're in Shitsville, Illinois.'

All eyes turned to Liz.

'It's just that I don't know exactly,' Liz stammered, 'I only found out about all this today. If Derek was here . . .'

'Of course there's a strong possibility you weren't being blackmailed at all,' Charles said decisively.

'You did notice that you came into a lot of money lately,' Frieda added.

'One hundred thousand euro,' Charles chipped in, for the benefit of everyone else.

Liz looked at him in astonishment, aware her neighbours were glancing at each other.

'I rang a pal in your bank,' Charles said.

Liz fidgeted.

'And Derek's disappeared, hasn't he?' Frieda said sadly. 'Which suggests he's something to hide. And, much as I hate to point out the obvious, Amanda's body was found in the place linked to your sister, right?'

Charles crossed his arms. 'I think it's safe to presume that whoever murdered Amanda was probably blackmailing her, too. Derek is gone, so . . .'

'He had a bang to the head, he's not himself,' Liz protested, checking through the kitchen window that Conor was still out of earshot.

Charles didn't seem to be buying it. 'We need to stop Derek, without involving the authorities and risking a criminal investigation into our private business. We have to meet like with like.'

'How are we going to do that?' Maud asked. 'We're just normal people.'

'There are always ways,' Kim said sullenly.

Kate, whose bleached-blonde hair was shaved on one side and long on the other, nodded mournfully.

'What does that mean?' Liz asked.

Frieda sighed heavily, picking between her teeth with her cocktail stick. 'Don't be so naïve, Liz. Everyone knows about that housewife from Clare, who was able to Google the word "hitman" and hire one.'

Even though the same thought had occurred to Liz, now that the offer to bump her husband off was being handed to her on a plate, she felt violently ill. 'I have to go,' she said, standing up quickly.

'There's an elephant in this room, and I'm just going to say it, OK?' George said. 'What if the gardaí put you under pressure later, and you crack and tell them what was said here tonight? If that happens every one of us is facing a hefty jail sentence.'

26

At the surveillance van with the waterworks' logo on the side, Alfie – dressed in Dublin Corporation overalls – rapped on the back doors and, when one opened, climbed inside and pushed through the black sheet blocking the view.

'I heard you've got me a new lead?' he said, taking a cap off and sitting opposite a fresh-faced officer in his twenties, who twisted around from a panel of screens and buttons to face him.

Alfie wondered why someone with his qualifications would want a thankless job working for a pittance in the police.

'That's right. We've picked up some very interesting email correspondence between the victim and one of the residents, who lived on the road behind her,' the officer said.

'Derek Carpenter?' Alfie asked. He hated computers, and didn't want to get into anything that would show up how little he knew about them, especially in front of someone who still had bumfluff on his face.

'No, not Derek. Here you go,' the officer said, handing the paperwork over.

'So what do these emails say?' Alfie asked with a lukewarm smile as he scanned them.

'It looks like Amanda Wells was paying one of the residents to dig the dirt on one of her neighbours.'

'What?' Alfie scanned the printouts and pursed his lips.

The officer shrugged. 'I thought it might be evidence of motive,' he said. 'Amanda Wells might have made herself some enemies.'

'It is. So I take it then that Derek Carpenter was the neighbour Amanda wanted the dirt on, right?' Alfie asked, rephrasing the question.

'No, actually Charles and Frieda McLoughlin were the subjects,' the officer said. 'And like I said, the neighbour working for Amanda wasn't Derek Carpenter, either. There's something else. There's also contact between this neighbour and a reporter called Niall Toland on the *Daily Record*, the one who got the tip-off about her body. They're only blank texts, but too frequent to be coincidental. It could be they were some kind of coded message – telling the other person to get in contact.'

'Which neighbour was Niall in contact with?'

The officer handed him a sheet of paper with the name and address.

'Ouch,' Alfie said, standing up too quickly and hitting the crown of his head on the roof. He rubbed it to ease the pain, and read the words on the paper. 'Amanda Wells is our victim, just remember that.'

He hopped out, banging the van door shut, pulled out his phone and dialled Niall Toland's number.

'Lunch tomorrow is on you,' Alfie spoke into the mobile. 'The usual place. If you put the receipt on your expenses I don't want my name down on any documentation. I may be retiring on Friday, but all these government bailouts have made shit of my pension, and I'm still bound by the Official Secrets Act. And while I'm on the subject of me giving you dig outs, I'm going to need to make our arrangement more formal. I quite fancy writing a column giving my opinions on the crimes of the week and what they say about society at large. You can run it by your editor today and let me know what he thinks when we meet.'

27

2011: Dublin, Ireland

The freelance reporter scanned the letter he'd just written one last time.

Mr Levi Bellfield Esquire,
HMP Wakefield aka Monster Mansion ;)
5 Love Lane,
West Yorkshire,
WF2 9AG
ENGLAND

Dear Levi,

I seen you on the box and wanted to write about how I believe you're INNOCENT of all them bus-stop murders. If you ask me you've been STITCHED UP due to unfair press coverage. I saw the girl you picked singing and dancing at the ironing board and on the CCTV with her short skirt and big smile, but what I

didn't see was the film of you jumping out of the
bushes to whack her over the head like they said you
did. So you had an empty flat fifty yards from where
she was last seen – BIG DEAL! So you trained whippet
puppies for coursing at Yately Heath where the
mushroom-pickers found her – BIGGER DEAL!! So
you drove a red car and someone in a red car tried to
abduct an eleven-year-old girl, the day before she was
murdered – BIGGEST DEAL!!!! It's all circumstantial,
and not hard evidence. If you don't mind me saying it,
you've been framed, mate. I read how your girlfriend
said you slashed photographs of blonde models in
magazines and said they were sluts, that does not
make you guilty of eight murders, it makes you
HONEST, ha ha! I heard your nickname is MR
TRUTHFUL, I rest my case your honour. I heard you
told your pal women were like pet dogs, well what I
have to say to that is it depends what they look like,
hehehe. They said your mam used to wipe your bum
until you were twelve, LUCKY YOU!!! As for the
story about you moving the mouth of the girl whose
drink was spiked and who you rode in the cubicle of
the club where you worked as a bouncer, ever thought
of a career as a ventriloquist, mwahha!!! They said
you were knocking down girls at bus stops and
reversing over them, what I want to know is did you
damage your sump, LOL! But seriously the last thing I
wanted to tell you is keep the chin up, mate. There is

absolutely NO PROOF to link you to that fourteen-year-old girl in 1980, other than her being in the wrong place at the wrong time, i.e. your school – PMSL! Keep the faith, you're the victim of a TRIAL BY MEDIA, mate, and when you get to sue the state for a MISCARRIAGE OF JUSTICE case, you'll be a millionaire, too. I would very much like to make your acquaintance, by the way, and if you could write back to me at the address on the back of the envelope, I would be much obliged.

    Yours sincerely, A.N. Other

PS Nice haircut

After folding the letter and placing it in the envelope, the reporter licked it closed and popped it in the letter-box. He'd lost count of the number of 'vile paedophiles' he'd lured into correspondence with letters just like this. He'd got splashes out of every one of them. He was working for the Irish edition now he'd moved over, but keeping his foot in the door of HQ with a story for the UK earned him lots of brownie points, and in the current climate that was no bad thing.

28

The Grimsby Family Circus big top was pitched in a field off the M50, a ten-minute walk from Nuns Cross. Liz couldn't quite believe she'd come to the circus, of all places, with the day she'd had, but she couldn't let Conor down. After he'd spotted it was 7.00 – the time printed on their tickets – he'd become distraught in Frieda's place, claiming that Liz had 'tricked' him, and that she'd never had any intention of bringing him to the circus. If a normal kid had behaved like that, they'd have been branded spoilt, but Conor's two settings were black and white. Anything in-between and he floundered. He could handle the world when there were rules. It was spontaneity and change and chance that made him have a meltdown. He never got out of bed until the clock read 7.30 exactly. If an earthquake had struck, he'd have stayed put – virtually paralysed – until the time was right. Car journeys were only doable if he knew where they were going and they took the same route as the previous time they'd been there. His mum and dad had told him he was going to the circus – so he was going to the circus.

'If you don't tell me where Dad is, I'm going to run away,' he'd sobbed, becoming inconsolable in Frieda's garden.

Liz had lost track of the time, exhausted from all the trailing about, but she jumped at the chance to flee the barbecue, shocked to discover that she knew so little about the people she'd signed up to a lifetime of debt to live alongside. She needed a trip to the circus like a hole in the head, but she didn't know what tomorrow would bring, and she knew that if she cancelled the excursion, Conor would think he'd done something wrong and blame himself for whatever life threw at them next. She had to keep some sense of stability and continuity in his life, now that it was set to change so much.

Clutching his hand, Liz handed over the tickets, hating the way that the woman at the counter with false eyelashes was staring. Conor had started 'stimming' – flapping his hands, jerking his head and rolling his eyes. He did that when he was in ecstasy. It was all the flashing neon. His fingers felt like they'd been connected to an electric current. She used to say, 'Quiet hands,' to him to make him stop, so ignorant people like the one in front of her now wouldn't gape. But not any more. Other mothers didn't tell their children to stop being happy.

'Thanks for bringing me, Mum,' he said. 'I wouldn't really have run away. I'd have come back after checking if Dad was here.'

Her heart surged with equal amounts of love and sadness. He was such a special, sweet boy, with more empathy in his little finger than most 'normal' people who could make eye contact. He was the gentlest person she'd ever seen around babies and animals. How could Derek have brought such dangerous people into their son's life? It just didn't add up. She knew he loved Conor as much as she did. That niggling voice struck up again. Maybe Derek was innocent . . .

As they neared the ringside flap, the music blaring from inside became deafening. The stink of elephant dung and musky perfume was overpowering. Conor stopped walking, his body tensed. Liz sensed he was summoning up all his courage. She reached into a pocket for a set of earplugs and popped them into his ears. Autistic kids had amplified hearing. A psychologist had explained that this was why they found concentration so difficult.

'Imagine trying to focus on anything in a disco, other than the noise and lights, because that's what's going on around them.'

Worried he'd want to go home before they'd even got in, and then spend the night regretting it – and not wanting to set him up for failure – Liz looked around for something to distract him for long enough to allow him to overcome his fear of noise. She spotted a tent with a fortune-teller's sign, and recognized the name.

A round of applause broke out from the ringside. According to the ringmaster's megaphone, the trapeze artist had just performed some kind of big-deal, mid-air somersault. Conor put his hands over his ears.

'Hey, why don't we go in there for a bit, it's quieter?' she said, removing one of the hands he'd sealed to his ears, and pulling out the earplug so she could speak to him. She nodded in the direction of the little tepee.

His face broke out in a relieved smile. Liz had never had any time for clairvoyants before Ellen disappeared, but over the years she had turned to every kind of psychic going, wanting to find some little grain of hope.

'Can you ring Dad, in case he's decided to go home first to get my homework done and doesn't know where we are?' he asked, shouting through the noise.

'There's no signal here, son,' Liz lied, ducking and pushing the flap of the tent aside to see if anyone was in there.

The sight of Dolores, Liz's co-worker in Supersavers, sitting at a little round table with a tasselled scarf knotted at the back of her scalp and big jangly earrings on made Liz smile for the first time all day. Dolores had mentioned getting a nixer here as a medium. A lump rose in Liz's throat. She watched as Dolores, eyes closed, chanted to a woman sitting opposite her at the table with her back to Liz.

Goosebumps spread across Liz's skin. After about a minute of convulsive movements, Dolores slumped like she'd been zapped with a bolt of lightning. Her head flopped forwards.

With a jolt, she sat upright suddenly, her eyelids opening, strands of her long henna-coloured hair coming undone.

Liz let the flap drop down quickly and waited until the woman had emerged before hurrying in with Conor herself, a queue forming behind her.

'Tarot, palm, angel cards, ouija board or crystal ball?' Dolores asked without looking up.

'None,' Liz answered, sitting down opposite her. She reached out for Dolores's fleshy hand, big gold signature rings on every one of her red-taloned fingers, like a set of knuckledusters.

Dolores looked up in surprise. 'Hello, chuck,' she said cheerfully. 'What are you doing here?'

'I need you to get in touch with the dead for me,' Liz said, fumbling for the locket she wore permanently around her neck, clicking it open and pushing it across the table.

Dolores grinned as if she believed Liz was winding her up, and then started to cough convulsively.

'It's not Derek, is it?' Dolores said, when she'd stopped spluttering. She still hadn't glanced at the picture in Liz's locket. She looked embarrassed, and then tried to hide it, leaning over to get at her handbag on the ground and mumbling about needing a sweet for the tickle in her throat.

Liz checked to make sure Conor hadn't made a mental link between the words 'dead' and 'Derek', remembering that he'd asked if Derek was dead earlier.

'Can we go now, Mum?' he said, with a glazed expression.

'Tell me that's not why you're here?' Dolores prattled on as she sat up. 'Derek's all right, isn't he? I mean, I didn't ring after you left the shop this morning because I knew we'd have heard if there'd been any developments . . . you know . . . for the worse?'

Liz pulled a 'not in front of Conor' expression and reassured her that Derek was fine. But Conor was starting to scratch the back of his hand. The skin was already broken and red raw from where he had worn it down during his last meltdown.

Liz separated his hands, and put them on the sides of her own face. It was her way of saying, 'Not much longer.'

Conor started to talk to himself, another one of the figaries that set him apart. Liz stood to wrap her arms around him; jitters had started making their way down his arms. He was starting to unravel, focusing on the sawdust on the floor, she realized. Sand and snowflakes had the same effect. The sight of multiple particles triggered his anxiety about change.

Liz stood to take Conor's hand and walked him over

to the flap, telling him she'd just be another minute.

Dolores picked up the locket and tilted her head as she looked at it, casually sucking the sweet she'd retrieved. Her eyes darted from Liz's face to the picture of Ellen admiring herself in the mirror. She'd been so vain that Liz had snuck up behind her to snap her pose. Ellen wasn't one bit impressed. Her expression said it all: a mixture of indignation and surprise. Liz had cut out the background – their bedroom – and just kept that image of her sister's gorgeous face to fit it into the necklace.

'It's to do with Derek and something that might or might not have happened years ago,' Liz whispered, checking over her shoulder to make sure Conor couldn't hear.

He was rocking on the balls of his feet. Liz spoke quickly, glancing at him regularly to check he was OK: 'I need you to ask her some questions for me, like what happened, and who killed her . . .'

She strained over her shoulder. 'Deep breaths, darling. Not much longer.' She turned back to Dolores again. 'I need you to ask her . . .'

'Ask her what?' Dolores said, sounding incredulous.

From the flap in the tent a voice called, 'Get on with it.'

Liz glanced at Conor again as she struggled to find the right words. Every time she thought about the last time she'd spoken to her sister, she felt as angry as she had back then.

213

'If Derek did it,' Liz whispered, brushing away a tear.

'What if the answer hurts you badly?' Dolores asked softly.

Liz looked away.

Dolores didn't take her eyes off Liz. 'Don't blame yourself. You did nothing.'

'I found out too late,' Liz explained urgently. 'I can't turn back the clock. I didn't know he was capable of that . . .'

'It's not your fault.'

Liz leaned her head on her hands. 'I keep thinking I've got it wrong, everyone's got it wrong, Derek wouldn't—' She looked up. 'I mean he couldn't. Can you just ask Ellen . . .'

'This is taking the piss,' a voice called from outside. 'The lion-tamer's show is about to start.' A string of heckles followed.

'Ask her,' Liz said, determinedly.

Dolores sat back and shook her head.

'Please,' Liz said.

But before Dolores could answer, Conor screeched, 'Dad!'

Liz turned.

Conor's face was animated, pointing to the flap. 'Mum, I just saw Dad looking in at us!'

Then he bolted out.

29

Jo sat in the *Daily Record* boardroom, at the far side of a glinting mahogany table from the reporter named Niall Toland, whom she'd first laid eyes on in the mountains that morning. The two men on either side of him had been introduced as his editor and his lawyer. The paper was pitched at middle Ireland, which meant it put human-interest stories on the front page instead of celebrity sex scandals. But by all accounts the 'compact' (the word 'tabloid' would have upset mid-market readers) had been haemorrhaging sales ever since middle Ireland was decimated by the recession. Not that you'd have guessed it from the flash boardroom with floor-to-ceiling windows. Still, Jo knew from experience that the same hunger that drove the redtops to get the story at any cost drove the broadsheets and the compacts, too.

Niall was in his late thirties, slightly unkempt-looking owing to his head of bushy curls, and bordering on obese. He was wearing a faded white shirt with a criss-cross of rusty stains that looked like ketchup on it, and one of the flaps was not tucked in. Jo longed to tell him to wipe the smug look from his face, that her wanting to speak with him wasn't a feather in his cap.

'Considering I requested an informal meeting, you seem to be taking this pretty seriously,' she said, looking from the spindly lawyer with officious round spectacles to the bear of an editor with the well-known face. He'd been a prop forward on the Irish rugby team in the nineties, and had a pundit's spot on a TV sports show. His opinions were invariably inflammatory, and he never called a match result right.

'Any suggestion that we would interfere with a live criminal investigation has to be taken extremely seriously in the current climate . . .' the editor replied, before hesitating. 'Sorry, what would you like us to call you?'

The hack grinned and looked down, like he had just got some private joke.

'"Chief" is fine,' Jo said. 'I thought the practices that closed the *News of the World* were a one-off.'

The lawyer started wringing his hands.

'That is what you're referring to?' Jo asked the editor.

'Yes, well, no,' the editor stammered. 'I mean, yes, of course, they were a one-off, but no, I didn't think a discussion about what happened to Milly Dowler was on today's agenda. It had nothing to do with us. It's of no interest to us. Our business is—'

The lawyer gave an exaggerated cough. The editor stopped talking. They all had the look of people kicking each other under the table.

Jo stood, and walked behind them to the window looking out on the city's skyline. 'You've got a bird's-eye view from up here,' she said, keeping her back to them. 'From up here everything's got perspective, hasn't it? You get to see the wider picture, the potential ripples and ramifications—'

'What's the point of this?' the lawyer asked.

'I sent a detective here today to find out where Niall got his information about the body in the mountains, and when. It will aid me in my attempt to establish the victim's last movements. That officer was given the runaround. If I leave here without that information, I'm going to make sure, Niall, that you are charged with being an accessory to murder.'

'Don't be ridiculous,' he answered, straining round to make eye contact. 'Everyone knows a journalist can't reveal his sources.'

His accent was northern Irish. Jo guessed Monaghan. Leaning both hands on the back of his chair made him squirm uncomfortably, which was exactly how she wanted him.

'There were other questions which you also refused to answer,' Jo said. 'As far as I'm concerned that means you are protecting a killer.' She paused and looked at the editor, though the question was for Toland. 'I'd have thought that, given the closure of the *News of the World*, you'd have considered it your duty to help me find who killed Amanda Wells. Newspapers have to pull up their socks on issues like journalistic integrity these days, don't they?'

'Of course, we'll help you wherever we can,' the editor replied.

'But I can't reveal my source,' Niall clarified, looking at him, 'under any circumstances.'

'What would your readers think if they knew you were refusing to help me find who killed a woman?' Jo asked. 'Because that's what you're doing.'

'My conscience is clear,' Niall said. 'I did what I was supposed to do. I passed the information on to your lot, and it turned out to be true. You should be thanking me. Chief.'

Jo stood up straight and folded her arms. 'Let's try this again, shall we? Do you know who your source is?'

'I don't want to say.'

'It doesn't mean you have to say who it was,' the editor coaxed.

'Fine. No.'

'So you trusted an anonymous source without reservation?' Jo asked incredulously.

The editor did not looked pleased.

'I checked the information out first, and when it turned out to be true, I passed it over to the gardaí.'

The lawyer's eyes darted over to Jo.

She'd copped it all right. 'Does that mean you went up to the mountains and established the murdered woman was there, first, contaminating a crime scene, before ringing it in?'

'Now I'm a suspect, is that it, chief?'

'I'm not ruling anything out. You knew where we'd find Amanda's body. You won't tell me how. From where I'm sitting you're acting like someone with something to hide. If you had something to do with what happened to Amanda, you've just given the perfect excuse if your DNA's found up there, haven't you?'

He laughed and it made Jo see red. The lawyer lifted a hand to indicate that he wanted to get a word in, but Jo got there first. 'I can have you brought in to the station now, and have your computer and every computer in here seized to find out what information you're withholding, or you can cooperate and help me find the killer.'

The editor leaned forwards quickly. 'There won't be any need for that.'

'What did your source sound like – accent . . . age . . . class?' Jo pressed.

'You really expect me to compromise his identity?'

'Good, we're getting somewhere.'

Niall rolled his eyes.

'Did you tape the call?' Jo asked.

'Yes,' Niall said.

'I want that tape,' Jo said. 'I can go to court to get it, or you can cooperate with my inquiry.'

'It won't be any use,' Niall protested, 'because he always uses a voice distorter.'

'Always? How many times has he been in touch?'

'Twice about the body in the mountains.'

'The first time to tell you where the body was?'

'Yes.'

'The second time for what?'

'To give me a follow-up story on the killer. That story is running in tomorrow's paper.'

'He rang you at home or work?'

'He rang on my mobile.'

'Both times?'

'Yes.'

'How would he have got that number?'

'I've no idea. It's not top secret.'

'And the calls you recorded took place when?'

'Sunday evening and today.'

'Sunday evening!' Jo exploded. 'We didn't get there until this morning.'

'For all I knew it could have been a hoax.'

Jo sighed heavily. 'What did he say at seven thirty on Sunday?'

Niall shrugged. 'He told me where the body was.'

'That's it?'

'Pretty much. Oh, and he said she was one of the missing women.'

'And today, what did he say?'

'He gave me information on the killer.'

'You can tell her,' the editor prompted. 'She's going to read it tomorrow anyway.'

Niall crossed his arms.

The editor smiled. 'I can tell you that Niall's source has told him that the prime suspect for Amanda's murder has gone on the run.'

Jo blinked. 'That's news to me.' She hoped it would get them off the scent. The last thing she wanted was to have to run a media gauntlet at the moment. 'Did you corroborate that information with a second source, Niall?'

'Of course.'

Alfie, Jo decided, sighing.

'I always knew that Derek Carpenter would strike again,' Niall said.

'I thought reporters were supposed to be unbiased?' Jo pounced.

'Let's just say I've experienced Derek Carpenter's temper for myself.'

Jo clicked her fingers, remembering something Sexton had told her about Carpenter attacking a reporter. 'You're not the one who was assaulted all those years ago . . . ?'

He gave a self-satisfied smile. 'It's amazing how many people remember that. I still get asked about it.'

'Does that make you feel important?' Jo said.

His expression changed.

'To find yourself right in the middle of the story?' Jo went on.

He shrugged. 'You get used to it. It's an occupational hazard.'

'You probably feel the missing-women story is personal now, don't you?' Jo went on. 'Like you have a duty to help put that bastard behind bars? Makes a good sound bite, doesn't it?'

The lawyer looked pointedly at his watch. 'Look, I've got to be somewhere . . .'

'I'm not the one keeping you,' Jo said, glancing at her phone, which had just beeped with an incoming text. She hoped it was from Foxy, and was letting her know that Liz or Frieda had showed up at the station. But it was from Rory, asking about dinner.

'I want to know where this is going, too,' Toland said. 'There's another big breaking story I've got a lead on. I'll miss my deadline if I can't get a move on.'

'Is it to do with the missing women?' Jo asked.

Niall was too busy texting himself to answer.

'No, nothing to do with it,' the editor said. 'A baby was snatched from the Central Maternity Hospital this morning. Niall got the tip-off.'

'Again?' Jo commented. 'You're on a roll.'

He looked away sheepishly.

'What about the other conversations?' Jo asked. 'What else did the source tell you?'

'What?' Niall asked.

'You said the source had contacted you twice about the body in the mountains. What else did he contact you about?'

'Nothing,' he snapped. 'That was just a figure of speech. Twice, that's it. Look, I have to go.'

'One last question: Did you, or will you, pay the source who gave you the information on the body in the mountains?'

He didn't answer. The editor shot him a look.

'Course not,' Toland replied, a little too quickly.

Jo's phone beeped again. This time the text was from Foxy: 'No sign of Liz in station and no lights on at her home,' she read. 'Amanda's secretary has arrived, and is waiting for you.'

'I've to make a call. I'll be back,' Jo said, leaving the room.

Niall sighed heavily.

Outside she rang Foxy. 'Well, what about the team watching the house? Did they see Liz go out?'

'Alfie called off the surveillance, Jo. He didn't want to put Derek off coming home.'

Jo hung her head back briefly, then wound up the interview.

Phoning Sexton as she walked back to the station, she told him to head to the Central Maternity Hospital to interview the mother whose baby had been snatched. She said she would clear it with the DI over in Pearse Street.

'What's it got to do with Amanda Wells's murder?' Sexton asked.

'That's the point – absolutely nothing,' Jo said, 'except that the same reporter got the tip-off on both.'

'Maybe he's very good,' Sexton suggested.

'Or maybe he's very well connected with sources in the underworld. I want to find out who he's mixing with, Sexton. I don't trust him. If he got the tip-off before we were contacted, the same way he did with Amanda Wells, he's probably connected with some real low lifes. Can you ask that new mum if he's been in touch? If she says no find out if she's had any contact with a man with a northern accent. If she says yes ask her if she'd place the accent in Monaghan. And get a time.'

30

Sexton hated cruelty. He was inured to every kind of horror a city could dream up, and then some. He hadn't flinched when it had fallen to him to carry in his arms a two-and-a-half-year-old girl whose face was in the belly of her granny's bull mastiff, and deliver her to the back of an ambulance because the paramedic was too traumatized, and the little girl's granny couldn't tear herself away from the dog she was trying to console.

When he'd had to wrestle a flick knife from a heavily pregnant woman carving the word 'Rat' into the forehead of her boyfriend's dead drugs rival – laid out in his coffin at the time – he'd done the needful, too.

But when a victim's suffering was prolonged, it got to him every time – hit him in the throat and made his eyes sting. Like now. He looked away quickly, and took a big gasp of air even though the woman he'd come to see had her eyes closed.

'She said she's going to stay put until the baby's back,' the nurse whispered. 'We've been trying to get her out so we can give her head a scan. She had a nasty bang when she fell.'

They were standing in the sacristy of a tiny room-turned-chapel in the maternity hospital, peering through a chink in the door at the woman in her dressing gown on her knees.

'I managed to persuade her own mother – the newborn's granny – to go home and get her a change of clothes,' the nurse continued. 'She's going to have to sleep on a couch here tonight.'

Sexton rubbed his jaw as he glanced at the woman, who was in front of a statue of Our Lady, and muttering constantly.

'Is there a husband, or a partner?'

'He said he'd lose it if he didn't get out there and start looking. He went to the station to find out what he could do.'

'We're doing everything we can.'

'But the poor little mite was only five pounds. I presume that's why she was picked.'

'What do you mean?'

'We tag them on the ankle. They slip off the smaller ones all the time because their joints are so malleable. The hospital's divided into zones. At any point we can see on the computer what zone an electronic tag is in. We don't allow the mothers to carry the babies if they leave the room. That way if we see anyone carrying a baby in the corridor we know something's up. Babies can only ever be moved in the cots. That's how we keep track of them. We found the tag under the mattress in the cot.'

'I need to talk to her,' Sexton said.

The nurse nodded, and opened the door for him, explaining in a hushed tone, 'The baby's name was Hope,' as they approached.

'Is,' Sexton answered determinedly.

The woman looked up as they neared. Her eyes opened wide at the first sight of them, but dimmed when the nurse shook her head. She looked down at the ground again.

'Maureen, this is Detective Inspector Gavin Sexton. He wants to talk to you.'

Sexton slid on to the bench alongside. He suspected he was in for several months of waking up in cold sweats. His own wife, Maura, had been pregnant with a little girl when she'd lost her life. Jobs like this brought it all back.

'I didn't even get a photo,' Maureen said. 'The signs all say no mobile phones, so I didn't turn it on. All the girls do, but I was afraid it might interfere with the equipment.'

Sexton put his hand on her shoulder. 'I'm not going to ask you to go through it all again. I've read your statement, and there's only one thing I need to clarify.'

'The harder I try, the harder it is to remember Hope's face.'

'There was nothing you could have done. This was done to you. You said the man who brought the flowers told you they'd need water. I want you to try and remember exactly what he said.'

She closed her eyes. 'He came in as I was nursing her. He said she was a beauty and that I needed to put them in water. I said I'd do it later, but he insisted. I wanted to get him out of the room. After that a nurse woke me up. I was on the floor.'

'Did you hear any kind of an accent?'

She shook her head fretfully.

'Any tattoos or distinguishing features?'

'Not that I saw . . . I wasn't looking.'

'What age would you say he was?'

'Thirty-something, it was hard to tell.' She put her hand up to her mouth. 'I just can't be sure. I mean, I saw him, but I wasn't looking at him. I didn't realize how important it would be. Oh God—'

'You said you put the baby in the cot, right?'

She nodded. 'He handed me the vase, and asked me to fill it. He said if I left them to sit they'd wilt, that making sure they got water was part of the service. I said it wasn't a good time. He said it would only take a sec. That was it. It only took three minutes in all, because the nurse came with my painkillers on the hour.'

'That's all I wanted to know.'

She gripped Sexton's wrist as he stood. 'I was

adopted,' she explained, making eye contact for the first time. 'I had the best parents any kid could want, a better start than if my real mum had kept me. But I still grew up believing that if I'd been loved, my real mother wouldn't have let me go. Hope is the only blood relative I have in the world that I know of, and I just want the chance to show her she's loved.'

Sexton nodded. He knew. He didn't believe Jo would have sent him here unless she strongly suspected some link with what had happened to Amanda Wells, and even though Jo didn't believe Derek Carpenter had murdered Amanda, just suspecting there might be a connection between the cases made Sexton want to bring Carpenter to book every bit as much as Alfie did.

31

Frantic, Liz sprinted into the crowd, spinning as she tried to squint through the darkness of the big top for any sign of her son. She couldn't see a thing or make her calling of Conor's name heard over the drone of four daredevil motorcyclists whizzing around a wrought-iron ball at breakneck speed – inches from collision with each other.

'Conor!' she screamed. Her heart was pounding so hard it felt as if it was going to burst through her ribcage.

This was real fear, not like when Ellen vanished. Much as she had loved her sister, this was different. This was her, Liz's fault. This was stomach-rising-to-her-mouth panic. All his life, she'd dreaded losing Conor – every temperature he'd had as a child she'd been paranoid had meant meningitis; every blind cord was knotted and tied up out of reach; she'd never kept bleach under the sink or left the garden gates open. *Why hadn't she walked away from Dolores and gone straight home when he'd started to get upset?*

Dance music pumped from speakers, and the throttle and roar of the motorbikes disorientated her to the point of dizziness. The crowd's faces were just a sea of black. She tried scaling the rows of seats layered on scaffolding, roaring, 'Conor!' over and over as she moved.

A woman in a shiny pink leotard carrying a tray of candyfloss and popcorn tried to grab her sleeve and usher her outside.

Liz pulled free and pushed her way past the legs and shoulders towards the sawdust centre, vaulting the barrier and shouting her son's name. She bobbed on her feet at different angles to try and be heard. Two burly men in bomber jackets appeared from nowhere, and she ran towards one of them, slapping him on the chest to get his full attention.

'My son . . . help me . . . find him . . . Conor.'

He answered in a language she didn't understand, pushing her back by the shoulders. He meant 'Calm down', or 'Stop', or 'I don't speak English'; something that only made her freak out more, because she had to make him understand how bad things were.

'My son's disappeared,' Liz said, slapping him harder. 'He could have been kidnapped. You look that way, I'll go here. Turn the lights on.'

The other one moved behind her and joined his arms around her waist to reef her off his mate. Liz turned her head sideways and bit hard into his arm.

He shrieked.

The ringmaster shouted something at them in the same language, gesticulating at the bikes. A clown appeared behind the flap the bikes had driven out of and shouted in English to get her out before there was an accident, and then she was being dragged backwards into the changing area.

Liz screamed Conor's name, and then, 'Police,' but everyone – the brightly dressed dancers, the acrobats in tights – moved away like her brand of crazy was contagious. She felt like she was in a scene from a horror movie.

With a thump, Liz landed on her back as she was shoved roughly into the car park. She tried to talk through her sobs, to beg them to let her back in because she needed to find her son, but even the woman who'd taken the tickets and had seen her with Conor pulled the shutter of her hatch down at the sight of Liz running up.

Zigzagging through the parked cars, Liz scanned inside each for any sign of Conor or Derek, and had just sprinted back towards the entrance to make another attempt to get in when an arm jerked her neck back and a sweaty hand covered her nose and mouth. A smell of salt and vinegar crisps was making her gag, and because she couldn't breathe she thought she was going to choke. All the self-defence classes amounted to nothing. Her handbag, containing the can of Mace, fell to the ground. Then everything went black.

32

'Amanda's secretary is in interview room one,' Foxy told Jo as she entered the lobby of Store Street Station. Jo checked the clock on the wall against her watch, thinking it couldn't be 8 p.m. already. According to her watch it was five past.

'Alfie's on the warpath,' Foxy said. 'That's why I've set you up down here. But it's only a matter of time before he finds out you're back.'

Jo clicked her fingers. 'Liz's son said they were going to the circus,' she said, remembering. 'Find out if there's a circus . . .'

'She was there all right,' Foxy said. 'A fortune-teller called Dolores, who also works with Liz in Supersavers, has just rung in claiming Liz all but admitted Derek murdered her sister, and that the kid saw his father. We're searching the tent and setting up roadblocks around it.'

'We're going to need to organize that tap on Toland's phone,' Jo said. 'He told me he had a conversation with his source today. If the killer's keeping in touch, we need to know what he says.'

Foxy scratched his jaw. 'Alfie's already got tapes of two conversations with the source. He's on good terms with Niall Toland.'

Jo blinked.

'He got them unofficially. He has them, but he doesn't, if you know what I mean. I'm arranging transcripts.'

'Toland went on and on about protecting sources,' Jo said, indignant.

'It's late, Jo. I need to get home to Sal. I can stay another hour, but that's it.'

'Of course, sorry.'

Foxy put his hand across the interview-room door to stop her pressing down on the handle. 'There's something else breaking. Alfie had the Carpenters' house turned over as a result of the fortune-teller's call. They've found an old school uniform and a matching shoe to the one linked to Ellen in Derek's home office in the garden.'

Jo winced, then had a thought. 'Hang on, he wouldn't keep those if he was guilty. He'd have got rid of them years ago.'

'Are you suggesting that they were planted there by the real killer?' Foxy asked incredulously.

Jo sighed deeply with frustration. 'I don't know yet.'

Foxy shook his head like he'd given up and lowered

his arm, and she stepped into the interview room.

'Tim Casey, this is Chief Superintendent Jo Birmingham,' Foxy said.

Jo was still trying to come to terms with the news as she sat down opposite the black-haired secretary in his early thirties and cautioned him. He bore a passing resemblance to Derek – was much the same height, and broad, but thinner, and he had the overly groomed appearance of a man who moisturized his skin and plucked his eyebrows. But despite the resemblance, dressed in his trendy floral shirt, with slim hands that looked manicured, he was the precise opposite of a tradesman like Derek Carpenter.

Jo had been surprised to hear that Amanda Wells's secretary was a male, but not taken aback. Amanda was a professional woman who'd lived alone and had virtual friends. She'd had a last meal that had turned into a row with a younger man, who hadn't come forward, which may have meant there was a romantic interest between them. A male secretary fitted the profile of a career woman who liked to be in control.

Jo held out her hand and offered Tim a stick of gum. He shook his head.

'You look like I feel: wound up like a spring,' she said, folding a piece into her mouth. 'What's the matter?'

He touched his forehead. 'I've never been in a police station before; not like this, anyway.'

'You and Amanda weren't close, then?'

'What does that mean?'

'Just that I presume you've never had a boss murdered, either,' Jo said, chewing. 'I'd have thought your first remark would have been about how tragic it all was, and how you'd do anything you could to help, but maybe I'm just an old romantic.'

He reached into a pocket for a hankie, and ran it over the back of his neck.

'What was she like?' Jo asked.

His eyes narrowed. 'She was a tough nut . . . in work.'

'How long did you work for her?'

'A few years. I used to have my own business, but it went to the wall. She offered to give me something to tide me over.'

'Big step down for you, wasn't it? To go from being the boss of your own company, to a woman's secretary. What was your business?'

He kept his head lowered. 'I'm a plumber by trade.'

'A plumber?' Jo asked.

'There's nothing out there. Nothing.'

'Yeah, but here's what I'm trying to figure,' Jo said. 'Why does an alpha female like Amanda, a career woman with her own business, a "tough nut" to use your phrase, hire a plumber to do the job of a legal secretary?'

A flash of something crossed his face.

Jo tilted her face.

'Was she a tough cookie outside work?' Jo knew she was on to something. 'Socialize together, did you?'

He shifted position on his chair. 'Occasionally.'

'What about Friday night?'

He shook his head vigorously. 'The night she died, no way.'

'You know more than I do if you know for certain that she died on Friday night. I'm still trying to find out the time of death. Anything you want to tell me?'

He moved sideways in the chair.

'I see you're wearing a wedding ring,' Jo said.

'Um humm.'

'Kids?'

'One.'

Jo turned to Foxy, and realized he was thinking what she was. 'Remember I asked you to bring in the restaurant manager for a line-up?'

'Hours ago? I sent him home . . .' Foxy said.

Jo glared. Foxy knew the question was designed to freak the interviewee out.

'. . . because he lives in an apartment across the road,' Foxy said with a wink.

'Give him a shout,' Jo said, turning back to lean across the table. 'If you're lying to me . . . if you're covering up the fact that you met Amanda on Friday night, now's your chance to tell me. Because if that restaurant manager picks you out, you're going to be in a hell of a lot more hot water than if it's just a simple case of trying to hide your bit on the side from your wife. It's going to look like you're covering up because of Amanda's murder. Do you understand?'

His eyes filled. 'It's not the way it looks.'

33

'It looks like he was having an affair with her, they had a fight over the fact that he had a wife, he took the row to heart and killed her, and he tried to frame the suspected serial killer, who he knew was in touch with her – Derek,' Jo told Foxy on the far side of the interview-room door, keeping her voice hushed. 'It looks like that's why he didn't come forward.'

'Come on,' Foxy said. 'He hasn't got it in him. We've got Derek Carpenter by the short and curlies, and you want me to tell Alfie that a bloke who works as a secretary, someone with manicured hands is replacing his prime suspect, Derek Carpenter, someone who worked in an abattoir and who saved as a trophy the last outfit his wife's dead sister was seen wearing?'

'It doesn't matter, what you or I think. It's what a jury might think if a barrister can plant the seed of reasonable doubt. Now organize that line-up and with any luck . . .' Jo jabbed her thumb at the interview-room door, '. . . Amanda's mystery man will keep Alfie off my back long enough for me to listen to the tapes he got of Niall Toland's recent calls.'

Jo watched nervously as Foxy told James Harkin, the manager of Genesis, where Amanda had eaten on Friday night, what was required of him in 'the bunker' – a windowless room in the bowels of the station – where line-ups were held.

She sat at a desk in front of a long rectangular wall-panel of one-way glass. Controls on the desk allowed her to be heard inside when giving directions through a microphone, and to record proceedings. Even with the advances in electronics, eyewitness testimony would be required for court, another irony of the system . . .

'If you recognize the man, step up to him and put your hand on his shoulder like this,' Foxy told Harkin in the line-up room.

Harkin, who was gripping his overcoat in front of him like a barrier, nodded. Jo sighed. It was one of the few issues on which she agreed with the civil-liberties brigade. Expecting witnesses to come face to face with suspects in this manner and to physically touch them was archaic and confrontational.

'OK, let's do it,' she directed, pressing the microphone button.

A door to the right opened, and eight men filed in. A line-up could consist of anything from six to ten men, but they all had to be of similar build and colouring.

Amanda's secretary, Tim Casey, was third from the right. Most of the rest of the motley crew consisted of men who'd been sitting at the bar next door. Jo also recognized the barber from the shop across the road, and one of the bus drivers from Busáras, opposite.

'That the plumber who specializes in client's pipes?' Sexton commented, entering the room and standing behind Jo. 'He looks like a metrosexual.'

'Very funny,' Jo said. 'How did you get on at the hospital?'

'The guy who delivered flowers snatched the baby,' Sexton said. 'Here's my notes.'

Jo took the stapled sheets and folded them into her jacket pocket, then went back to watching Harkin survey the men's faces, willing him to pick Casey. All of the men were looking straight ahead. Casey was sweating profusely from his forehead, and wiping the beads dripping down his face with the back of his arm.

'This is taking the piss,' Alfie said, bursting through the door like a man possessed. 'We need Derek Carpenter in there, otherwise there's no point.'

'I disagree,' Jo said, her jaw tight. 'Why would Tim Casey say he was with Amanda on Friday night if he was not?'

Alfie opened his mouth to say something, but Jo shushed him as through the glass Harkin walked up to Tim Casey, extended an arm and placed it on Casey's shoulder.

'It doesn't mean a thing . . . ' Alfie said. 'You know what they've just found on the CCTV tapes? Liz Carpenter's car emerging from the car park where Amanda's car was last seen, that's what! You need to . . .' He stopped short himself when Casey covered his face with his hands and started to blub so hard he bent over.

Jo leaned forward and pressed the microphone button. 'Interview room one,' she told Foxy, who'd walked in to send the others home.

'I'll do it,' Alfie said. 'If someone has to rule him out of Amanda Wells's murder, it's going to be me.'

34

Liz had given up trying to work her hands and feet free of the binds. She lay, staring at the ceiling, exhausted. There was no way she could get out of them without help. Her throat was so dry. *Where was she? A box-room? A baby's nursery?* There was a Moses basket and a cot and a nappy-changing table. Everything was dazzlingly pink. But it was too cold here for a baby. She didn't know how long she'd been unconscious, or who'd taken her here. She couldn't remember how she'd arrived. She was sore all over.

Had Derek taken her? Had he been at the circus? Had Conor managed to find him? Dark thoughts raced relentlessly through her head. *Was it better that her son was with his father or out there on his own? What should she pray to God for? If Conor had met his father at the circus was that good or bad?*

Who was Derek? Or, more to the point, what was Derek? Did he have some kind of condition? Was he a psychopath, a sociopath, a schizophrenic, bipolar?

The panic attack came thick and fast, and her breathing became more rapid. It was almost impossible to inhale through the tape covering her mouth. She made a conscious effort to focus on the air travelling in through her nostrils, to try and slow her ribcage down.

Hearing something move overhead, her gaze shifted back to the ceiling. *Where am I?* She shivered. The air in her nostrils was musty like it hadn't been lived in, and goosebumps prickled on her skin with the cold. A shaft of light flooding in through a crack in the curtains from street lamps outside glowed yellow, just the way it did in Nuns Cross.

Her eyes swept across the ceiling, searching. Then a noise. *What was it? Who?* Her head shot from side to side. Her heart beat so loud in her ears it almost drowned the sound out. She made out the evenness in the weight, and the space between the sounds. *Footsteps*. Someone was walking up there in the attic. She strained to listen. Then a different sound, one she recognized. The springy creak her own attic hatch made when it was being opened. Derek had converted theirs and some of the neighbours'. Someone was coming down the ladder. Liz held her breath and calculated. The steps were too heavy to be a woman's.

Suddenly the light went on overhead, and she squinted as her eyes stung painfully. A figure in the doorway. A man moving towards her, too small to be Derek. Relief flooded through her veins, and she hurt her face trying to smile through the tape as she realized through the bursts of vision that she knew the man walking towards her. It was her former neighbour, Paul. *Was this his house? He and Jenny hadn't had children, so why was she in a baby's room?* The last time Liz had seen Jenny in the shop, she'd overheard her mention, while talking on her mobile, that she and Paul were going to try IVF. But that had been weeks not months ago. *What was Paul doing in the attic?* Liz started to squirm and moan through the gag.

'This is going to hurt,' Paul said, putting his hands on either side of her mouth. 'Please don't shout, I'm not supposed to be here. The bailiff would not be happy.'

Liz smiled as he pulled away the tape. She was next door, then. Thank God. Her smile dropped as another thought occurred to her. *Did Paul take me here?* He'd lost a lot of weight, and at only five foot five, being skinny made him look as wiry as a jockey. He was wearing a frayed T-shirt and dirty jeans.

'Paul,' she said hoarsely once he'd stripped off the tape, 'how did I get here? Who brought me? Did you see him? Was there an old man? Was it Derek? What are you doing here?'

'Jeez, Liz, one question at a time, and not ones you already know the answer to. You were brought here by that arsehole with the clamping truck. I heard him talking to our other neighbour, that wanker, Charles McLoughlin, telling him he was holding you here to lure Derek out in the open. They don't know I'm here, nobody does. I haven't seen Derek or an old guy. And last, but not least, what do you think I'm doing here? This is my home, Liz.'

'You have to help me, Paul,' Liz said. 'Untie me quickly. Conor's in danger. He's out there somewhere. He's so vulnerable. Even if he's with Derek, and if he keeps him safe, there are people who want to hurt Derek. They're desperate. They could do anything, anything! Look what they did to me. I'm not just talking about neighbours. I'm talking about the people he used to work with. They want to kill him. They tried to get to Conor in school. But it's Derek they really want. My son's hurt nobody. He's never had to fend for himself like this. He's on the autistic spectrum. I'm so scared for him. Please, we have to hurry. I didn't want to go to the gardaí, but I have to now. There's a number for one of them in my pocket; we have to ring her.'

Liz paused only to draw a breath, but long enough to realize Paul was not reacting. He moved to the pocket she gestured to with her head, and reached in to remove the card.

'Jo Birmingham,' he read, and then blew out a spurt of air like he'd just run a race. 'Who helped my family in our hour of need, Liz?' he asked.

Liz swallowed.

He gave her a strange smile that made her skin crawl.

'Jeez, just kidding. At least you brought us some hot

drinks round on the day of the nightmare. I'll tell you this, you find out real quick in a situation like that who your friends are, you know? But I don't think you can ever really know your neighbours.'

Tears welled up in Liz's eyes. 'If you could just untie me, Paul? I know I should have done more for you, and Jenny, Paul. I should have offered to put you up, or something. Where have you been staying?'

He didn't so much as turn around. 'The health board put us up in a hotel. What do you think of that, Liz? It's cost more than our month's mortgage to keep us there already. The country's being run by a bunch of con artists. The pressure was too much on Jenny. IVF causes the hormones to go mental. Then, between me losing my job and us losing our home, we split up.'

'I'm sorry, Paul. If you untie me, I'll call the gardaí myself. I should have called them already but I thought I could sort things out. This has gone too far.'

'You know what I miss most about not having a home, Liz? It's the little things like being able to stick on a kettle and have a cuppa, or have the space for somewhere to keep the crap, you know what I mean?'

Liz started to cry. 'I feel so bad that I wasn't there for you. Please, untie me, Paul.'

'No need to feel guilty. I'm on the up,' Paul said. 'I've got a new business, and I'm going to get my house back, this house.'

'What kind of business?' Liz sobbed.

He sat down on the end of the bed, tapping a temple. 'All kinds of stuff. Using my loaf mostly, on projects I was already working on. I'm trying to look at things laterally, with one aim in mind: how to make money, real money. No more shit PAYE-be-robbed-blind by the government every budget, and have your pension plundered because it's considered fair game, too. No more prehistoric newspaper man deciding your job's gone because he's got a bad bout of constipation one morning. The other kind of money. The kind that made developers rich during the Celtic tiger days. Free money. That's what I'm talking about.'

Liz shook her head. 'I really need to use the bathroom, Paul. If you could just—'

He kept going. 'You take a newspaper, for instance, Liz. Say a reporter writes something that libels someone: you know, gets something wrong, impugns a person's reputation. Well, that person can get hundreds of thousands of pounds from the newspaper to settle the case. That's the kind of money that could turn a reporter's head, make it in their interest to get it wrong, if you see where I'm coming from?'

'You used to work on a newspaper, didn't you Paul?' Liz said quietly.

'That's where I cut my teeth for this new world, learned how to look at things as if everyone's lying, so to speak.'

'Please, Paul?'

'Everyone in this country is on the take. But they expect the rest of us to work till we drop so they can line their pockets. Well, not me, not any more. From now on it's strictly get-rich-quick schemes only for me.

'I have to give some credit to Amanda, of course. She gave me the idea after she hired me to find out what skeletons existed in the closets of that prat Charles McLoughlin. She didn't plan to profiteer in a traditional way from the information. She just intended to keep it to use when she was ready.

'I never realized just how skilled I was. You know what the big lesson I learned when I was a journalist was? The truth doesn't exist. You take the travel writer who gets a free holiday from the holiday company to write a piece about a resort. You think they're going to criticize the company that's picking up the tab? Or the political reporters having lunch with politicians, or the crime writer who has to get to know the cops to keep them sweet to get the inside track, or even the soccer correspondent who has to get the interviews with the big stars who'll remember the bad stuff if he writes it. Only one newspaper ever wrote the truth, and they shut it down. The *News of the World* exposed the real truth. And because it pissed off all the celebrities who demanded publicity when they were trying to make it, and wanted to turn it off when it suited them, they all came crying to Lord Justice Leveson.

'Everyone's pretending to be something they're not.

They shut the *News of the World* down over it. The double standards people live by make me sick. Even your Derek's a hypocrite. He wants everyone, even you, to think he's this ordinary family man, but what he really is, is a liar. He lied to you about your sister, for instance.'

'How do you know that?' Liz said, sobbing uncontrollably.

'Unsecured broadband, tapping into voicemail, pinging – it's not rocket science. Just common sense, really. It's not hacking at all, it's just homework. I let Derek know I knew his secret.'

'What does that mean?' Liz drew a breath.

'See, Derek had this incredible opportunity to make money. I knew he'd found out someone in work was doing something they shouldn't. I told him: "You don't have money but you can get it. Tell Mervyn's you want money to keep your trap shut." Derek was supposed to give it to me. It was my idea, but he got greedy and wanted to keep it all for himself.'

'A hundred thousand euro?' Liz asked.

'Yeah.'

'He got it from Mervyn's?'

'That's right.'

'So did someone from Mervyn's take Conor's books?'

'I guess they wanted to show him how easily they could get to his son.'

He took Jo's card out of his pocket and examined it.

'So this is the copper who's investigating, is it? Jo Birmingham.'

Liz's head turned to the door, following the sound of a distant wail that made every instinct in her body bristle because of its unmistakable pitch.

'Would you excuse me for a second?' he said, heading back into the landing. Liz listened as he climbed back up the ladder, and thudded across the ceiling.

Liz strained to hear, because it couldn't be coming from the attic. But there was no doubt about it. Paul had a baby up there.

35

2011: Wapping, London

They were like the good cop and bad cop when they sat alongside chatting like this, the pair of corporate middle-management heads sitting in front of Scoop posing as Mr Ordinary Joe on the tube. They didn't even know Paul was behind them, not that it would have mattered. Neither of them had ever acknowledged him when he'd passed them before in the building, over on business from Ireland. But that was the culture in Wapping. If someone was paid more than you, they didn't need to say hello.

'It's toxic,' the bad cop said, 'doomed.'

He looked more like a civil servant with his respectable haircut, boring glasses, and fuddy-duddy suit. He'd the eyes of someone who'd rip your throat out, if required.

His younger companion, on the other hand, was much more upbeat.

'Don't say that,' he said. 'We still set the news agenda every week.'

'Yes, but for the wrong reasons,' the bad cop said. 'Look at the impact already on sales and advertising. The victims of seven eleven . . . nine eleven, you can understand it, it's sick. The corner shops are refusing to stock us, and I don't even want to think about what lawsuits are coming down the line.'

Paul did not want to hear this. He'd been watching developments from the Dublin office and knew he'd have to fly over to get a real sense of what was going on. In Ireland, a politician could be caught red-handed trying to pick up a rent boy in Phoenix Park and he didn't have to resign. A former Taoiseach could be branded a liar in a payments-to-politicians scandal, but could keep all the perks of his former office. Not like in the UK, where heads were expected to roll.

Now he was here, having followed the good and bad cop, and was listening to it first hand, he was getting the kind of headache he hadn't had since his mother had done a runner. Ten years he'd been working his backside off to get where he was. His life was nicely sorted now, thank you very much. He had his own place, his own car, a clean bird who'd married him, had learned to read and write, and had money in his pocket. He wasn't going back to being nothing, or having nothing. His days of needing hard drugs to get through were over. The only smell that came close to giving him any kind of high these days was the smell of newsprint.

'Bet you the old man will shut it down,' bad cop

continued. 'What option does he have? He needs to make a stand before the poison spreads.'

Good cop was getting agitated. 'And to think it all comes down to one person driving it,' he said. 'It had all but blown over. The investigation . . . the committee. People weren't interested.'

'Until Milly,' bad cop clarified.

'But how can someone as troubled as Sean Hoare hold an organization hostage?' good cop agreed.

'He's put all our jobs on the line,' bad cop said.

Paul was getting a crick in his neck.

He wondered if they could feel the holes boring into the back of their heads.

'Who knows what's around the corner. The storm clouds hanging over us could well blow over if circumstances take an unforeseen turn.'

The bad cop gave his first smile. 'If things were to change . . . in the blink of an eye . . . we could maybe go back to normal.'

'Exactly . . .' said good cop. 'And not be on the brink of losing our livelihoods.'

Paul had heard enough. He plugged the earphone of his iPod into his ear and selected his favourite download: Eminem, 'Stan'.

It didn't matter how many times he'd listened to it over the years, it was still as true as the first day he'd started. You only got one shot, and you never let it go.

36

'Whose baby is it, Paul?' Liz asked. 'You can't keep a little one in an attic like that. A baby won't survive. Is Jenny up there too, taking care of it?'

'I had to hide her up there with everything going on around here. And I already told you that Jenny left me, Liz. It's hard enough to make a marriage work when times are good. And can you stop talking about the baby? Or I'm going to have to tape up your mouth again. Someone's coming to collect the baby. No harm will come to the baby. It's just another of my new easy-money business ventures. I was planning to get it for Jenny to persuade her to come back, but then I decided she needed a home to come to in the first place, so I turned the plan into a money-making one. If that clamper guy hadn't had the brainwave to use my house to keep you here, you'd be none the wiser.'

'I can take care of it while we wait, Paul. You can't take your eyes off a baby; anything could happen. They can get too warm, too cold, they can choke on vomit. Bring the baby down, please.'

'Forget about the baby, Liz, I mean it. Besides, kids adapt. You should have seen the shit hole I grew up in.'

'I'll pay you every penny of the hundred thousand euro Derek extorted from Mervyn's Meats. Just get the baby down. You said you didn't want to harm it. All you've done, so far as I can see, is blackmail Derek.' She paused. 'You're probably the one blackmailing the others, too, right?'

He licked a finger and air-chalked it up.

'There's a lot worse crimes than that going on in Nuns Cross, Paul,' Liz went on. 'Amanda's dead. My son's out there somewhere. I've been kidnapped. If that baby goes back to its mother unharmed, what you've done is nothing in comparison. Don't ruin your life by letting something happen to it.'

Paul didn't answer. He didn't get a chance. A figure had appeared in the doorway and, before Liz could react, something glinting in the way only metal can had been drawn up and brought down on Paul's head. He collapsed on the spot.

Derek, paler than she'd ever seen him, paced over to her, a gun in his hand.

37

In the detective unit, Jo took the earphones from Aishling and sat down at her computer, clicking on the first conversation between Niall and his source, which the others had already listened to.

A distorted voice said, 'YOU. A. HACK?'

Jo's eyes moved to the clock. It was half nine. Dan would be like an Antichrist. But there was no way she could leave now, not with Alfie still in the interview room with Tim Casey. She held the earphones tight to her head, keeping her back to Aishling, with Sue and Joan hovering nearby, waiting for a word.

Jo closed her eyes to concentrate. She knew they all wanted her to give them the nod that it was fine to go, but the truth was she needed them. She listened to the familiar sound of a keyboard clattering on the tape, followed by a slurp, and someone gulping. She pictured Toland slugging from a mug of coffee.

'I don't do crank calls.' That same northern brogue.

'I. NEED. TO. TAKE. PRE.CAU.TIONS.'

'I always protect my sources.' Toland again.

'UN.TIL. A. COP. OFF.ERS. YOU. A. BIG. SCOOP. AS. A. TRADE. OFF?'

Jo raised her eyebrows.

'You've been watching too many Lou Grant repeats,' the reporter said. 'What's your information, mate? I'm busy here.'

'DO. YOU. PAY?'

'No.'

'FOR. A. SPLASH?'

Toland hesitated. 'It depends. I'd need to know what's involved before I could put a value on it.'

A hand on Jo's shoulder. She glided the mouse over the pause button on the screen, and slid the headphones back on to her neck, wearily.

'Sorry, Jo,' Joan said. 'It's just . . . do you mind if I go, too?'

'It's up to you,' Jo said. She put the headphones back on.

'THERE'S. A. BOD.Y. IN THE MOUNT.AINS.'

'Tell me something I don't know,' Toland answered.

'ONE. OF. THE. MISS.ING. WOM.EN.FROM. THE. NINE.TIES.'

Toland stopped typing. It sounded like his lips were now pressed right up against the receiver. 'What?'

Jo guided the mouse to a new window and Googled the word 'voice distorter' as she continued to listen. She clicked on to the top hit, which gave details of a spy shop that also sold bug detectors, surveillance microphones, and night-vision and pinhole cameras. The tape reeled on.

'A. WOM.AN. BUR.IED. AT. THE. SALL.Y. GAP. YOU. GOT. A. THOM'S. THERE? SUS.PECT. LIVED. IN. NUNS CROSS.'

'How does he know so much about the street directory?' Jo asked, lifting one earphone off her ear, turning around and looking for Foxy. He'd mentioned that he needed to head off. But the electoral register was generally only used by people in the commercial sector, for sending out personalized junk mail, she knew.

'Maybe he's a cop,' Foxy answered, appearing in front of her and buttoning up his coat.

Jo put the earphone back in place, listening as paperwork got shuffled about, something banged down, pages flicked, and then Toland spoke again, 'This better not be a hoax.'

There was a sharp intake of breath and Jo suspected Toland had just spotted Derek Carpenter's name listed in Nuns Cross.

'HOW. MUCH?' the source asked him.

Toland didn't hesitate. 'We don't pay for stories.'

'TWO. FOOT. BE.HIND. A. HEAD.STONE. IN. MEM.OR.Y. OF JIMM.Y. COLE. A. DRI.VER. WHO. WENT. OV.ER. EDGE.'

The line went dead. Jo pulled the headphones off.

'What do you think?' Foxy asked.

'We need to put Toland under surveillance to see if he drops money off somewhere. He told me he hadn't paid up yet. But he's agreed to it in principle on the tape.'

'There's no way we'll get a budget for monitoring him twenty-four seven without Alfie's backing,' Foxy said. 'And he's not going to want us watching his man in the press.'

'The thing is,' Jo said, thinking aloud, 'Toland's source used a lot of jargon – "hack", "scoop", "splash".'

'And he knew Toland would have a Thom's on his desk, as most journalists do, and he asked for money,' Sue chipped in.

'Right,' Jo said. 'I think we're talking about a journalist.'

'Toland himself?' Sexton asked, taking an interest. 'How would he have had a two-way conversation with himself?'

'It would explain why he took such precautions with his voice,' Foxy said.

'Or he has an accomplice,' Joan suggested.

Jo turned as someone tapped her sharply on the back. It was Alfie. She couldn't be sure if he'd overheard.

'You can forget about Tim Casey being in the frame,' he said. 'I've grilled him. He met some mates in the pub after Amanda stormed out. I've confirmed it with them. I heard you interviewed Niall Toland. Maybe he did it.'

'Don't be like that, Alfie,' Jo said, mocking him back. 'It wasn't personal.'

'I'm glad you take that view, because tomorrow I intend to interview Dan.'

Jo swallowed. 'What? Why?'

'Don't make me spell it out. Dan has a history of dodgy snouts.'

'I'm not with you,' Jo said. She knew Alfie was referring to some bother Dan had had over failing to keep a file on his agents, but she wanted him to spell it out. The relationship between a garda handler and an agent had to follow a strict protocol because of previous abuses. Anyone giving information to the gardaí was assigned a handler who protected and paid them, not unlike a journalist and their source. As criminals were the only ones with information worth reporting, it had led to no end of trouble, because many were allowed to perpetrate bigger crimes than the ones they were ratting up, and the state was not only turning a blind eye, but paying them for the privilege. Dan had always been anal about protecting his sources.

'There was a file in Dan's cabinet that indicated he'd registered Derek Carpenter as a tout. Maybe there's a reason Dan let him off the hook,' Alfie said.

Sexton had answered a ringing phone, and he covered the mouthpiece and turned to Jo. 'Sorry to interrupt, but Liz Carpenter's neighbour is downstairs.'

Jo nodded and looked at Foxy. 'Go home to Sal.'

She turned to the others. 'You lot can go. I'm sorry this case has taken over your lives too.'

38

Frieda McLoughlin was led into interview room two by her solicitor – a thin woman in her forties with a reputation for representing guilty parties – and a man Jo presumed to be Frieda's husband, based on the hand-holding. Their fingers weren't knit like lovers', they were cupped like friends'. Frieda displayed none of the bolshie confidence Jo had witnessed in Liz's house just a few hours earlier. Her face was drawn, and the vertical worry lines between her eyebrows seemed especially prominent.

Based on the swagger, Jo was chalking Frieda's husband down as someone full of self-regard. He put a hand out to Jo, announcing, 'Charles McLoughlin,' with a practised handshake that squeezed slightly too hard. His hair was dyed too dark for his face, suggesting he was a vain man, too.

'I know you only asked to speak to my wife, but it's my house as well,' McLoughlin said. 'We wanted to get this matter sorted out tonight once and for all. My wife is stressed out of her brain by it.'

'Find another couple of chairs, will you?' Jo prompted Sexton, as he handed her a stack of printouts. He'd been the one to offer to stay behind. Jo glanced down at Amanda Wells's recent emails, which had been printed out, thanks to being synchronized with her iPhone. Jo still hadn't had a chance to read them. She licked a finger as she thumbed through the printouts, leaving Charles to quiz his brief quietly. Jo folded a corner down on one of particular interest.

As Sexton exited again, Jo went through the rigmarole of reassuring the solicitor that the interview was 'routine' and 'preliminary' – the usual bullshit to keep her at heel. She did not offer her client a cuppa. Tea was for victims, and the vulnerable, and despite Frieda's wet-rag appearance, Jo was convinced she was neither. But given developments, her interest in this woman had shifted considerably. What Jo needed to know now was where Liz Carpenter and her husband and son were.

Sexton carried two chairs in under his arms, negotiating the door with his foot. They screeched as he shunted them into position around the small square table in the centre of the room. The solicitor took the one to Jo's right, Frieda sat opposite, and her husband was on Jo's left. Sexton sat by the door.

'My client is greatly upset by the—'

'Your client has a tongue,' Jo interrupted.

Frieda looked up sharply. And there was a glimpse of the woman Jo remembered.

'We don't have time for the usual niceties,' Jo told the brief. 'I'm tired and hungry and I'd like to get home. This is not a formal interview, as you know. This is informal, and it's voluntary. I have chosen not to caution your client, and your presence is completely unnecessary. I'm doing you a big favour by allowing it to take place so late, as it is. If there's any legal issue, it's your prerogative to intervene. But I can tell you now, unless your client has something to hide, something pertinent to my investigation, you're wasting your time here. I won't have you waste mine, though.'

The brief knew better than to argue.

Jo looked straight at Frieda. 'We found the deeds of your house in Amanda Wells's car,' she said. 'I take it, therefore, that Amanda was your solicitor. Have you any idea why these documents would have been in her car on the night she was murdered?'

Frieda threw a look of astonishment at Charles, who'd leaned forward to grip the edge of the table. He took a deep breath. 'Amanda represented a lot of the residents in Nuns Cross, because hers was the nearest practice to the estate. As a matter of fact, she was right there when the builder opened the show house, giving free advice to prospective buyers and offering a cut-rate commission to handle the sale. Subsequently, we weren't happy with the way the sale was dealt with, and we'd threatened legal action.'

Jo considered. 'What was the problem?'

'The builder didn't have proper planning permission when he built the estate,' Charles said.

'You're joking,' Sexton blurted. He looked down quickly before Jo could catch his eye with an admonishment.

'Any solicitor worth their salt would have seen it,' Charles went on. 'It was a right-of-way issue. Amanda must have known.'

'Known what?' Jo pressed.

Frieda frowned.

Charles turned his palms up. 'That anyone who pleased could take a shortcut through the estate from the neighbouring convent grounds if they wanted, and be perfectly within their rights to tramp through our gardens to get to the main road.'

'The estate's walled, isn't it?' Jo prompted.

'Not where Paul and Jenny Bell's old house borders the convent grounds,' Frieda blurted. 'That's why we need the right-of-way issue resolved. To stop them coming through.'

'Who?' Jo asked.

'Hood rats,' Charles answered. Frieda shot a reproving look at her husband. Jo watched the way he checked to see if she'd noticed. She held his stare but moved on.

'How did Amanda respond to your threat to sue?' Jo asked.

Frieda sat up straight. 'We'd made up with Amanda

since,' she said in a tinkly voice. 'It was all water under the bridge.'

'You dropped the case . . . ?' Jo asked.

'Not exactly,' Charles said, watching his wife. 'You could say it stalled. We had some . . .' Jo noted the worried glance he'd thrown at Frieda as he seemed to struggle for the right word '. . . problems of our own,' he continued.

'Nothing we couldn't handle,' Frieda clarified quickly. 'Nothing at all, really.'

'What problems?' Jo asked Charles.

When he didn't answer Jo turned to Frieda. 'What problems?'

Jo wasn't prepared to wait for an answer requiring the kind of thought the couple were clearly giving it.

'One of my officers has been going through Amanda's recent business activities,' she said, banging the printouts on the table, and then leafing through for the one with the bent corner. 'I see she was in the process of remortgaging your home. Can you tell me about that?'

'What? Let me see that!' Charles said.

Jo put a hand up to stop him reaching over. 'I take it that means no?'

He leaned forwards. 'I'd no idea. We'd given absolutely no authorization for that. I've heard of rogue solicitors – the same as everybody has – remortgaging their clients' properties to line their own pockets. That's the only thing that could have been going on. If that's what Amanda Wells was doing, I can tell you this, she'd have been struck off.'

'Or killed?' Jo asked.

Charles sat back quickly.

'Do you have our deeds now?' Frieda asked. She checked on Charles. 'Will they be needed as evidence?'

'Sorry?' Jo asked.

'I mean, we are planning on selling up. They won't be held up by a court case, will they? Court cases can take years . . .'

Charles sighed. His back slumped in the chair.

'Can I remind you that I'm investigating the murder of your neighbour, Mrs McLoughlin?' Jo said. 'You seemed very friendly with Liz Carpenter this afternoon. Do you—'

Jo didn't get a chance to finish.

'I barely know her,' Frieda said, looking instantly sorry she'd said anything.

Charles reached under the table for his wife's hand and, based on Frieda's wince, squeezed it too hard.

'Like you barely knew Amanda Wells?' Jo said. 'There was an open bottle of wine in Liz's kitchen,' she went on. 'Were you having a drink together?'

'Yes,' Frieda acknowledged, clearly frustrated.

'Liz Carpenter, the woman you barely knew, but drank with in her home this afternoon, might be in danger. I need to get in touch with her. Have you any idea where she might be?'

'No, none at all,' Frieda said, softening her voice.

Jo was growing more annoyed. 'She never mentioned friends or family to you over the years?'

'The Carpenters kept to themselves, actually. I was afraid of him, if you want to know the truth. Even Liz seemed . . .' She stopped.

'What?' Jo pressed.

'She said something today about wishing Derek was dead.'

'Is that right?' Jo said.

'Then at the barbecue . . .'

'What barbecue?' Jo asked.

'We had one earlier.'

'And Liz, the woman you barely knew but drank with in the afternoon, was there, is that right?'

Frieda blinked, then gave a dismissive wave. 'Yes, I think so.'

Jo ignored Sexton, who was looking from side to side, like he wanted to get in, and asked, 'Yes, or no?'

'Yes.'

'Is it appropriate to have a barbecue after your neighbour has just been murdered?'

'It was prearranged.'

'You couldn't have called it off, in the circumstances?'

Frieda mumbled something inaudible.

'Who went?'

'Just other neighbours.'

'And what time did she leave?'

'Who?'

Jo stood up and leaned across the table, exasperated. 'The cat's mother! Who do you think? Liz! Was her son with her?'

Frieda looked at Charles. 'I'm not sure.'

'You're not sure, Mrs McLoughlin?' Jo repeated, glancing at Sexton, who was standing up, too. 'How many neighbours were at this barbecue?'

'Um . . .'

'What am I paying you for?' Charles demanded, losing his cool with his legal eagle.

Jo put her pen down on the table and a hand out to Sexton to tell him to sit down.

'Two, three . . . ten?' Jo continued to press Frieda.

Charles jumped to his feet. 'Too much for this, that's for sure . . .' he told the lawyer.

'Change of plan,' Jo told the solicitor, before turning to Charles. 'It's now clear you've withheld information about Liz Carpenter's last known movements. You have the right to remain silent. Anything you say can and will be used against you in a court of law. You have the right . . .'

39

July 2011: Watford, Hertfordshire

Sean Hoare glanced at his reflection in the back of a silver-plated soup spoon as he waited in a restaurant for his Wapping contact to show. Considering his doctor had declared he 'must be dead', because of the state of his liver, he didn't look bad for his forty-eight years, if he said so himself. He still had a full head of hair, which looked jet black when slicked flat with his trademark Brylcreem, a throwback to the years he'd spent in Wapping. He still had all his own gnashers, which could be bleached and zoomed as white as a set of milk teeth these days. And the mischievous twinkle in his brown eyes had never dimmed – which was saying something, given the fact that he'd been out of a job for the last few years.

But his luck was changing: his phone had been hopping all week. The establishment – the BBC, the Guardian, the Telegraph – all wanted him now. It was a long way from the six Shafta Awards, marking his contribution to the worst stories in tabloid journalism, which he'd won as a showbiz correspondent over the years. The one about Posh and Becks buying a private island off Essex was probably his most colourful work of fiction.

Since making the switch from writing stories to supplying them to the New York Times, *he'd been making headline news all over the world. His latest contribution in the secrets-of-a-tabloid-hack vein had been published the previous week, and the fallout promised to make it his most controversial yet. It had the legs to run and run . . .*

Placing the spoon back in line with the knife, he reached for the carafe of sparkling water. His throat was as dry as sandpaper. He checked the other diners out as he topped up his glass. He'd picked an out-of-the-way restaurant for the meeting, but if he recognized anyone, he was out of here. The move from writing stories to becoming one had made him as paranoid as hell. Whistleblowers didn't exactly have a great survival rate in London. The former KGB informer, Alexander Litvinenko, who'd accused the Russian secret services of staging terrorist acts to bring Vladimir Putin to power, had died of radiation poisoning after a meeting in a sushi restaurant on Piccadilly. And Bulgarian defector Georgi Markov, who'd exposed corruption in Prime Minister Todor Zhivkov's private circle, had been assassinated with a poisoned pellet fired into his thigh from an umbrella as he crossed Waterloo Bridge, back in the seventies.

It wasn't just dissidents who'd had personal safety issues. Sean, for one, hadn't bought the supposed suicide of the former UN weapons inspector, David Kelly, in Oxfordshire. The circumstances surrounding the death of the man who'd leaked Tony Blair's weapons of mass destruction dossier had left more questions than answers.

So Sean had taken precautions himself. He'd made sure to leave his mobile phone at home in case anyone tried to 'ping' him. The irony wasn't lost on him. The current story that had everyone on the far side of the Atlantic talking, but had silenced whole swathes of the press at home, revealed how, for a three-hundred-pound payment to the Met, an individual's movements could be tracked and pinpointed to within a few yards by a simple triangulated calculation of which three masts their mobile phone signal was pinging off. Only people on very good terms with their consciences could afford to carry a mobile these days.

He ran a napkin across his brow and along the back of his neck. He knew exactly how much power the Murdoch media empire wielded with Downing Street and the Old Bill.

Sean needed to keep his head down for a while. The last thing he wanted was a prison sentence. Not that he had any regrets for coming clean about the real story behind all the News of the World *scoops. All he'd ever wanted from his old bosses was fair play. For years it had suited the paper to treat Sean's drink and drug problems as an occupational hazard. Everyone knew the only way to infiltrate the world of models, rock stars and actors was to take pills, drink too much, and snort cocaine with them. His expense account had been designed to cover the cost of doing things that no sane man would attempt. Once upon a time, the paper had promoted him for being prepared to go above and beyond the call of duty to rub shoulders with celebrities. That was how he'd ended up spending about a thousand pounds a week taking three grams of cocaine a day and drinking Jack Daniel's for breakfast.*

But all that came back to haunt him when Princes William and Harry twigged that their phone messages were being listened to by the newspaper. Sean had stood up for the royal correspondent as the newspaper tried to distance itself from methods that had once been par for the course when breaking or stacking up a story. Sean's drinking and drug use turned into a reason to fire him. But their cover-up was built on a house of cards. How could you blame one rogue reporter when you needed two people – one to ring and tie up the line, and the other to ring a couple of seconds later in order to get straight into the mailbox, enter the security code and listen in?

'Ready to order, sir?' the waiter asked.

Sean studied him, and wondered why he looked so familiar, and then shook his head. 'I'll wait for my friend.' He surveyed the menu, glancing over the top of it from time to time to try and work out if he did know the waiter after all.

He didn't want to put his contact in any jeopardy by being seen with him. He still had friends in the newspaper industry, people in the inner circle who looked up to him for taking a stand, and were willing to give him a steer about how his revelations had gone down, and what Murdoch's next move might be. Up to now, News Corporation had only tried to smear the New York Times, claiming Sean's story was published because of corporate rivalry alone: attempting to assassinate his character by dismissing him as a troubled crank.

The funny thing about it was, they'd treated his dubious moral repute like a badge of honour when he'd worked for them. He'd been actively encouraged to practise his 'dark arts' – hack phones, blag his way into people's confidence by pretending to be anything or anyone other than a journalist, ping, or bribe anyone who had a price. The right source in the police could give you anything – run a car reg to tell you who was driving behind you, a social security number to tell you what they were earning, even give you their last credit-card transaction. He had contacts in the banks, the internet companies, the phone companies. The better *the stories, the more readers the newspaper gained. The more readers it had, the more advertising it got. The more powerful it became, the more money it had to sluice around. Even the Green Book – containing a list of phone numbers, and tips about the movements of the Queen, Prince Charles, senior royals, and their friends and contacts – had been acquired from a cop on security detail for less than two grand. Everything and everyone had a price.*

Even the Old Bill were covering their tracks.

'Sir, I've been asked to give you a phone message. The person supposed to be meeting you has sent his apologies.'

Sean looked up in surprise. The waiter had returned. He definitely knew him from somewhere. The voice and the face were from so far back, he couldn't put them in context.

'Have we met?'

The waiter shrugged. 'Not that I'm aware of, sir, but you meet a lot of people doing what I do. Would you like to order now?'

Sean wished he could place him. 'Did the caller give his name?'

'He did, sir, but I'm afraid I didn't catch it.'

Sean shook his head. Something was wrong. The waiter took the menu from him, and walked away.

It was funny the way things turned around, Sean thought, grabbing his coat.

But six years after being sacked, Sean had assumed

the high moral ground by holding his hands up to everything he'd done. Life was a lot easier on this side of the story, free of the stresses put on reporters to come up with an exclusive at any cost.

He sat back down to sip some water, trying to settle his nerves. When he looked back now, he could see that the problem was that the culture that had developed in the newsroom was not so much morally dubious as barking mad: young female reporters had been made to wear lingerie so they could get into swingers' parties; a reporter had been required to sit in a glass box in the newsroom for twenty-four hours to emulate a stunt performed by magician David Blaine. And when the competition ratcheted up, the insanity knew no bounds. When pictures appeared in a rival newspaper of a reporter swimming in the water with a bottle-nosed whale beached in the Thames, the News of the World *powers that be had dispatched a reporter to the North Sea to help find the whale's family, rather than be outdone.*

The public would have to decide for themselves who was telling the truth and who was lying.

He put his arms in his coat. Complete strangers probably knew more about his secrets than his nearest and dearest. A person's life could change in the space of a few minutes. Or end.

Sean hurried home, aware that at this rate the stress of paranoia would kill him, if nothing else.

40

It was Charles McLoughlin who cracked – before Jo had finished advising him and Frieda of their rights.

'We didn't even bring her there. We just went to check she was OK . . .'

'Shut up,' Frieda snapped.

'Who?' Jo asked.

'Liz,' Charles said. 'George wanted to keep her somewhere to lure Derek back. He was trying to buy Liz's car off her because he'd seen it out real late on Friday night. He was convinced Derek must have used it to get rid of Amanda's body. He thought if we had it, we'd have forensic evidence against him we could use to blackmail him back. Derek's behind all this. He's the one you want—'

'You stupid, useless . . .' Frieda blurted, cutting him off.

'Get her out of here and charge her with obstruction,' Jo told Sexton.

Sexton advanced and restrained Frieda, who tried to resist. 'Coward,' she screeched at Charles.

'She's going to need you more than he will,' Jo told the solicitor, who was bustling out after them.

Charles sat down and put his head in his hands.

Jo stood up. 'Where is Liz now? Is Conor with her?'

He shook his head slowly. 'I can only tell you what George told me. He's the one who followed her to the circus. He said she got separated from the kid. He got her into the car and brought her back to Nuns Cross. This is all Derek's fault. He's the one holding everyone to ransom. He assaulted Amanda. He's the reason it snowballed. If he hadn't . . .'

Jo leaned in. 'Where is Liz Carpenter?'

'We were just trying to put things right, trying to contain the situation by keeping her in one place. We would never have hurt her,' he said, covering his face.

Jo slapped her hand on the table. 'Where is she?'

'I don't know. George took her to the vacant house in Nuns Cross. But when we went back to check on her, just before we came here, she was gone. There was so much blood.'

41

After leaving Frieda with the duty officer, Sexton left the station and jostled his way through Molloy's pub, around the corner on Talbot Street. Swallowing his first sip from a pint of Guinness, he cleared the fluffy moustache with his lip as the gargle slid down his gut, taking some of the day's tension with it. He'd been gumming for a jar, drained from watching Jo try to prove Derek Carpenter's innocence. Locating a group of colleagues, he used his free arm as an oar and headed for them.

Sue pulled a seat out from under the table when she saw him coming. She was the one who'd nudged him on her way out of the incident room to tell him to be sure to join them. She wasn't bad-looking. He wondered if he'd a chance with her. He had to be moving on from Maura's death if he was starting to fancy women again, which was good.

'Cheers,' he said, clinking glasses.

'Oi, oi, here comes trouble,' she said, nodding

towards someone and then lowering her gaze quickly.

Sexton turned to see Alfie, emerging from the Gents with a stagger. He crossed paths with a lounge girl carrying a tray laden with drink balanced precariously in her hands. The girl stopped in her tracks and cursed at Alfie, who appeared not to have noticed. Some of the booze swilled on to the tray. The way she glared and was still roaring after him suggested Alfie had pinched her backside. She had black mascara and a silver tongue-piercing. Some of the rougher-looking male customers at the bar were starting to take an interest.

Sexton headed over, putting his hands on Alfie's shoulders and apologizing to the girl on his behalf. She wasn't impressed, but she moved off. Sexton took the whiskey chaser from one of Alfie's hands, leaving a full pint in the other.

'I think that's enough of that for one night, my old son.'

'Don't tell me Birmingham's here?' Alfie responded. 'I was just starting to unwind. Here, you know what she needs, don't you?' He leaned in to whisper it to Sexton in no uncertain terms.

'Leave it,' Sexton said, trying to back up as he continued on his path towards Sue, but aware that Alfie was following.

'She's made a balls of it,' Alfie said, speaking to the back of Sexton's head.

Sexton kept going, though on this occasion he agreed.

Jo's efforts to prove Dan infallible had made her incapable of logical thought. She was like a bloody terrier – the most stubborn woman he'd ever met when she got an idea in her head about something. That had good points and bad. On this case it was definitely the latter. She'd been exactly the same when it came to entertaining the prospect that Maura might have been murdered.

'I've met her type many times over the years,' Alfie ranted. He made a talking hand. 'They sit in front of HR talking about how they've been bullied and intimidated by a man, when they'd rip your throat out, given half a chance.'

'Jo's all right,' Sexton said, trying to shake him again. 'She's under pressure.'

'And I'm not? I'll tell you her problem. She doesn't see it out there on the streets as being a case of them and us. She wants it every way. You know how hard it is. Even if you manage to convince a jury, life doesn't even mean life. They're back out on the street again in the blink of an eye these days, between bail, remission, and early release.'

Once again, Sexton tended to agree.

'It doesn't matter, anyway,' Alfie continued. 'I'm relocating the incident room to Rathfarnham tomorrow. It should never have been opened in Store Street in the first place.'

'Have you told her?' Sexton asked, turning.

'Not yet. Thought I'd surprise her.' Alfie tapped the tip of his nose. 'That's the difference between you and her. You know if our lot don't stick together and occasionally get "creative"' – he made rabbit ears around the word – 'it's all over.'

'What does that mean, Alfie?' Sexton asked, reaching into his pocket for his own phone, which had started to ring.

Alfie was too busy clicking his fingers like he was playing maracas at the lounge girl, who was ignoring him, to answer.

Sexton put one finger in his ear and held the phone up to the other one as he answered. 'What?' he shouted. 'What?' He glanced at the phone to double-check that the caller had hung up. He recognized the number as one of the incident-room phones.

Sexton turned back to Alfie and returned to his stool. He wanted to make sure that it was the drink talking, and that there was no question of Alfie doing something stupid like planting evidence.

But Alfie was on the phone himself, shouting to give him a second as he pushed towards the exit.

Sexton knew he should have put his pint down and walked the five minutes back to the station to find out who wanted him, and for what. But he had booked a table for two with the girl who'd stayed the night with him on Sunday. He'd met her in a taxi queue a few hours earlier that night. He'd been one ahead of her, and she'd jumped in beside him uninvited and asked if he fancied sharing the fare. His place had been first on the drop-off, but they'd had such a laugh in the back of the cab he'd asked her in for a coffee. He'd nearly fallen over when she'd agreed. The sex had been incredible, the way it always was between strangers. No baggage. He hoped she'd show. He liked the fact that there'd been no pressure on them to get to know each other before the reward at the end of it. He'd no number for her – she'd refused to give him one – but he'd made her promise to meet him in his local Chinese. He wasn't even sure of her name. She'd given him two different ones at various stages in the night, and he was pretty sure she'd been lying both times. She didn't look like a 'Rachel' or a 'Roz'.

Sue nudged his arm with hers. 'There must be a development,' she said. He followed her gaze to Alfie, who'd re-entered and was waving frantically for Sexton to join him.

'Fuck it, anyway,' Sexton said, draining his pint. 'That's my chance of a new relationship out the window.' He headed for the door.

42

At 10.45 p.m. on the button, Jo stepped out of her banged-up Ford Escort outside the vacant house beside the Carpenters' at Nuns Cross. Sexton hadn't been able to hear her over the unmistakable racket of a pub when she'd phoned half an hour earlier. If he was drinking there was no point in getting him to accompany her, anyway. She was pissed off. She had a home life, too, which as usual was suffering. But it was impossible to scarper on a case like this. It had to take priority. This was life-and-death stuff. She'd brought a pair of rookies and contacted a profiler. He lived nearby and was parked up outside the house already, on the phone.

She hurried towards the house, just as a white transit Tech Bureau van rounded the corner. Jo turned to wave. Flynn, the forensic photographer, was behind the wheel. He was in his forties, with a beer belly and a cheery face. Flynn pulled in and Jo leaned through the passenger window on both elbows after giving a nod to the young female officer in the passenger seat beside him.

'This the one?' Flynn asked.

'Yeah,' Jo said. 'I called in Eamonn,' she said, waving the profiler over.

Flynn moved around to the back of the van, opened the door, reached in and handed out sets of white overalls. 'Can a leopard change his spots?' he asked Eamonn as he joined them.

'I thought we weren't sure if we were dealing with a leopard,' Eamonn answered, looking to Jo for confirmation. She nodded.

'You were in Amanda Wells's place, too, weren't you?' Jo asked Flynn. 'Find anything of evidential value there?'

Flynn shook his head as he pulled up his jumpsuit. 'It's clean as a whistle around there. There was no sign of a struggle. I wouldn't say Amanda Wells had so much as a nosebleed as long as she lived there.'

'Maybe the killer realized how hard it would be to get the body out of this place,' Jo said, nodding in the direction of the gates.

'And there I was, thinking solicitors were feeling the pinch as much as anyone now that the arse has fallen out of the conveyancing business,' the female officer with Flynn said. 'How much do you reckon a house here would set you back?'

'Depends when you bought,' Jo guessed, putting her legs and arms into the suit and pulling the hood over her head. 'At the height of it, you could have named your price.'

'Not that you'd be able to shift one now,' Flynn said, taking a shell case from the back of the van, opening it to check the contents, and then banging it closed.

The sound of a vehicle screeching into the cul-de-sac made Jo look up. Alfie was sitting in the passenger seat of an unmarked car. He did not look happy, to put it mildly.

'I'll follow you in,' Jo said. 'Best to go in through the back if we're going to keep Alfie from losing it.'

Flynn nodded and headed off with the rest of the team as the car pulled in at the spot and Alfie lowered his window. Sexton was in the back, Jo realized.

Alfie was munching from a grease-stained brown-paper bag of chips.

'Get in,' he told her through a bulging cheek.

43

When Jo was in the car, Alfie turned on her. 'What the hell do you think you're playing at, Birmingham?'

The driver – young, male – stared straight ahead, playing invisible like an old pro. Sexton, who also had a bag of chips on his lap, offered her one.

'Give me a break,' Jo said, turning her nose up at the stink of alcohol. 'How could you call off the surveillance without consulting me? It's short-sighted . . . it's irresponsible . . . and if it transpires someone else has been killed, it's bloody criminal.'

Alfie threw his hands up, like he'd just given up chasing someone who'd nicked his wallet. 'Just answer me one question,' he said. 'Why are you so dead set on ignoring the facts staring you in the face? If I didn't know better, I'd say you've an agenda.'

'There's no need for—' Sexton tried to cut in.

'I'm sick of your snide insinuations about Dan,' Jo reacted, reaching for the handle.

'I've been going out of my way trying not to spook

Derek Carpenter,' Alfie said to the driver in mock-amusement, 'and she swans in here bringing the technical squad, a profiler, and a pair of uniforms with her.' He turned back to Jo. 'Why didn't you leave the siren flashing, or organize a parade to march through Nuns Cross while you were at it, just in case the residents didn't notice you? I'm sure the garda band would have obliged. Isn't it bad enough that you blew our one chance of snaring potentially the biggest serial killer in this country's history by letting him slip out of our fingers in the first place?' He scrunched up the bag of chips.

'You might want to brush up on the guidelines we follow when we get information pertaining to the possible commission of a crime,' Jo said, slamming the door after her.

'What are you blathering on about now, Birmingham?' he said. 'What are you doing here?'

'I'm here for the same reason you are: to investigate an allegation that Liz Carpenter was being held against her will in that vacant house, and to oversee the collection of any forensic evidence from the scene.'

Alfie's scrunched-up face suggested he was surprised. He started to cough as his last mouthful of food went down the wrong way.

'I presumed someone had notified you, and that that was why you were here, too?' Jo asked.

'I'm here because one of the neighbours spotted

Derek Carpenter going into that house,' he said, pointing to Number 30, the one on the corner right next to the Carpenters' place.

44

'One of the neighbours spotted Derek and rang in the information,' Alfie explained after Jo had updated him on what she'd learned from Charles McLoughlin during his interview.

They were standing at the entrance to a pink nursery where Flynn was dusting surfaces with Luminol, while his colleague, who had already flashed a UV torch around, was carefully bagging a stack of miniature blood-soaked blankets, which Jo observed were too small for the bed.

'Which neighbour?' Jo asked.

'I don't know,' Alfie answered impatiently.

'It's important.'

'Oh, now the neighbours are in on the plot to frame Derek, is that it?' Alfie asked.

Jo knew better than to argue with a drunk. She tried to ask Eamonn for his take, but he put a finger to his lips.

'Shhhh.'

Jo drew a breath. Treading the egos in this case was like trying to negotiate a minefield – blindfolded. She closed her eyes in frustration as Alfie answered his phone and rattled off exactly how much shit Derek was in now, and then she tried to work out if Charles McLoughlin had had something to do with whatever had happened in that room. The part he'd admitted playing in the abduction of his neighbour was minimal. But was that because he, or his awful wife, had gone further and had killed Liz themselves? And where were Liz and her son?

'Make yourself useful, and go and find out who used to live here,' Jo told Sexton, who'd been standing to one side with his hands in his pockets. 'And see if you can find out who it was on the estate that spotted Derek.'

He nodded, and headed off. Jo sighed. What she really needed to know most was whose blood was on the bed. And that, like establishing Amanda's time of death, was not going to happen fast.

'OK, in my opinion it was an accident,' Eamonn said.

'Oh, right, how do you make that out?' Alfie asked.

Jo rolled her eyes.

Eamonn looked at him warily. He pointed into the room. 'A seasoned killer, such as a serial killer, would have gone for a clean kill.'

'Like suffocation or strangulation?' Jo asked.

'Exactly.'

'What about a sadist?' Jo asked.

Eamonn peaked his hands against his lips. 'Even so, someone accomplished, so to speak, would have learned not to kill somewhere like this. It's too risky.'

'This is juju,' Alfie said, heading for the toilet. 'I need a pee.'

'Not in here, you don't,' Flynn called after him.

Alfie clicked his tongue and headed for the stairs.

'So you mean we're talking about an argument that's got out of control?' Jo clarified. 'Only, whoever inflicted an injury – presumably on Liz Carpenter, who we've been led to believe was tied up here – must have had mens rea: they must have intended to kill if they caused her to bleed while she was tied up.'

Eamonn shook his head. 'I said the injury was caused by an accident. A row escalates. I'm saying that I think what happened here involved the precise opposite, that I see no sign of a row.'

Jo rubbed her eyes and tried to think of what else could have happened. 'But how do you accidentally stab someone tied up, who can't defend herself? If you're saying there was no struggle, how could she have just fallen on a knife?'

'It's simply my opinion.'

'Yes, and don't get me wrong, I value it. So please, your opinion is what I want.'

Eamonn pointed to the bed. 'Let's say we're dealing with a straightforward killer who wants rid of this person held captive here. He comes in, let's say carrying a knife. If his aim is to do away with the woman, and the weapon he plans to use is a knife, why didn't he move to the victim's neck . . .' Eamonn sliced a finger across his own neck '. . . and slash her throat?'

'How can you be sure he didn't?' Jo asked.

'The blood pooling was in the middle of the bed,' Eamonn pointed out.

Jo rubbed her forehead. 'What if he came in and stabbed her in the heart? Maybe she was lying further down the bed, or maybe she wriggled away from him.'

'But she couldn't.' He indicated the footboard at the end of the bed. 'The stomach is not somewhere I've ever seen someone stabbed when lying prostrate. The heart, the neck, even the face – but the stomach only if the victim is upright, otherwise it's about the least likely spot to aim for. And as for it happening here? Never. That window looks out on the street outside. What killer would take the chance of being seen or heard?'

Jo jumped when Sexton put his hand on her shoulder. He was watching one of the rookies, who'd been checking the rooms, start to climb a set of attic steps that they'd just pulled from the ceiling in the landing.

'The house has been vacant since the owners, Paul and Jenny Bell, were evicted,' Sexton said, reading from his notebook. 'Paul was unemployed. Jenny was a hairdresser. They had no kids.'

'OK, thanks,' Jo said, making a mental note to look into Paul's background.

'Oh, and there's a reporter on the doorstep asking questions,' Sexton continued. 'Alfie's dealing with it.'

'What?' Jo said.

'Yeah, he's with the *Daily Record*, apparently.'

'Please don't tell me it's Niall Toland?'

'Afraid so,' Sexton answered.

Jo sighed. 'You said no kids, right?' she asked, glancing back at the pink nursery as she moved to the front door. 'This is a crime scene, Alfie,' she called down when she saw Toland inside the hall and on the wrong side of the cordon. Jo was livid. Alfie hadn't even made Toland suit up.

'Don't move,' she told Toland, taking the stairs two at a time.

'He's just leaving,' Alfie answered, flushed.

Toland was animated, protesting that it was a matter of public interest.

'I said stay put,' Jo warned. 'And I'll have your shoes,' she said, pointing.

Toland looked at her like she was joking, and attempted to take another step back towards the door.

'She's right,' Alfie said, stepping sideways to block his path.

'You go and get him some overalls from the van so he can walk out without causing any more contamination,' Jo told the uniform standing outside the door.

'What was all that shite you fed me about not wanting to scare Derek off?' Jo asked Alfie. 'You brought a bloody reporter to the scene!'

'I didn't tip him off,' Alfie said.

Toland avoided both of their eyes. 'I can't reveal my sources,' he said sheepishly.

A panicked shout for help from upstairs made them all stop and turn.

45

Even if she hadn't known whose office she was in, Liz would have guessed that it had belonged to a woman. The beam of Derek's torch had glided over leopard-skin cushions and a crushed-velvet throw on a leather couch. The walls were covered in Amanda's framed qualifications.

Sweat droplets trickled down Liz's back as she tried to keep her breathing steady. *Derek and Amanda must have been more than neighbours before he killed her*, she thought. *Maybe that's how he got a key to her office and the code for her alarm. Is he going to shoot me here?*

'Sit down,' Derek said.

Liz kept her hands in her pockets so he wouldn't see them trembling as she lowered her bum into the seat. 'Where's Conor? Where is he?'

She knew Derek wouldn't hurt their son, even if she'd just seen him smash Paul's head in. Paul had still been breathing when they'd left him. The wound to his head mightn't have been deep, and Liz knew scalp injuries were notorious when it came to blood loss, but left unconscious and unable to help himself, Paul might well bleed to death. And there was a baby back there . . .

'Quiet,' Derek said.

Derek had refused to let her help Paul or take the baby, saying only that if she attracted any attention they might never see Conor again. So she'd shut up and had done exactly as he asked, slinking under the cover of night through the culvert and into the convent grounds to get out of Nuns Cross.

'I need to use the bathroom.'

'You know where it is,' Derek said, holding the door open for her and pointing the torch out into the corridor. 'But I can't put on the light, love, sorry. And I can't give you this either.' He held up the torch. The gun was tucked under the belt of his trousers.

Liz pushed through the door, into the corridor, squinting to try and get her bearings as Derek shone the light.

'Love . . .' he said.

How could he still call her that? She froze, but didn't turn.

'I know you're scared, I can hear it in your voice. But don't worry, it's nearly over.'

To her amazement, he let the door to the office close. Liz hurried into Amanda's loo to keep up the pretence, as she tried to work out in the pitch black if the window, which she remembered seeing in here on Friday, could (a) be opened, and (b) was big enough for her to fit through. She'd started patting the walls – feeling around frantically for the window – when she heard the office door beside her creak open again. Derek was calling quiet reassurances through the door, telling her to let him know when she was ready, he'd hold the light for her. Liz flicked on the faucet so he wouldn't hear the sound of her lowering the toilet seat down so she could stand on it. It banged on to the porcelain but she kept going. Her teeth chattered as her hands moved to the window and established its dimensions. It was much smaller than she remembered, tiny. She could feel the embossed frosting in the glass, it was no more than one foot across and two high. She'd never fit through it, but Conor might . . . if she could get Derek to bring him here. She flicked the handle, and her heart soared when she realized it wasn't secured and opened perfectly.

Liz climbed back down, upending what must have been a basket of loo rolls – based on the things rolling about on the floor – and only barely managing to stop a vase of some description from shattering on the tiles.

'You OK in there?'

She started to hyperventilate.

'Yep,' she called back, 'coming.'

I can't go anywhere without Conor.

With the thought came clarity. The panting began to slow down to deep breathy puffs in and out. *There was no point in trying to escape because she didn't want to yet*, she thought. Not until she knew what Derek had done with Conor. Her only hope was to try and talk to him. Finishing up, she washed her hands under the tap, holding her wrists under the cold water and splashing her face. Then she slid the bolt back across and pressed the door handle down.

Derek held the door open for her, and then opened Amanda's office door. In the beam of the torch she saw he'd rolled up the rug on Amanda's salvaged wooden floor. Her heart stalled. Was he planning to move her body in that? And then something else in the centre of the floor caught her attention.

Liz stared. There was a handle set into it.

'I know you probably have a lot of questions, and I'll answer every last one of them, but not now, there isn't time.'

He looked like death with the light shining up from under his jaw, the play of shadows in the hollows of his eye sockets and cheekbones making him resemble a kid mucking about at Halloween. He also had that skittish air of someone with a fever, she noticed. Something was up. Something more than panic. There was a sheen on his skin like varnish. She remembered the antibiotics he'd been getting in the hospital, and wondered if it was possible he'd had an internal bleed.

Derek reached over his shoulders, pulling his sweater over his head stiffly. A T-shirt he was wearing underneath, which was covered with damp patches, rose slightly, revealing bandages that must have been put on by nurses after his accident. He patted some strands of flyaway hair back down.

'Is it just me or is it hot in here?' he asked.

Liz was freezing. 'What's wrong with you?'

He swiped the back of his hand across his forehead. 'I'll be fine. Just feeling a bit, dunno, weird.'

Liz wondered if he'd collapse. If so, it would be the second miracle of the night.

The possibility that she might yet escape with her life sent a rush of adrenalin coursing through her veins. 'Whatever you've done . . . whatever it is you're going to do . . . I know you love our son . . . just tell me where he is,' Liz said, her voice breaking.

But Derek was too focused on that handle to answer. He pulled it up and a hole appeared in the floor.

46

'Amanda had me fit it up during the renovation job,' Derek explained about the trapdoor. 'There was a whole basement level that had fallen into complete disrepair because of the extent of the damp. She said it could come in handy for storage space, so I dry lined it, and got Tom to plaster it. I even offered to put in proper stairs so it wouldn't be hidden, but Amanda wanted the access to be concealed because of the documents she was keeping down there. I assume she didn't want everyone knowing about it. Solicitors need to keep a lot of important documents secure.'

Liz remembered the banging noise she'd heard from Amanda's office when she'd been hiding in the loo on Friday, and realized that it could very well have been that lid. She could see a ladder set against one of the shaft walls behind the trapdoor, which sat open at a ninety-degree angle against the floor. She could tell, as the torch flashed around it, that if Derek stood in the hole at his six-foot-two height, the top of his head would probably only just be below the hatch.

He lowered himself to the floor so he could lie flat and extend an arm into the hole to guide his torch around the inside, glancing up as if he seriously expected her to lean over and share his appreciation, like a kid who'd found a cave full of treasure.

Liz took a few steps closer. The beam of light was bouncing a lot further than she'd anticipated in his dark cave.

'I know it's not much to look at, but you have to see it from down here to appreciate it. You'll understand when you get in, because from this point on, it's our bolthole. It's fully stocked with food and water – I cleared out all of Amanda's files to make room. It's wired up, so there's power in there, too. I had to paint it myself because she was so paranoid about anyone else knowing about it. There's a generator and a heater. If it came to it, we've enough supplies down here to survive for a month. It's aerated, too, so you don't have to worry about smothering. I've run vents up. It's even got a toilet. Hey, I've even got a mini-fridge down here, full of Bud, and a portable DVD player. Oh yeah, there's a water cooler, too. It tastes a lot better than what comes out of our tap. You never know, you might not want to come back up to the land of the living. You still can't put the light on, though, because Conor's asleep down there . . .'

Taking a deep breath, Liz aimed the sole of her shoe

at the open lid of the trapdoor and kicked it, sending it smashing against Derek's head.

He let out an almighty roar. Kneeling down on her hunkers, Liz lifted it so she could smash him again.

'Dad, are you OK?' came the words from below in the split second before her arm crashed down.

With that, the bunker flooded with sudden light.

47

Liz's heart stalled.

'Ow, my fucking head,' Derek groaned. Liz watched in horror as he rolled over on to his back, his hands moving to his head. 'What happened? I spring-loaded that to stop it from happening.' He moaned. Liz scrambled towards him and managed to grab the gun from his belt.

Darth Vader appeared at the top of the ladder. 'Dad, is there blood? You know I'll faint if there's blood. So is there?'

'Sorry for waking you,' Derek grunted.

'Oh, hi, Mum. You have got to see in here, it's super cool. It's like a regular tree house, without the tree, I mean. Are you OK, Dad? Good news, there's no blood. Can you see any, Mum?'

'Go back down and put on *The Clone Wars*,' Derek said. 'We'll be down in a second.'

When Conor disappeared from view, Liz said in a hushed tone, 'If you think you're going to bury me and my son alive, you're sadly mistaken.'

'What the fuck is wrong with you?' Derek hissed, checking Conor was definitely out of earshot before easing himself up on to his elbows. 'I'm trying to protect you from the people who want to get at me, and you're trying to kill me?'

'Why didn't you tell me about Ellen?'

Derek moaned and rolled over on to his side. His hair was damp with perspiration. He looked terrible, paler than marble.

'I tried. I told you I thought I was protecting you . . . us . . . at first. The more time went on, the harder it got. I'm sorry.'

Liz kept her eyes centred on his head as he tried to sit up. 'Don't move. I will use this gun, I mean it. I don't want you to talk any more, either. I don't want to hear any more of your warped logic.'

'If you're planning to kill me, go right ahead. You won't be able to shift my body, which means you'll have to walk our son out past me. The alternative is you lock me in there and take Conor, but if you head back out there alone, I know both of you will be killed,' Derek said with another deep groan. 'Mervyn has paid people to kill me, and they will wipe you out without so much as a second thought to get to me.'

He curved his back and knelt shakily.

'I said, don't move,' Liz warned.

'Use it, then, I wouldn't want to live without you and Conor anyway.' He lunged and grabbed her by the wrist. Derek knocked the gun from her hand and kicked it out of the way. He wrestled it free, and then, wrapping his two arms around Liz's upper body to restrain her, he manhandled her on to the ladder. Gripping her tightly, he pulled her down into the den.

'Are you two fighting?' Conor asked when they landed with a thump, Derek on his back and Liz on top of him. She shrugged Derek off her angrily.

'No, son,' Derek answered, getting up slowly. Clutching his head, he climbed up the steps and out, lowering the lid closed behind him. She heard him wedging something against the trapdoor, and guessed he'd pushed whatever it was under the handle to prevent her getting the lid up as soon as he was gone. She tried to visualize what it could be. It didn't matter, it wouldn't take much to shake it free.

In any event, all hope of that happening evaporated with the sound of a deadweight thud directly overhead.

48

Back home by half eleven, Jo did her best to wipe up the food Harry was firing from his plate, while negotiating the binging microwave, supposed to be defrosting some steaks for dinner. Harry shouldn't have been up at all, but Dan had said he hadn't wanted to wake him after he'd fallen asleep at four without any dinner. The result was that Harry was up, wide-eyed and bushy-tailed. Jo had the phone squashed between her shoulder and ear waiting for an update from Tallaght Children's Hospital, where the baby they'd found in the attic had been rushed by ambulance.

'She's stable,' the doctor told Jo. 'We'll know a lot more in the morning. Let's just say it's a good thing you found her when you did. She wasn't malnourished, but she was very, very cold.'

Thanking her, Jo sighed as she hung up and rang Foxy to tell him the news. She was about to ring Sexton too, but spotting Dan's impatient expression at the sight of her on the phone she snapped it shut instead. This was always the hardest part of the day for her, and considering this one had started in such a gruesome way, that was saying something. Every night when she got in, the first thing she had to deal with was guilt. It required a mental shift: she had to force herself to put work to one side and concentrate on her family. Jo permanently felt bad that she wasn't spending enough time with them, that the house looked like a bomb had hit it, and that she was failing so miserably on the home/work balance front. She even felt guilty that she felt guilty, and couldn't just enjoy this precious part of the day at home.

Tonight was no different. The kitchen sink was piled with dishes, and she groaned at just how manky the floor was – in dire need of a hoover and a mop. She cursed at the sight of a bag of groceries she'd bought on the way home the previous night and hadn't emptied yet. It had fallen over on its side, and a box of eggs had broken and seeped into the sliced bread. She pulled a face as she deposited them in the bin. It wasn't as if she could ask Dan to get his finger out. He could barely get from A to B, and was hypersensitive as it was about the role reversal induced by his injuries, which was putting enough strain on their marriage. Sourcing a bloody cleaner had proved impossible, because their home was too out of the way, and nobody who was prepared to work for what they could afford to pay drove a car. And as for the laundry . . .

It wasn't that Jo wasn't willing to get stuck in each

night, just that because she was wrecked she begrudged any time spent on the house, because it was attention diverted from the few precious hours she got to spend with her sons, and that made her grumpy. She'd passed a bearded electricity guy reading her meter on the way in, reminding her that everyone was in the same boat. The days of unions and rights were gone, everyone was working around the clock, and a person had to be grateful for any job in the current climate.

'Here you go, son,' she told Harry, swapping plates and giving him a chocolate pudding and a spoon.

Jo leaned sideways, pulled the microwave door open, muttering, 'Blast,' when she realized she'd managed to partially cook the steaks. She glanced around for a cloth. The inside of the microwave looked like someone had heated tomato soup for too long: there were red splodges and splashes all over the walls and door.

Harry stretched his arms, dropping the spoon and sending chocolate spattering on to the floor. He needed bathing, too.

'Poor love,' she said, giving him another spoon and kissing him on the top of his head.

'Mmmm, microwaved meat,' Rory teased, looking over her shoulder at the sorry plate of leathery-looking steaks giving off a foul smell. He was in his pyjamas, but had got up to say goodnight.

Jo made a 'blah blah' motion with her hand, and began to empty the dishwasher, keeping one hand in the small of her back, and grumbling under her breath at the amount she'd still to do.

It wasn't fair to ask Rory to give her a dig out: as he was sitting his Leaving Certificate, it would only eat into his study or sleep time. But she was going to have to broach the subject of hiring one of those come-in-and-blitz-the-house firms to appear every quarter at some stage with Dan, even if it meant forking out five hundred euro for the privilege. She'd happily go hungry for the joy of sitting down in a clean house at night.

Dan banged the bottom of the kitchen door open with one of his crutches, and heaved himself into the room.

'Oi,' he asked Rory, 'since when has becoming a MasterChef judge been an option on the college application form? Are you still hungry?'

'Nope. I'm full,' Rory said, eyeing up Jo's steaks. 'Think I'll leave you two lovebirds to it.'

'Night,' Jo called after him.

'In fairness, he's right,' Jo told Dan, wiping chocolate off her own face with some kitchen roll. 'I've made a pig's ear of it, again.'

'You can't be good at everything,' Dan said.

'Thanks, love,' Jo said, leaning in for a kiss. Right now she felt pretty crap at everything.

'I'm sorry I'm so late,' she told him. 'It's this bloody case.' *How often have I used that as an excuse?* she wondered, hoping against hope the guilt was making it seem more often than it actually was.

Dan had been organizing knives and forks from the cutlery drawer to set the table when she got back. She wondered why he was now lighting a candle in the middle of it, as he moved piled-up laundry from one side to the other. Jo was not going to sit at a table piled with clothes. She began to tell him as much, but he dropped a clattering knife, and started lowering himself to pick it up.

'Here, let me,' Jo said, anxious to help.

'I'll manage,' he said, losing his grip on his crutch, and trying to manoeuvre the knife into a position he could reach with his foot.

Jo backed off helplessly, and got distracted by the sight of Harry firing more food from his spoon for fun.

'Happy anniversary,' Dan said, sounding like he was talking to himself.

Jo turned around, and pulled a face. 'Oh Jesus, love, I'm so sorry. I've been too busy, I forgot.'

He loped off towards the sitting room, muttering, 'I remembered because I've got nothing better to do. Your present's on the bed.'

Jo hated that he looked so hurt, and followed him. 'I didn't mean you're not busy, Dan. Come on, give me a break.'

He waved a hand over his shoulder to tell her she was digging herself into a bigger hole and to stop, but that was like waving a red flag, because it felt to Jo as if he couldn't be bothered to argue.

'Dan, can you just listen to me for a second?'

'I'm not one of your underlings.'

'I wasn't for a minute suggesting you were.'

'There you go again with your bloody patronizing tone.'

Jo reached for his hand and sighed. 'Fifteen years, eh, who'd have thought?'

'Thirteen really, if you count the two I wasn't around.'

If he'd intended to hurt her, it had worked. Jo stood up to walk away before she said something she regretted. But Dan came as close as he could to an apology. 'Don't bother cooking tonight. I've been picking all day. I could do with a drink, though. Did you get a bottle of wine? I left a message when I couldn't get you, asking you to pick a bottle up on the way home.'

'I'm sorry. I've been chasing my tail all day. I didn't realize I'd a message.'

'Doesn't matter. I'm only fit for bed.'

'Right,' Jo said. If he was planning on hitting the scratcher, she was going to have to bring up the subject of Derek Carpenter straight away, though the timing was terrible. Harry started to wail before she got a chance. He'd fallen over. Jo stopped what she was doing and picked him up. She tried to wipe him clean as he laughed, and couldn't resist giving him a tickle. As soon as he was sorted, she followed Dan into the sitting room. He was aiming the zapper at the box. *EastEnders*, or some similar shite, that he had actually gone to the trouble of recording, she realized. He would have baulked at the idea of watching a soap when he'd been working. Now he sat through complete dross with a glazed expression.

Jo sat on the couch. She really needed to talk to him before he got too engrossed. She picked a last bit of food from Harry's hair as he ran past towards a football and kicked it, and then chased it again.

'How's the pain today, love?' she asked, attempting a none-too-subtle shift of gear.

He shrugged, and kept staring at the box. 'The same.'

'I need to talk to you about the case. It's important.'

He aimed the zapper and pressed the mute button with a sigh.

'Alfie Taylor wants to interview you tomorrow about Derek Carpenter, over that girl we found in the mountains today. You remember . . . ?'

It didn't seem like news.

'He found out you registered him as a tout. I presume he wants to know why, and what information Derek had to give. I need a heads up.'

'It's confidential.'

Jo stared at him in disbelief.

She couldn't hide her exasperation. 'I'm supposed to be your bloody wife.'

'When it suits you.'

'What does that mean?'

He didn't answer, and Jo knew she couldn't pursue it

without raising her voice, which she wouldn't do in front of Harry.

She took a breath. 'On the phone earlier, you said Ellen was a bit of a tearaway. The only logical conclusion I can draw from your complete lack of concern about this is that you believe Ellen could have run away.'

He didn't answer. Inasmuch as she knew this man, that was the equivalent of an affirmation. She wanted to grab him and shake him. 'I know you registered Derek Carpenter as an informant, but as he was a suspect in Ellen's disappearance, you must have had more to base the runaway theory on? A diary, something like that?'

'Not a diary. Ellen hadn't come home a couple of times in the previous week. She refused to tell her family where she'd gone, just claimed to have lost track of time and fallen asleep in a friend's house. Her friends covered for her at the time, but after she disappeared, they admitted they'd no idea where she'd been.'

'I have to presume that Derek told you this. But what information could he have given you about the case that could be trusted?'

'I told you, I gave him my word. I'm sorry.'

'This is madness.'

'Derek Carpenter took me into his confidence,' Dan said.

'Took you into his confidence?' she repeated slowly. 'He was a murder suspect. It was your job to get him to talk.'

'I was younger then.'

'Oh, God,' Jo said, closing her eyes. She stood and started pacing. 'Didn't you wonder what Ellen's shoe was doing in the mountains when it was found? How could you not entertain the possibility that Derek might have been trying to cover up his own involvement?'

'I was confident he was telling the truth,' Dan said. 'Derek told me he planted the shoe there himself, because of all the speculation about a serial killer dumping bodies in the mountains at the time. He wanted people to believe that Ellen had been targeted by the same man.'

'And you took that as gospel? I don't believe this,' Jo cut in, the panic beginning to well up in her throat.

'Would you if I said that someone else corroborated this version of events?' Dan asked.

'As long as it wasn't Liz.'

'It wasn't Liz,' Dan answered.

Jo blinked. 'Not Ellen?'

No answer.

Jo let out a grunt of aggravation. 'Do you know where Ellen is now?'

'No. I helped her to leave the country, but I haven't had any contact with either of them in twenty years, apart from a few weeks back, when Derek Carpenter rang to give me details of a drug-smuggling operation in the company where he worked, the details of which I've passed on to the drug squad.'

315

'Mervyn's?'

'Yes, the meat plant, that's right.'

'I knew Mervyn was hiding something,' she said, talking as much to herself as him. 'Drugs – yes, yes, that has the ring of truth.'

'Since you've guessed that, I don't feel I'm breaking a confidence this time,' Dan said. 'The drugs are being smuggled in animal carcasses. It's a massive operation, and Derek's information is invaluable. He's going to be put in a witness-protection programme for his own safety.'

'Alfie thinks he's gone to ground because he's got something to hide,' Jo said. She paused. 'Hang on, did Derek ring you directly?'

'Yes.'

'And you rang him back? There was more than one call to and fro, right?'

'That's right. Why?'

'No wonder Alfie's like a dog with a bone between his teeth. He's been tracking your bloody phone. He probably thinks that if you're in touch with Derek you know where he is. Do you?'

'Give me a break!'

'You're being an absolute . . .' She turned away rather than say the word.

When she looked back, there was fire in Dan's eyes.

'Ditto,' he said.

49

Foxy had been in bed when Jo called to update him. He hadn't been able to sleep, anyway. His wife, Dot, had gone out socializing and he couldn't relax until she got home safe. He checked the display on the alarm clock – 11.39 p.m. – and then went back to mulling over what Jo had said. On the face of it, her claim that she was nominating Niall Toland as a suspect, and presuming his source on the tape to be someone who was in cahoots with him, just seemed a step too far to Foxy. Maybe Alfie was right, and Jo was incapable of impartiality on this case. But something about the second conversation Toland had had with his source had been niggling at Foxy, too. It was only a partial recording, much shorter than the first. Jo hadn't listened to it yet, as far as he was aware.

Foxy tried to work out what it was about it that seemed so odd. It was something to do with the power shift between the journalist and his so-called source. Toland had gone from being the one calling the shots in the first conversation to accepting everything the source told him in the second. Foxy was prepared to admit that this might have been because, having discovered how useful the source was to him, Toland wanted to keep him onside. But something about it wasn't right. Foxy had even asked Joan, who'd typed the transcript for Jo, to redo it, because she'd taken it upon herself to guess what the last broken word uttered by the source was.

The conversation had started with the source asking Toland how it felt to land such a big scoop. Toland had replied, 'Great.' The source had asked if he was ready for the next one, and Toland had answered, 'Absolutely.' Foxy thought it weird that Toland seemed so nonplussed by the source's announcement that the killer had gone on the run. He didn't ask any obvious questions like who the killer was. There'd been some more toing and froing between them about something completely tangential – a football-match score – and then when Toland had said, 'Thanks for this,' the source had uttered his last words, 'Don't thank me, that would be your mis—' At this point the tape ended, presumably because – based on the high-pitched tone – one of the parties, Toland probably, had hung up. Joan thought the source had been about to say, 'That would be your mistake.' But Foxy was still not sure. It sounded slightly awkward. Wouldn't it have been more natural to say something like 'It would be a mistake to do that', or 'That would be stupid'?

'Maybe he just got his words muddled up,' Joan had argued.

Foxy sat up at the sound of Dot turning the key in the lock downstairs and banging the front door shut after her. Lowering his feet into his slippers, he rose to head down to help her up the stairs. Then he had a change of heart, sat down again, and lifted his legs back under the covers. Dot would want a nightcap if she heard him up. The racket might wake Sal, their teenage daughter, who had Down's syndrome.

He listened intently as Dot heaved herself up the stairs, puffing and panting. Sal was a good sleeper, but considering the length of time it was taking Dot to get up the stairs, it wasn't beyond the bounds of possibility that Sal might yet stir. He considered going out to help Dot, but again decided against it. She'd shouted at him for doing something similar on previous occasions. He reached over to turn off his bedside lamp, closing his eyes so she wouldn't give him every spit and cough of the night when she got in.

Dot had been renewing old acquaintances in the last few months, claiming she wanted to catch up with people she hadn't seen for years before they both headed off together on a round-the-world cruise – supposed to be like a second honeymoon, but without the renewing of vows – to mark his retirement. But he knew it was just an excuse to drink in a way she couldn't at home because he didn't – or at least he hoped that's what it was.

Foxy didn't want to jinx things by challenging her. Their marriage hadn't exactly been without incident. It didn't change the fact that she was the only woman he'd ever loved or wanted. The bedroom door opened wider and the room brightened as Dot flicked on the overhead light.

'Can you turn that off?' he asked, worried the brightness travelling down the landing would disturb Sal. She liked to sleep with both bedroom doors left open.

Dot snapped it off again, grumbling something about him being an old grump, and then tried to stifle some giggles as she banged into, or tripped over, one object after another as she tried to strip. She stank of sour booze and smoke. And she didn't smoke.

Foxy stretched an arm out and turned the bedside lamp on again.

'Jesus,' she snapped, squinting, 'can I not have a bit of privacy?'

She had managed to get her skirt and blouse off and had only half hoisted her nightdress up. Her face was a mess. Her false eyelashes were coming away at the corners, and her lipstick had smudged into the wrinkles around her mouth like red stitches.

Foxy sat up. 'Here. Let me,' he offered.

She held her arm up and walked her hips as he pulled the nightdress back down. 'Did you get the tickets today?' she asked as he lifted the corner of the duvet for her to get in.

'Yes. I tried to ring you to let you know, but your mobile was off.'

'I must have been having my face done. I decided to go for collagen treatment so I can look my best before we head off. The surgeon was very nice. He was Indian, I think. Too young for me. You should try it. Honestly, there were more men than women in the waiting room.'

'How much did that cost?'

'I can't remember.'

'You can't keep spending money like it grows on trees, Dot.'

'Oh, don't be such an old fart,' she said. 'Life's for living. We'll be dead long enough.'

She hopped up out of bed again, and started to sing 'Moon River', pursing her lips, walking her shoulders and cocking her hips. She still harboured a dream of becoming a professional singer.

'Would you like to dance, beautiful?' he asked her, feeling his heart lift as her face lit up. He adored her, but he had an ulterior motive – to stop the racket.

It was while her arms were wrapped around his neck that the penny finally dropped. What if the word that Joan had assumed was 'mistake' was actually 'missus'? And the full sentence: 'Don't thank me, that would be your missus . . .'

As he recalled, Alfie had mentioned when he'd asked Foxy to put the tapes into the logbook that Niall Toland had probably cut the phone call off early because he

321

was shattered, being a new dad. It might be nothing. He made a mental note to mention it to Jo in the morning. Right now his own missus was his only concern. Dot had fallen asleep in his arms, and was snoring her beautiful head off. Something else occurred to him as he tucked her in. Men didn't launch into a heartfelt discussion about a match with someone they didn't know. Sure, they talked football basics to strangers as a conversation starter, but an in-depth analysis of the match, and knowing which team they supported, implied friendship.

He was starting to come around to Jo's way of thinking, despite all the odds. Foxy would get her to listen to the tape tomorrow for herself, but right now he was certain that Toland and his source knew each other.

50

Jo was burning the midnight oil, sitting up in bed, chewing the top of a biro with a pad of foolscap balanced against her bent knees. Rubbing her eyes, she yawned and glanced at the pertinent points in the statement Sexton had taken from the mother reunited with her child. She was absolutely convinced Niall Toland knew a lot more about what had happened to Amanda Wells than he was letting on, and the logical inference was that it was because he was in closer contact with the source and the presumed killer than he wanted anyone to be aware of. *Just how well connected with the underworld was he?*

The painkillers Jo had taken before coming to bed had made her drowsy. She hated taking them as regularly as she did, and knew she was on a collision course with an ulcer, but her headache was even making itself felt in the nerves of her teeth. She'd managed to reschedule the appointment with Dr Griffen, her ophthalmologist, after ringing earlier to offer a grovelling apology for the 'no show'. But using the job as an excuse for never being where she was supposed to be was starting to wear thin. Other people managed to juggle their personal and professional lives, so why couldn't she?

Jo stole a glance at Dan lying alongside, his legs over the covers, one arm behind his head, wearing only his boxers. He'd been monosyllabic since their stand-off, and was staring at a late-night movie on the TV in their bedroom. The room was lit by a blue glow, and the lap-top screensaver kept flicking to life at the slightest vibration from its perch on the locker beside Jo's side of the bed. She hadn't bothered to put on the bedside lamp. It only made her eyes feel more tired. She wondered how much longer she'd have to wait before it would be safe to broach the subject of Ellen Lamb with Dan again. Giving each other the silent treatment was juvenile and exhausting. His face was stony, and he looked too thin. He'd lost a lot of weight since the shooting, and didn't sleep soundly any more either, not like he used to.

His anniversary gift – a skimpy black silk camisole and matching knickers – sat in its gift box on the dresser. Jo had put the bunch of flowers left on top of them in water before getting in to bed. The bloody flowers had marked her white shirt. But annoyance had quickly turned to guilt, long since replaced by fury at the fallout from their row. That was the reason why she'd opted for a pair of comfy, and profoundly unsexy, fleece-lined pyjamas, designed to send out an un-mitigated signal he should make no attempt to touch her. She didn't want presents, she wanted him to trust her and to talk to her, the way he used to.

Jo studied the rough map she'd sketched of Nuns Cross, outlining the five cul-de-sacs and writing the owners' initials in the boxes she'd drawn for houses, along with a note about their occupations.

She'd got all forty residents' names from the electoral register, an alphabetical listing of the addresses and occupants. The information wasn't going to pass any scientific test – a search in the land registry would have given her the actual deed owners – these names could be renters for all she knew. For now, she was prepared to take a punt that anyone who'd listed Nuns Cross as their address to vote was the probable owner. She'd also looked into each resident's occupation by running their social security number through the system, and had run searches on all of the names, looking for previous criminal convictions. As it happened, of the forty residents listed, Derek Carpenter was the only one with previous.

She rubbed her face in frustration. She could almost hear Alfie now, claiming that with enough strands of circumstantial evidence, you could fashion a rope. There was only one resident she'd no occupation for, and it was the former owner of the vacant house in

Nuns Cross: Paul Bell. Jo needed to find out more about him. She glanced up at the telly impatiently. The noise was starting to get on her wick, and affect her concentration. She wished Dan would turn it off. He sensed her bristling, and turned it down.

Jo stared at the computer screen as Paul Bell's social security number returned the details of his last occupation – journalist. She sat up straight, and felt her heart speed up. She scrolled through the details to establish where he'd worked, and saw he was a former member of staff at the *News of the World*.

Jo's eyes darted to her shirt lying on top of a wicker laundry basket in the corner of the room. Flicking a corner of the duvet back, she stood and headed out to the hall, grabbing the stained shirt she'd dumped earlier. Carrying on down the stairs of the dormer, she stopped at Dan's flowers in the hall and held the shirt up to the stalk containing the lily. Rubbing it to and fro, she made exactly the same criss-cross pattern in precisely the same colour as she'd seen on Niall Toland's shirt when she'd interviewed him in the station.

Jo hurried back to the bedroom and retrieved the mother's statement Sexton had given her, running a finger down the lines. Other than the flowers, there was nothing tangible to link Toland to the baby bar her hunch. But it was as strong as they got.

'What's the matter?' Dan asked.

'I think it's the reporter,' Jo said, feeling a rush of

adrenalin. 'I think it's two reporters . . .' she continued aloud as her brain teased things out. 'Niall Toland's not being led around by the nose by the killer. Derek Carpenter is.'

'Derek didn't do it,' Dan said.

'I know,' Jo snapped. But if her own husband didn't trust her enough to tell her what was going on, why should she be bothered to discuss it with him any further? Reaching for her dressing gown, she hurried out to the hall to make some calls as Dan pulled the duvet up to his chin and turned his back on her.

Sunday

51

Four thirty in the morning, and Paul Bell sped along the narrow military mountain pass, taking regular over-the-shoulder glances into the back seat while scanning every angle for somewhere to pull in and dump the woman's body. He smoothed his hair with a set of chewed fingernails as he tried to calm Niall Toland down. Panicking wasn't going to help the situation. But lying stretched out across Niall's legs, her torso gripped between his arms, was one of Paul's neighbours, the solicitor, Amanda Wells. Paul had arranged to meet Niall at Paul's old home in Nuns Cross, to discuss their plot to kidnap a baby and cash in on the newspaper reward. He hadn't been back since the eviction, but he'd thought his old house would be perfect for meetings because it was at the end of the cul-de-sac and bordered a culvert to a convent and he needed somewhere to keep the baby. Thanks to an ancient right of way, it was also the only spot where you could get in and out of the gated community without going through the key-pad entrance. But they'd found Amanda's lifeless body waiting for them, as well as a bag containing medical paraphernalia – a hypodermic syringe, empty vials, a canister of pills he didn't recognize, in an old Henry Norton's bag. Her clothes had been soaked in blood.

Paul cast another quick look back. Black mascara tracks streaked down Amanda's face; her signature flaxen-gold hair was matted with vomit. And Mr Nine-to-Five Toland was in some kind of crazy state of denial, wailing and refusing to accept that the dead woman was dead.

Paul's knuckles were white on the steering wheel, and he was leaning slightly forwards, with his lights on full, trying to stay clear of the ditches on either side of the winding road. If he went off it, which, given the banshee noise levels emanating from the back, was not beyond the bounds of possibility, they were going to have to carry the body somewhere to dump it and walk the fuck back.

The mist was so heavy, it was like driving with a set of net curtains over the windscreen. He honked hard whenever he hit a complete blind spot, before hitting enough straight road to take another quick look back.

'She just opened her eyes and looked at me,' Niall screamed, between howls.

'Don't be stupid, she's dead as fuck,' Paul shouted back.

Niall swiped at the tears and snot streaming down his

face. 'She's not dead, she just moved, or had a fit or something. What did you do to her?'

'How many times do you want me to tell you: NOTHING!'

Niall went into a complete meltdown. 'You said you wanted to talk about the story of my career. You said it was about finding a missing baby and getting the kind of money that could set me and Monica and our son up for life into the bargain. That's why I let you come to visit Monica in hospital. You did not say anything about dumping a woman's body in the mountains. You lured me into this under false pretences. You killed her. You're on your own.'

Paul gritted his jaw. He'd got to know a lot of journalists over the years. The only reason he'd selected Niall as a partner on his big idea to scam a newspaper out of a reward was because he'd found out Niall's girlfriend was heavily pregnant. It had given him access to the Central Maternity Hospital to scope it out. The reason he'd needed a journalist in the first place was (a) to convince an editor that finding the baby was worth a reward, and (b) to write the story about the stooge who'd be entitled to the reward. Paul knew most of the hacks in town from his own time on the scene, but he'd passed up on the dodgiest ones for the chance of getting one with a pregnant girlfriend onside. If he'd known Niall was such a pussy, he'd have opted for someone who appreciated that sometimes, regularly, life did not go as planned, and would have taken his chances going in and cold-delivering the flowers when the time came . . .

'Turn back, I want out,' Niall roared.

'Listen to me,' Paul shouted over the din. 'I didn't kill her, so we've got nothing to worry about. The plan we had for tomorrow doesn't have to change. You're going to get your baby story, and we're going to share the reward like we arranged. All you have to do is keep it together. Think about it, how much longer do you think you've got in newspapers? The story's changed by the time newspapers are printed. It's instant on smart-phones, tablets and computer screens. Newspapers can't compete with that. Advertisers are moving to Google and Facebook because they know everything there is to know about their clients. They reckon by 2043 there'll be one newspaper reader left out of 312 million people in the States. You and Monica have got to be prepared, to protect yourselves for the future. You've got a kid to think about. You don't want to end up like me. I lost my job, my home and my wife, because I wasn't prepared. All we have to do is be clever about it and we can still pull it off, and make a few quid while we're at it. Maybe Jenny will even come back to me, and I'll be able to afford to get us our pad back.'

Niall didn't answer. He was sobbing too much.

Paul decided now was probably as good a time as any to pitch his idea about how to get them out of this hole.

'I've got a plan.'

'I don't want to hear it. I want to go back. You said the big story was going to be about a missing baby. You said all I had to do was persuade my editor as soon as the baby was snatched that it would be worth getting in with a reward offer.'

'Right, it is. But first we've got to do this missing-woman story. Just think about the difference having that money's going to make. The minimum your paper will offer is six figures. I know how it works, remember?'

Paul's hooded blue eyes narrowed as he went back to monitoring the situation from the rear-view mirror, his right foot pumping the accelerator. He slammed on the brakes as the car went into a skid and juddered to a halt, inches from a boulder. He banged his head off the steering wheel in the process. He took a deep breath and put the car back in gear, starting her up again. He had to focus.

'Listen. One of her neighbours, and mine, was wanted way back in connection with the missing women. You know him too – Derek Carpenter.'

'That bastard?' Niall asked, drawn in.

Paul pounced. 'I'll bet he's the one who killed her. So what I'm saying is, if we dump her somewhere linked to him, the cops are going to assume he did it. Right?'

'If Derek killed her it would explain that Henry Norton's bag being there,' Niall answered.

'Did you bring it?'

Niall nodded.

'Then we've got a prop,' Paul said. 'Do you remember the exact spot where that evil bastard dumped his sister-in-law? I mean the exact spot.'

'Of course,' Niall said. 'Take a left at the cross. Oh, sweet Jesus, did you see that? Did you? She just moved again.'

If he didn't know better, Paul could have sworn he'd seen a flash of something in the mirror that time. Amanda's body had jerked or stiffened, like someone having an epileptic fit. But it had to have been some kind of reaction to the motion. He was sure she was gone. A trickle of foam had dried in one corner of her mouth.

Niall moaned. 'You have to turn back, she's not dead.'

Paul kept talking so Niall would stay with him. 'If we nail that bastard Derek Carpenter for those women he killed, you'll end up a hero,' he said. 'Trust me, she's dead as fuck.'

This time Toland didn't answer.

It was seven thirty that evening, and Paul had a problem. Call boxes were a bugger to find these days – it was only a matter of time before they became a thing of the past, too, but coin boxes were not an option, supplying the precise opposite to what Paul needed because he had to use a voice distorter – privacy.

Paul had had to drive down to the sticks to find one isolated enough to let him talk in peace. The cops would find the number eventually, so it was vital he wasn't seen.

People were a lot wiser since the controversy. Personally, Paul didn't understand what all the fuss was about. He'd watched the hounding of his old editor on TV, the way the cameras had jostled her, the smart-arse solutions in the last edition of the newspaper's cross-word encrypted by furious staff, the secret recording of her last address put up on YouTube. It had made him really angry. He'd shouted the real questions at the box when Mr Know-All and himself a member of the press, Jeremy Paxman, had appeared.

What about all the paedophiles caught trying to ren-dezvous with kids they'd duped online? What about the match-fixing exposés that saved punters losing their money to the bookies? What about the sex-offenders' register – how do they think that had come about? What about Fergie charging for access to Andrew? The footballers in romps with hookers?

Everyone was so high and mighty now about privacy and not wanting to peep under the covers. But they were the ones who'd bought the papers to read the stories. Half the country was listening in on their other half's messages, finding out what they were up to. They didn't call it hacking, they called it homework.

Paul hoped people were happy now they'd castrated their right to know what was really going on. The days of exposing double standards were over. The irony was that most still hadn't even changed the default security code on their mobiles.

Personally, he didn't see the problem with accessing Milly's phone in the first place. What if they'd found her? Saved her? That was the point, wasn't it? So what if they'd run a few stories on the back of what they'd heard? Newspapers were in the business of making money. The cops didn't have the million-pound offers of rewards, that's where the newspapers came in. The hacks were helping them. That's why the relationship had become so symbiotic.

What if the *News of the Screws* had found Milly? Would anyone have remembered then that the press had hacked her phone in the process? Nobody would have cared about police corruption or press tactics; the end would have justified the means.

He dialled Niall's number.

'You a hack?' Paul asked when the call connected, just like they'd eventually agreed.

The next morning, Paul met Niall in a laneway near the maternity hospital. Paul was getting the same buzz in his florist's overalls as he had back in the days when he'd been a wine waiter in the Dorchester. But Niall's lip was practically quivering as he handed over the bouquet he'd bought. He was bobbing on the balls of his feet, looking anxiously this way, and then that, wiping the beads of perspiration breaking out on his forehead. Paul wanted to slap him one. He was the one with two layers of clothes on, and taking all the risks!

'We shouldn't have met so close to the building. It's asking for trouble,' Niall said.

Paul rubbed his hands together. 'You need to get out more, mate. This is the fun part.'

Niall stared at him like he'd lost it. Paul remembered how that look made him feel when he was a kid. Nothing and nobody was going to turn back the clock. He was somebody now.

He reached out for Niall's shirt to swipe away some pollen stains but the smudge made them worse. He squeezed the top of Niall's arm tight.

'Cheer up. What doesn't kill you makes you stronger.'

Tuesday

52

Dr James Griffen's face was about an inch from Jo's. Squinting with one eye, he stared through a lens into Jo's left eye, stepping sideways to do the same to the other. He was as bald as an egg, with rangy limbs and an abrupt manner. His office contained only qualifications on the wall and clinical equipment. There were no photographs of family, no golf trophies on his shelves, no signs of any life outside work.

Jo had had a frustrating morning, as her team tried to track down Niall Toland and Paul Bell, but there were still no leads, and still no sign of any of the Carpenters. Given all of the blood found in Paul Bell's house, Jo prayed that Liz and her son were still alive somewhere out there. As well as the McLoughlins they now had George Byrne in custody, charged with kidnapping, but none of them seemed to have any idea where Liz was now.

The lack of developments had, however made it easier for her to slip out to see Dr Griffen, who had agreed to squeeze Jo in, between scheduled appointments at his consultancy rooms in the Eye and Ear Hospital.

'Thanks for fitting me in,' Jo said.

'I'm not going to mince words,' said the doctor, stepping back and flicking the light on again.

Jo's throat closed to about the size of a straw. She wished there was someone with her to pat her hand so she could take the news in better, and to tell her everything would be all right, so she could tell them not to say that, and get that rush of anger from sensing someone else's pity. It would have stopped her feeling sorry for herself. She hadn't told Dan about this visit.

She sat up in the exam chair, and transferred her feet to the ground. 'When have you ever?' She wished he would look at her; instead he was sitting behind his desk making copious notes with a flash gold fountain pen, and speaking to her like she was an afterthought.

'You need new cornea transplants. You've been luckier than most, up to now. I have some clients who've required three surgeries in the same number of years.'

Jo took the seat in front of his desk.

'How soon?'

'Straight away. They've deteriorated dangerously. The left one's at the end of the road. The right's showing worrying signs. I'm putting you on the donor list.'

'Jesus. Can I put it off till things calm down a bit in work?'

Griffen put his pen down. 'Do you want me to ask the donor families to hold off making a decision until your downtime? Have you any idea of what they go through? Eyes and hearts are the hardest for them to part with.'

'It just seems very sudden. What do I do now?'

'You go home and pack a hospital bag. Give this to your employer.' He handed over the sheet he'd been writing on.

Jo took it and stared.

'When the call comes, you need to be ready.'

'Give me a guestimate? I've got a three-year-old. His father can barely get out of bed in the morning without help. My teenage son is doing his Leaving Certificate this year. I'll need to make arrangements.'

'Tomorrow, the next day . . . it's impossible to tell. Listen to the news. And count your blessings that there's a bank holiday weekend coming. From where you're sitting right now, the more casualties on the roads the better.'

53

Sitting on the edge of Chief Superintendent Jo Birmingham's bed, Paul pushed off his trainers at the heel with his toes, peeled off his sopping towelling socks and dropped them on the floor. He flopped back on the pastel-coloured eiderdown, arms splayed, bare feet planted firmly on the ground. Every part of him hurt, but at least he'd finished the job now.

As clean-ups went, this one had been hell. Every lunge had reverberated through his aching ribcage as he'd gone down on all fours to scrape and swipe up the endless gunge and grease. He'd lost count of the number of old newspapers and towels required for the mop up. It was close to 12.30 p.m. now, and he was absolutely exhausted, weak as a bloody kitten. Still, it was worth it.

He'd blagged his way into her house, past her disabled husband, telling him he'd been booked to clean the oven. The husband had put up a bit of resistance, claiming to know nothing about it. But Paul had assured him it was all prearranged, had even cracked a joke about not knowing what his own wife was doing half the time. Hubby dearest had headed out a few minutes ago, telling Paul he'd a physio appointment and asking for his details, wanting to know how long the job would take, and only leaving when he couldn't get his wife on the phone (because Paul had used a jammer to block the phone signal).

The key to a good blag was finding out the subject's weakness, and then playing to it. Paul had been here last night, pretending to read the electricity meter, had cased the place over to establish his bearings, seen how untidy it was through the lit windows as he'd prowled around virtually invisibly in the dark, and had come up with a ruse that would enable him to blag his way in the door. He'd put himself in the shoes of a working woman who was time poor.

'If I am finished before you get back, I'll just wait outside until you come back and pay me,' Paul had said.

The hubby made sure to let Paul know they were both coppers who lived here before finally getting into the taxi waiting at the bottom of the drive, taking a little boy with him.

Paul could not believe his luck. If he'd known hubby was heading out, he'd have waited until he was gone, and then broken in. He needed to establish where exactly the cops were in their investigation so he could find out who had nearly smashed his loaf in last night, and try and track down Liz.

There was only one way around what he'd told her. He'd been careless last night, letting his tongue run away with itself. Jo Birmingham's name was on the card that Liz had had in her pocket. Paul had got the address from a contact in the mobile-phone service provider after citing the number on her card. An hour in front of Jo's computer was all he'd need to establish where the investigation was at. Blagging his way into a station would have been a hell of a lot more difficult, though stranger things had happened. It wouldn't have been impossible – contract-cleaning firms were always looking for staff.

Her laptop was on her bedside locker, and since her hubby was gone, the only thing missing was a gift wrap and a bow. It would give Paul exactly the kind of heads up on the investigation he needed, and now that the baby had been found in his house, the shit could potentially hit the fan.

He pitied her with a high-flying job like that, being married to the type of man you'd catch watching *The Oprah Winfrey Show*, or *Dr Phil*, or whatever people who'd nothing better to do did. Mr Jo Birmingham was in desperate need of a shave and a haircut, and a shot of self-esteem.

Not like Paul. 'A brilliant self-starter.' That's what it had said on the reference they'd given him after they'd shut the newspaper down. The secret to being a good blagger was just telling people what they wanted to hear. A woman like Jo Birmingham worked all day, therefore the last thing she'd want to do at night was clean her oven. Her crippled husband wasn't about to do it, there was too much role reversal in this house as it was.

He'd used the oven-cleaning trick countless times before. All you had to do was get down on your hands and knees and scour and scrub for the too-posh-to-push kind of women who thought it beneath them. The best bit was he'd never even needed to invest in any equipment: he could get on the bus or train carrying a bucket, oven-cleaner spray and rubber gloves. Even a recession couldn't change the habits of some of the domestic slatterns he'd come across.

She was sexy, this cop, Paul thought, letting his head drop to the side as he took in the furnishings. She had good taste. He'd been through her knicker drawer, found something new he'd have made her wear if he was giving her the seeing-to her husband couldn't, or wouldn't.

He wondered if she was better on the job than on the job, so to speak. He'd presumed she'd link from the Henry Norton's bag to Derek and Ellen, but no, Derek was still out there somewhere. It didn't matter anyway, he'd be coming into a tidy sum soon enough: the baby story had run that morning, and the reward had been offered before the baby had been found. If they could just find out where the investigation was at, they might, despite last night's catastrophe, pull it off.

Paul felt his eyes starting to close. He hadn't slept a wink because of all the activity in the house and the headache from the blow to his head. He'd woken up minutes after having his head koshed, and found Liz gone. He'd set off looking for her; she couldn't have got far with her rescuer. But when he'd got back to the house the whole estate had been buzzing from all the garda activity around his place. Sitting on Jo Birmingham's bed now, his last thought was that he'd better get up before he fell asleep . . .

With a sudden sharp intake of breath, Paul realized he must have drifted off – he didn't know for how long. As he blinked he tried to work out how long it had been.

'I said get the fuck up, you wanker,' a man's voice growled.

Paul squinted against the sharp overhead light. The butt of something was banged into his ribcage. A crutch.

'What are you doing?' the copper's husband said.

Paul turned and saw the cripple standing over him, with the little boy in one arm. This was going to be easy. He stood and lunged.

54

Alfie was already waiting at Roly's Bistro in Ballsbridge when the *Daily Record* editor pointed over for the benefit of the waitress checking the bookings at the door. He recognized him from the telly. He could waffle for Ireland a lot better than he could scrum half.

Alfie sank his fork into a cube of deep-fried Brie and put it into his mouth, watching out of the side of his eye as the editor – in an expensive three-piece, pin-striped suit – approached.

'I'm not late, am I?' the editor said, slinging off his suit jacket and passing it to the waitress.

'I was too hungry to wait,' Alfie answered through his bulging cheek. He mopped up the beetroot with half a bread roll lathered with butter, and bit into it. 'I wasn't expecting you. Where's Niall?'

'He's running late on a story. He says he'll join us as soon as he can, if he can.' The editor shook out the napkin and spread it across his lap as he sat, and then reached for the menu before continuing, 'I wanted to talk to you personally, explain why your proposal just wouldn't work in the current climate. It's an absolute nightmare out there for newspapers right now. Nobody wants to pay for news anymore.'

'I read his story about the baby snatched from the hospital,' Alfie said, wiping the corners of his mouth. 'Is it true you're paying a woman half a million quid because of the information that led to the baby's safe recovery last night?'

The editor looked pleased. 'That's right. We put out the details of our plan to offer a reward in an advertising campaign on the radio every half hour, in the hope of reaching people before baby Hope had to spend a night without her mum. We never expected the campaign to result in a breakthrough so quickly, but we couldn't have hoped for a better result. This story is going to run and run, and we've got the inside track. The phones have been hopping all morning with businesses wanting to take out advertisements. You can't put a price on that kind of branding.'

'What do you know about the woman who provided the tip? Only, I didn't get a chance to read about it yet.'

'Helena Moriarty?'

'Yeah, the one who won the money.'

'Well, Helena's one of life's salt-of-the-earth busybodies. She's in her fifties, from Tipperary town, a member of the Irish Countrywomen's Association, who just happened to be in Dublin shopping for the day when she noticed a man in a maternity shop practically buying the place out. Helena became suspicious because he'd no girlfriend or baby with him. He bought a cot, a pram, a buggy, a potty – everything he'd need to get a child to the age of three, and he paid in cash. In her interview, Helena said it struck her as strange because normally the nesting instinct kicks in before a new mum gives birth, and they buy little bits in the run-up to the baby's arrival. She'd heard about the missing baby through our radio appeals on the drive to Dublin, and she asked the man if the baby's mum was at home minding the tot. He told her to mind her own business. She got such a bee in her bonnet that she followed him to Nuns Cross, saw him go into number thirty and then rang us. Niall called in to your lot, leading to the discovery of the baby. She's now been reunited with her mum, and we've a photographer headed over to the hospital right now to take some shots of them together for tomorrow.'

Alfie looked over the editor's shoulder to see if there was any sign of his steak. 'What was Helena's surname again?'

'Moriarty,' the editor said, 'Why?'

'You've been conned, my old son,' Alfie said giving him a wry smile. 'It was just old-fashioned police work that brought us to Nuns Cross last night. Niall had nothing to do with it.'

The editor opened his mouth to say something, but it

turned to a cough and he reached for the jug of water. 'You're wrong. Niall got there at the same time you did.'

'That's right, he did,' Alfie said, raising his eyebrows. 'Has Helena been paid the half million quid yet?'

A waiter arrived over with a bread basket and tongs. The editor closed the menu and handed it back to him, not taking his eyes off Alfie. 'The seafood chowder, please.' He reached for the newspaper, and folded the rustling pages open to the one he wanted. 'You're saying Helena had nothing to do with what happened. That all these claims she made weren't true?'

'I'm saying that last time I met Niall out and about in town, he was with his girlfriend Monica Moriarty from Tipperary,' Alfie said, chewing steadily.

The editor sat back and waited for the waiter to move off after topping up his glass.

'Cheer up. I presume the old chestnut that reporters don't reveal their sources must be bullshit in the current climate. Management must have ways of establishing who they are. Do you record calls to the office, for instance?'

'For training purposes,' the editor said.

'What about mobiles?'

'We pay the bills, we can get the itemized printout, the texts.'

'Email?'

'It all goes through the company server.'

'You'll have a lot of material to go through, but at least you'll be saving the company half a million quid,' Alfie said. 'You did mention the newspaper was facing challenging times.'

The editor reached for his phone. 'I'm going to have to make a call.'

'What's the matter?' Alfie asked, smirking. 'You're like a hen on an egg. You're going to make my food go down the wrong way if you keep lepping about like that. Another newspaper might just click how badly you got it wrong.'

The editor blinked and put his phone down. 'That column you were so interested in: I've had a change of heart. When are you officially retiring?'

'Friday,' Alfie said.

'I think it could really work for us,' the editor said in a flat tone. 'I see it as a weekly comment box on the crimes that most sickened, upset, or intrigued you. We'd want it to be opinionated, and zero tolerance in style to fit in with our demographic.'

'I can do that,' Alfie said.

'And Derek Carpenter would be the perfect subject to kick-off on. Do you still think he's the murderer on the missing-women case?'

Alfie sat back, and smiled. 'Not a doubt in my mind. Niall's been stupid, and greedy, but he's not a killer. Derek Carpenter is. I said it from day one. I staked my entire professional reputation on it, to take on some of the younger guns who think they know it all, and it's about to pay off.'

The editor rubbed his hands together. 'If you pin those missing women to Carpenter you'll be the cop who solved the biggest crime in the country. We'd be the paper that supplied you with the lead. What do you think?'

'I don't have to think,' Alfie said after a mouthful of water. 'I've got two kids who want to go to university, and a wife who goes into decline if she doesn't get some sun in January. I'm fifty-five years old. It costs seventy euro to fill my petrol tank, and don't get me started on the cost of membership of Malahide Golf Club. What do you think I think?'

The editor extended a hand. Alfie answered it with his own. 'You tell Niall to be very careful whom he talks to in the future,' Alfie said. 'And since I've saved your paper a small fortune, and no end of embarrassment, I'll be expecting that to be reflected in my remuneration.'

The editor nodded.

Alfie sniffed deeply as a rare steak was put in front of him. His fork clanged off the bottom of the plate as he started to carve it up. He was going to put that bastard Carpenter away for life if it killed him.

55

Spotting the table the team were sitting at, Jo headed over to join them. She'd arranged to meet them off site at a Wagamama, after taking a call from Alfie on the way there. He'd informed her of his plan to relocate the incident room to Rathfarnham, with immediate effect.

'The first conference is at 2.30 p.m., if you want to attend,' he'd said. 'It's entirely up to you. I'm only extending the courtesy so you're not in the dark if you should have to take over next week, which I doubt will be necessary. You already know how I feel about the direction you've tried to push the case in, and I'm not going to repeat myself. If you do choose to come, you should know that I will consider your role purely observational until I'm gone. After that you can dance on my grave for all I care. But I'll be making it my business to have the case against Derek Carpenter bang to rights before then. From today we're shifting focus from finding Amanda Wells's murderer to finding Derek

Carpenter, and I've assigned another twenty-five officers to the case to that end.'

Jo had declined his offer to become a lame duck. However, as members of his team were still flitting in and out of the station organizing the transfer of paperwork, she'd arranged to meet the others in a nearby restaurant for a briefing, under the auspices of lunch, rather than have anyone accuse her of completely contravening the direct instructions of a superior.

She handed Foxy the *Daily Record*, and flicked her phone shut as Sexton stood to pull out a chair for her. Alfie had finished up their conversation earlier by asking where Dan was and why his phone was off, reminding Jo that he'd planned to interview him today. Much as it galled Jo to have to be the one to ring first after last night's stand-off, she'd been trying to get Dan ever since, and had just touched base with Harry's pre-school to learn that Dan had never arrived there with Harry. He hadn't showed up for his physio appointment, either. She'd a few missed calls from him in close succession on her phone, but he hadn't left any message. She wondered what was going on. If Harry was feeling ill, Dan would have called to ask for her view. Apart from anything else, she needed to talk to him about Dr Griffen's news. Considering the way he'd kept her shut out last night, she wondered what had changed since her husband had come back. She felt more alone than ever.

Foxy scanned the front page and curled his lower lip before passing it on to Joan.

'Have you seen this?' Aishling reacted, reading over Joan's shoulder. 'A woman named Helena Moriarty is getting half a million for finding the baby,' she said. 'She's a regular Miss Marple.'

'Half a million!' Sue asked, cramming closer for a look. 'I didn't think newspapers had cash like that these days,' she remarked through a bulging cheek.

'If there was a Miss Marple involved,' Jo commented, 'I think she's working for Niall Toland and his source. We're getting very close to the truth, I can feel it in my waters.'

Sexton put his hands behind his neck and stretched out his legs. 'If Toland took that baby, he deserves to be hung, drawn and quartered for what he put that mum through.'

Foxy gave Jo his theory about how Toland seemed to be acquainted with the source on the tape.

'We need to build a profile of this Paul Bell,' Jo said.

Aishling started an internet search on her phone.

'I just don't see how Amanda's murder and the baby snatch could be linked,' Sue said. 'They're such different crimes.'

'This is what Paul Bell looks like,' Aishling said, passing over her phone.

Jo took it and after one glance at the thin man with slits for eyes she clicked her fingers. 'He was the photographer up in the mountains with Toland at the crime scene yesterday morning. He looks really familiar.' She frowned; had she seen him somewhere else as well?

'Maybe he's one of those rogue reporters who knows how to gather information,' Sue said. 'My ex used to go around with a spy pen in his pocket. He didn't know how to turn it off properly, so half the time he was recording me.'

'Maybe,' Jo said, thinking to herself. 'Maybe it's not that crime that links Amanda and the baby. Maybe it's just money. It can't be sheer coincidence that Derek had just come into money, and that there was half a million quid riding on finding that baby.'

'Does this mean you want to rule Derek Carpenter out as a suspect?' Sue asked, astonished.

'He's not in the clear yet,' Jo said. 'How did he get Ellen Lamb's uniform?'

Jo turned to Aishling. 'We need to find the florist who put together the bouquet for the maternity hospital yesterday,' she said. 'Establish exactly what flowers were in the arrangement, and then try and narrow it down that way. We can check payments, phones, and possibly even CCTV to see if we can prove Niall, or Paul, bought them. Niall's shirt was covered in lily-pollen stains.'

'Got it,' Aishling said.

'Sue, can you track down the woman at the centre of

these claims in the paper, this Helena Moriarty?' Jo said, reading the name. 'And again, establish if there's any link to Niall Toland or to Paul Bell?'

'Sure,' he replied.

Jo stopped talking as her phone beeped. She put it down again without opening it, because it wasn't from Dan. It was Alfie. Jo turned to Foxy. 'Can you give me an update on the forensics? Any news from the lab on the ID of the blood in the room?'

'It's a close relative of Liz Carpenter's,' Foxy said.

Jo held her hair off her face. 'Christ, please don't tell me it was her son?'

'They're running comparisons as we speak,' Foxy answered. 'They also established that Derek's fingerprints were all over the Henry Norton's bag in Amanda's mouth.'

'What about Ellen Lamb's shoe? Any trace of DNA on it?'

'Derek's,' he said, looking apologetic.

'It doesn't mean anything,' Jo said defensively. 'Sisters share shoes all the time.'

'We'll find out the size they took in shoes,' Foxy suggested.

The waiter arrived over with the menu. Jo waved her hand that she'd pass. She'd eaten in Wagamama once before, at an officer's retirement do. She thought it a good idea to have a bit of everything, instead of sitting there for the entire meal regretting what you'd picked because everybody else's looked better. But she'd too much on now.

Spotting a bottle of white wine that had already been depleted, Jo motioned to it and raised a quizzical look.

'We're allowed one,' Joan said, pouring the dregs of the bottle into Jo's glass before clicking her fingers in the direction of a waiter.

'Not on my watch,' Jo said, putting the flat of her hand over the top of the glass.

'We really only wanted to get his attention,' Joan said, admiring the waiter. 'What do you think, Jo? Gorgeous, isn't he?'

The waiter, who was shining glasses with a white cloth, seemed to sense her interest and sent a winning smile in their direction.

Jo reached for the menu, and angled it for privacy against her face.

'No point asking her,' Aishling said. 'She's the only one here who's got a man.'

Jo was thinking, *If only they knew*. She might be the only one at the table in a relationship, but she was willing to bet every one of them still had more of a love life than she and Dan at the moment. She could count on one hand the number of times he'd drawn her into his arms since moving back home. She'd tried to put it down to the heavy painkillers he still needed, had even used his dented pride as an excuse, but she was as insecure as any woman when it came to her relationship. His gift of sexy underwear just emphasized how far apart they'd grown. They were too pissed off with each other to be bothered. She wondered if he was seeing Jeanie again, and decided against ringing him. After draining a glass of water she said, 'I'd better get a move on.'

'What about lunch?' Joan asked.

'Not if we're going to solve this case today,' Jo replied.

'Today?' Aishling butted in. 'You're joking?'

Jo didn't blink. 'I might not be here tomorrow.'

'You can't go till we bring Derek in,' Sexton said.

'You're presuming he's still alive,' Jo snapped.

56

Hawthorne had just finished a Y-incision on a young man's torso, and was walking both elbows to separate the ribcage at the sternum when Jo pushed her way through the weighted door, out of breath.

'Sorry for barging in. Your secretary said you'd be busy for the next couple of hours. I don't have a couple of hours.' She paused for breath, glancing at the clock on the wall. It was 2.30 p.m. Alfie would be starting his conference now.

The sound of ribs breaking was like a creaking door that needed oiling. The victim had been a bloated man, with short, shiny, chestnut-coloured hair and skin aged prematurely from the sun, Jo observed.

Hawthorne reached into the cavity and scooped out the heart, turning to the only other living person in the room, his assistant, Stephanie, studious behind a pair of big glasses that couldn't hide her glamour-model looks. Two more bodies were waiting for his attention on trolleys in the room.

She glanced at Hawthorne – who was talking into one of those Madonna headsets that ran between the ear and mouth – to see if he was put out. He was tetchy at the best of times. But he was too busy mumbling his findings into the microphone, something about the signs of external bruising on the thoracic cavity being consistent with the internal evidence. He ran a rubbery finger under a cross-section of the flesh.

'I need to establish Amanda Wells's time of death,' Jo told him. She was making a conscious effort to keep the language just about as formal as possible. Cage-rattling was her only hope of getting him to play ball.

'Stephanie, bowl, please,' Hawthorne said, snottily.

'I'm sorry, I know you're busy, but so am I,' Jo said.

He slapped a maroon stomach into the kidney-shaped bowl, snipping the tip with a scissors and squeezing the contents into the bowl. The smell was foul. 'Spicy . . . Indian, based on the vivid reds and yellows, I'd say,' he commented.

'Well?' Jo asked Hawthorne again. He had his back to her.

His young assistant glanced at Hawthorne to make sure he was concentrating on the innards. He was a control freak as well as everything else. Then she held up four fingers for Jo to see, making a see-saw motion with the other hand, and mouthed, 'Sunday morning, give or take.'

Jo's eyebrows soared. *Sunday! Why had nobody seen Amanda on Saturday?*

Hawthorne plonked the liver down in another of Stephanie's dishes. He incised the throat and checked the hyoid bone for damage. 'Strangled,' he said. 'Unusual in a man.'

Jo turned to leave. She couldn't afford to waste any more time here. She'd got what she needed.

'Amanda Wells's time of death's irrelevant,' Hawthorne said without turning around.

Jo stopped in her tracks.

'What?'

'The autopsy was a complete waste of bloody time. Her body may have been illegally disposed of, but that's not going to result in a life sentence. She wasn't murdered. She died of fright, as I suspected. There was no murder as such, that's why I've let cases of more importance take precedence.'

57

It was useless, Liz could not shift the trapdoor lid. She'd been trying all night. Her shoulders ached from barging it, and the bruises were turning into watery welts. She'd waited until Conor had drifted off to sleep before starting, but had woken him with the bangs. In desperation, she'd tried to get him to help, but it had been no good. Finally he'd gone back to the couch, plugged in the earphones of his iPod, and was now rocking to a silent rhythm, munching his way through a packet of his favourite biscuits like being here was the most natural thing in the world.

'Why do you want to get out, anyway?' he asked, speaking over the noise of his music.

'I'm just testing it,' Liz had lied.

'What?'

She'd walked over to him and removed one of his earphones. 'I'm just making sure Dad's den is secure.'

Liz sat down alongside him on the sofa, putting her

arm across his shoulders. 'We haven't had much of a chance to talk lately, son.'

'Everything's fine, Mum,' he answered in a jaded tone. 'No bullies.' He plugged the earphone back in.

'Except for the person who took your schoolbooks,' Liz said, taking it out again. 'They shouldn't have done that. You know how I feel about secrets.'

'OK.'

Where had he learned to do that? she wondered. Conor had the ability to move off a topic he didn't want to discuss by accepting it, without agreeing or disagreeing, down to a fine art. He had completely mastered the art of diversion so as to keep his feelings locked away.

'You win, Mum. It was some old geezer who said Dad owed him some money, and if I didn't give them to him, he was going to hurt him.'

'Sorry? What?' Liz asked.

'Um humm.'

Every maternal cell in her body tensed at the thought of someone putting Conor under that kind of pressure.

'What else did he say? Did he touch you?'

'I really like this song, Mum. Can I just listen?'

Conor had just played another one of his opt-out-of-the-real-world cards.

'Remember how we told you when you were little not to talk to strangers?' she said, softening her tone.

'I know, I know, he talked, I didn't.' Conor's voice sounded panicked.

'You're not in trouble at all, darling. It's just . . . there are bad people in the world.'

'You mean like the person who hurt Aunt Ellen, don't you, Mum?'

'He told you about that, too, did he?' Liz swallowed the lump in her throat as blood rushed to her head. She and Derek had never discussed what had happened with Conor; there had never been a right time. He'd never said the words 'Aunt Ellen' before. Nobody else had the right to broach the subject with him outside the family. If she'd had a knife and that man had been in front of her, she knew she'd have used it.

'Sometimes good people have to do things they wouldn't normally do – bad things – to make sure good people, and great kids like you, can get on with their lives in peace, even if it means their lives change for a while, OK?' Liz said.

'Right,' Conor said.

Conor rested his head on her shoulder and stretched his arms out. 'No, this is my Mum.'

'What?' she asked, confused by the remark.

'Gross! I told you to look at the place, not her, didn't I? Super cool, isn't it?'

Liz checked to see why Conor was babbling. His words made no sense. His extended arm was gliding the iPod around.

'What are you doing? Who are you talking to?'

'Just Jeff,' he said, about his best friend.

'What is he, psychic?'

'No, he's got Facetime credits.'

'What's Facetime?'

'Duh! Mum, you're such a dick. Sorry,' he added quickly, holding up the iPod to show her. Liz had saved for months to buy Conor's Christmas present, but that didn't mean she'd any idea how to use it, or what it could do. But now Conor's best friend was staring back at her from what Liz had always thought of as a jumped-up Walkman.

'Hi, Liz,' Jeff said cheerily.

58

In Mountjoy, prisoner Number 17582 was having a spectacularly bad day. First, the young screw with attitude had ordered a search of his cell, and had confiscated two of his mobile phones. That was going to stop him keeping abreast of his Dublin north inner-city runners tab. The bastards had been robbing him blind, throwing his Charlie around left, right, and centre to celebrate, so he'd had one of them shot in the back of the head and dumped in the canal as a warning. If they sensed he was in-communicado, they'd start to plan a reprisal.

Next, he'd heard on the prison grapevine that the slag who'd produced his four kids had just been jailed on shoplifting charges, resulting in his kids being put into care. And last, but not least, his drug-squad member on the payroll had tipped him off that some toerag named Derek Carpenter had fucked up the meat import-export route he'd had established to the UK – thanks to his old man's connections to Mervyn's Meats – by turning tout.

'This is your fucking fault, Mervyn,' he hissed down the

backup phone, which he'd taped behind the cistern. 'I'm supposed to vet everyone who works for you, so why do *you* keep hiring pensioners and people like Carpenter you haven't cleared with *me*?'

'Everybody's heard of Derek Carpenter,' Mervyn argued. 'He bumped off six women. I thought his reputation would keep the others in line. Pensioners will work for half nothing, as your old man knows. And I didn't think with those kinds of credentials Derek needed a reference.'

'Until you get the money Derek Carpenter stole from me back, I'm holding you personally responsible.'

'I told you, I know where he is. We just have to sit tight. He's holed up in the office of a local solicitor he's bumped off. I've told the boys not to move on him yet because it will bring too much heat.'

'Has he got any firepower?'

'He's got a Glock semi-automatic, otherwise we'd have moved in ages ago. That said, he's currently asleep on the office floor. Looks like he had one too many.'

'Get in there, you cunt, and get me the hundred thousand euro he robbed off me,' the prisoner said, frowning at the sound of a siren growing steadily louder over the phone. 'Tell me it's driving by,' he added, conscious Mervyn had started to pant like he was sprinting in a race.

'Torch it,' the prisoner shouted. 'Are you running, you stupid fucking cunt? Do not leave there before the pyrotechnic display, do you hear me?'

59

It was mid-afternoon. The last of Alfie's crew had all finally vacated the station, and Jo was relieved to be back at base. Aishling hurried up to her – one arm outstretched to hand her some paperwork – as she crossed the detective unit. Foxy was waiting in the doorway with the phone from her desk in his hand, telling her that there were two callers waiting on lines one and two.

'The chief state solicitor is on one, willing to discuss if you've got a case against whoever dumped Amanda Wells's body,' he said. 'And the chief of the drug squad is on two, to fill you in on what Derek's boss has been up to. Who'll I tell to ring back?'

'Neither, I need to talk to both of them now,' Jo said, taking the document from Aishling and trying to work out what it was. She had free rein to direct the investigation as she wished, but only until Alfie either located Derek and had him charged, or found out what Jo was up to and had her charged. The clock was ticking, but she had assigned fifty officers to work on the leads she wanted chased down, including locating Paul Bell, Niall Toland, and Bell's wife, Jenny.

'This is the bit of interest,' Aishling said, pointing to some handwriting on the official form, a two-tone, multi-paged document, the type that requires every letter to be capped and boxed, Jo observed.

Jo flicked it over and turned it upside to read the back, which was in English. It said 'Department of Education' across the top.

'What is it?' Jo asked.

Aishling took it off her, turned it back the way it had been, and returned it. 'It's an application form for a home-tuition grant for Conor Carpenter.'

'I don't speak Irish,' Jo said.

'Well, one of the Carpenters clearly does,' Aishling said, showing Jo how the side of the form least likely to be understood had been filled in.

From his seat on the far side of the room, and with his back to them, Sexton patted an extended arm in the air and, covering the mouthpiece of the phone he'd been talking on, yelled, 'Quiet!'

Jo looked over with curiosity. 'So, what is it? Quick, I need to take those calls.'

'Well, it may be nothing,' Aishling said.

'Go on.'

'The form was stamped on Friday by Amanda Wells.'

Jo's curiosity was stoked because Liz had made no mention of this meeting when Jo had quizzed her.

'A clerk in the Department had it couriered over to us because he saw what happened to Amanda on the news,' Aishling went on.

'Is there something in it?'

'Nothing. This is what's of interest.'

She handed Jo a white envelope that had been opened, with a letter inside. Jo pulled it out.

'Amanda sent it by registered post on Friday, and it arrived today,' Aishling went on. 'In it she states that she did not rubber-stamp a grant application for the Carpenters, should such a form arrive. She goes on to say she noticed the date of her stamp had been changed, but that she hadn't used it that day, and so it hadn't been changed by her, but she suspected one of the Carpenters might have had the opportunity.'

Jo turned to the form and glanced at the stamp, suddenly intensely interested.

'She said she didn't stamp it?' Jo clarified.

'Correct, which means one of the Carpenters must have, suggesting face-to-face contact with her on Friday, the day she was last seen.'

'Maybe Derek isn't in the clear yet after all,' Foxy said, sitting on the edge of Jo's desk and lifting the handset.

'You realize that if you're right, I'm wrong,' Jo told Aishling, adding, 'Get around to her office and bag and tag the stamp that was used. We'll get it fingerprinted, find out if it was Liz or Derek that used it.'

Foxy was jotting numbers on a pad, and murmuring into the phone that Jo would call as soon as possible. As soon as he'd hung up it rang again and he answered.

'The blood in the bedroom . . .' he said, putting Jo's phone down.

Jo turned.

He indicated with a set of walking fingers that she should close the door behind her.

'. . . belonged to Ellen Lamb,' he said.

Jo sat down. 'What?'

'The lab indicated it had to be someone close, so I organized collection of the original sample of her DNA. Legally, we're not supposed to retain them after a certain time, but . . .' He pulled a face so she could fill in the blanks.

'Ellen?' Jo said.

'She must have been alive all these years,' Foxy said.

Jo nodded, watching Sexton haring across the room outside towards her.

'Jo, they've found the Carpenters,' he said, bursting in the door.

'Alive?'

'All three,' he continued breathlessly. 'The control room in Tara Street took a 999 call twenty minutes ago from some kid telling them his friend Conor Carpenter was in Amanda Wells's office basement. An ambulance and a squad car were sent out, and they found the place on fire. Two units of the fire brigade had to be dispatched.

'They're taking Derek to the Mater Hospital. He's in a bad way. They were treating him for smoke inhalation in the ambulance but they're doing extra tests to see if there's more to it. It looks like a murder-suicide bid.'

'What about mum and son?' Jo asked.

'They've gone home.'

'Home? That's about the most dangerous place they could go.'

'No, we've got Derek,' Sexton said.

'Did anyone stop them?' Jo said, rushing for the door.

'Alfie's going to try and have Derek charged with attempted murder, Jo,' Sexton called after her. 'If he hadn't collapsed, he might have pulled it off.'

'Or maybe he was going to the rescue of his family,' Jo said.

60

'Do it,' Paul told Niall. 'You've got the gun. What's the big deal?'

The woman was kneeling on the edge of a disused quarry in the Wicklow mountains that rainwater had turned into a lagoon. Her hands were bound behind her back. She kept turning to see what was going on, her eyes out on stalks. There was a good forty-foot drop to the surface of the water and, based on how sheer the drop was, Paul reckoned the lagoon was at least as deep again. They didn't even need to use the gun. All they had to do was push her in. Her knees were less than a foot from the edge. One swoon brought on by an attack of vertigo, or a faint, and she'd be over the edge. Given the amount of blood she'd lost, her collapse wasn't beyond the bounds of possibility. They hadn't expected to have to bump her off, but what choice had they had? Events had taken yet another unforeseen turn.

'Why don't you do it?' Niall asked, the revolver

cocked limply against the back of the woman's head the way he'd been instructed. He hated heights himself, and kept turning his head sideways so he wouldn't have to see. His brain kept instructing him to get down on all fours. Paul was indignant. 'Do it.'

'You should do this one if only to prove the point.'

'What point? What are you on about?' Niall asked. He was more inclined to swing the weapon around in the other direction and blow Paul's brains out than shoot this woman he'd only just met.

'That people are all the same,' Paul said, 'that the impulses that drive cops and murderers, rich and poor, famous and ordinary people, are all exactly the same. That was the point the *News of the World* made every Sunday. That when you look through the keyhole of the ivory tower, people are just people.'

'Can you let the *News of the World* go? We've moved on.'

'Gentlemen,' the woman said, a quiver in her voice belying the apparent composure which the formality of the word had given. 'Nobody has to die,' she said. 'I'll get you the money you want today. Let's just go back to my hotel room.'

'How do we know you're not going to pull another stunt?'

'I'm twenty-eight stone. I don't pull stunts, and I don't do kneeling. Any second now I'm going to fall over the edge if both of you don't help me up. You don't want to kill me. You don't want to kill anyone. It's not like I can go to the police, as you know.'

Niall looked at Paul. Paul looked at Niall.

The woman started to sway.

'Would you have shot me afterwards, if I had done it?' Niall asked Paul, helping the woman back up.

'I was wondering the exact same thing about you,' Paul said.

61

Christ, Liz thought, flattening herself against the wall of the corridor, thirty metres from intensive care where Derek was being treated. There was a uniformed garda standing in front of the room. He was six foot five – at least – with a set of scrum-half shoulders in a short-sleeved blue shirt under his sleeveless stab-proof vest. Tackling him to the ground wasn't going to be an option, then.

She glanced back over her shoulder towards the communal TV room, where she'd left Conor. Their near-death experience hadn't knocked a stir out of him. He was too trusting to believe his father capable of hurting him. He'd run through Amanda's blazing office, his only concern afterwards that Derek, who he'd caught a glimpse of in the back of an ambulance, was all right.

But Liz had just about held it together. What Derek had done in the past had finally registered now he had tried to kill them, too. She'd done the mental maths in the minutes before help arrived. If she told her rescuers what Derek had tried to do, if he was convicted of all of his crimes and became Ireland's most notorious killer, it would shape the rest of Conor's life. She'd enough money to take off and start a new life for them.

There was only one loose end that needed tying up first: Derek. If he survived, it was only a matter of time before the gardaí got enough evidence to charge him. But if he didn't survive, the case against him would disappear into the ether. And that was why she was here.

By the time the cops came for her statement tomorrow, Derek would be dead – if she had anything to do with it. There'd be wires, or a drip, or switches she could interfere with. All she had to do to was get near him.

She walked up to the officer. 'I know it's not visiting time, but can I see Derek Carpenter? I'm his . . .'

She didn't get the chance to finish. A middle-aged man in a leather jacket had appeared from somewhere. 'You're Derek's wife, aren't you?' he asked, flashing a smile she didn't trust. 'I've some good news for you. Visiting hours don't apply in there.'

'Yes, I'm Liz Carpenter.'

'I was told you wanted to go home,' he answered, extending his hand. 'I'm Chief Superintendent Alfie Taylor. I've been very worried about you.'

'Sorry.'

'It's not your fault,' he said.

'Can I see him?' Liz asked.

'Sure,' Alfie said. 'Why not?'

'There's another member of his family in there at the moment – his sister,' the officer explained to both of them.

'His sister?' Liz repeated, her breath catching on the word. Derek's family were spread out all over, and not close knit. Apart from which, they couldn't have heard the news of what had happened so quickly. She tried to work out who else might have bluffed their way in there: someone from Mervyn's Meats who wanted their money back . . . their neighbour, Paul . . . or maybe the other neighbours had taken a contract out on Derek's life. Kim and Kate had the contacts . . .

She shouldn't argue, or look surprised. She should keep her cool and let them do the job for her.

'This is the lady now,' the uniform said as an obese woman emerged from the door behind her.

She looked at least twenty-five stone – dressed brightly in a huge floral dress and sneakers. There was something familiar about the size and shape of her teeth, set in a little smile in the middle of her gigantic face, that Liz couldn't stop staring at.

To her surprise, the woman took her in her arms and pulled her close. 'It's me, Liz,' she whispered, in a light American accent.

And then the ground come up to meet Liz as her breathing tried to keep pace with her heart. Ellen.

62

Sexton drove to Nuns Cross, as Jo was too preoccupied. The clock was against her. At any moment the call could come that a cornea donor was available or that Alfie had had Derek charged, and that would be it, she'd have to throw in the towel, let the case that had snow-balled against Derek Carpenter take its own course. She reached into her bag and took out a tube of hand cream, squeezing some on to her hands, rubbing them together and wondering how she'd got so bloody close to this case that it had shut out the rest of her life. She still hadn't managed to tell Dan she was about to be hospitalized. He was clearly determined not to talk to her until she'd apologized. That she would do as soon as the case was solved.

Gripping her hands, she tried to quieten them. They had a life of their own, and she kept rubbing her lap, tilting her head against the passenger window, eyes closed. It was a grey day, but her eyes were so sensitive any light had become unbearable. Her head was pounding in time to the wipers, which were slashing at the drizzle. Would Liz have gone to Nuns Cross with everything going on? She doubted it. If she was an innocent and in danger, that was the first place the people who were trying to harm her family would look. Jo willed her brain to work it out, to come up with the answer that she believed was staring her in the face.

Sexton was the first to break the silence.

'There's no shame in getting it wrong, Jo,' he said, glancing across.

'Can you just drive? Because I'm one hundred per cent certain that Liz Carpenter is not safe at home.'

'You can't still believe Derek didn't do it?'

Jo sighed. 'You've got very friendly with Alfie all of a sudden. He tipped you off about the fire at Amanda's, didn't he?'

He didn't deny it. 'Maybe Derek was planning to kill Liz and then do a flit. Maybe his injuries from yesterday's crash caught up with him. I don't know. And neither do you. That's all I'm saying.'

'And neither does Alfie,' she clipped, glad when her phone rang.

'Hi,' she said into her phone, pointing to the bus lane so Sexton could weave out of the traffic and inject some speed. They were hitting clear road in spots, but still had a fifteen-minute drive ahead of them.

It was Rory. 'Mum, something's happened to Dad,' he said breathlessly.

Jo felt for the handle on the passenger door. 'What?'

'I can't get the front door open. I can see Dad's legs through the letterbox. He's lying against the door. Harry's hysterical. I'm trying to talk to him through the letterbox . . . I'm going to break a window.'

'No,' Jo shouted. She didn't want Rory to see something that might haunt him for the rest of his life. 'Keep Harry talking. I'm on the way.'

'You're not here now, Mum. I might be able to help Dad. Just call an ambulance; I'm going in.'

63

A torch the size of a pen was being shone into Dan's eyes by a paramedic holding the lids open with his thumb when Jo and Sexton arrived. Jo jumped out before Sexton had brought the car to a halt, and almost lost her footing in her effort to get to Dan, sprinting over to the stretcher. Rory was rocking Harry in his arms. Harry's sleeping head was resting on his elder brother's shoulder.

'How is he?' she asked the green-suited paramedic.

'Sore,' Dan said, coming to.

'Thank God,' Jo said, leaning in to kiss his face. She cupped it with her hands. 'I thought . . .'

She sighed so hard she had to take a deep breath to refill her lungs.

'We'll take him in to get him X-rayed, make sure there's nothing broken, and no head injury. They may want to keep him overnight.'

'I'm coming with him,' Jo said.

'No,' Dan said. 'Stay with the boys.'

Jo looked over her shoulder, and realized she couldn't leave them.

'Did you see who it was?' she asked Dan.

'It was the oven cleaner you organized,' Dan said.

Jo didn't want to worry him by arguing that she had done no such thing. 'What did he look like?'

'Skinny. Slitty eyes.'

Jo blinked. It was Paul Bell.

'I came back and caught him in our bedroom, and I wasn't strong enough to stop him getting away,' Dan continued. 'I tried, but I had to keep Harry safe.'

Jo clicked her fingers remembering where else she'd seen Paul. It was at the electricity meter: he was the man she'd passed late last night. He must have been wearing a false beard.

Jo stepped into the ambulance to kiss Dan on the forehead, muttering sorry over and over into his ear. Then she walked over to Rory and hugged him as they watched the ambulance drive away.

'I'll put Harry down for a nap in a minute, son. Take him inside for now.'

Alone with Sexton, she told him, 'You were right about me getting it arse ways. If those journalists left Dan alive, they're not the killers. I've got it all wrong. Amanda Wells wasn't a victim. Ellen Lamb wasn't murdered. The only reason Amanda's phone was in her hand was because the journalists aren't the killers, they're just incompetent. That's why Amanda was holding her phone. They wanted it to lead us straight to Derek.'

64

Liz sat on the edge of Ellen's sumptuous hotel-room bed in the Shelbourne on St Stephen's Green, gripping her sister's hands. She didn't know how she was ever going to bring herself to let go again. Conor was fast asleep, tucked in under a snow-white, feather-filled duvet, and Liz was marvelling at her sister's complete transformation – her strawberry-blonde hair was gone, even the shape of her eyes looked different now her face had filled out.

Liz was in ecstasy, on a high from the rush of holding her actual, warm, living and breathing sister. It was the first moment of pure unadulterated happiness that Liz had had since Ellen had gone. Even Conor's birth had been tinged with sadness because Liz hadn't had her sister with her to share in the wonder of her perfect baby boy. She held on for dear life as she listened to Ellen explain why she'd let a lifetime pass since they'd last seen each other.

'Dad started abusing me when I was seven, I think,'

Ellen announced. 'A counsellor told me it was probably earlier, but that often victims block it out from their early memories to cope.'

Liz caught a breath. Her life had started to drain out of her from some invisible hole. Everything was sinking. The ecstasy of the moment vanished as she tried to process the unbelievable. She started to blink rapidly. Their dad had what?

Ellen's eyes had filled. She lifted Liz's chin with her fingers to make her lock eyes. 'By the time I got to sixteen, I knew that if I didn't get away from him, I'd either kill him or myself. I hated how he'd made me feel about my own body. Like it was always dirty. I hated myself for not having been strong enough to get him to stop. I wanted to die to escape the demons. I'd started self-harming. Each time I took the knife to myself the wounds got deeper. I knew I was getting braver, and part of me was scared I would go through with it. I had to go, so I went. I was out of choices.'

Liz puffed out her cheeks and tried to process the information again. 'Our dad?'

Ellen sighed. 'I know he never laid a finger on you, and I wasn't going to take the chance that you wouldn't believe me by telling you. I tried several times, but because he was dying and you and Mum were so intent on nurturing him, I just couldn't do it. My head was done in from it, not knowing whether to tell you, or to top myself. I thought if I killed myself and didn't leave a note, he'd have got away with it. But if I'd left a note telling you why, I'd have caused you even more pain than if I'd just come out with it. So in the end, running away was the only option.'

'Our dad?'

'There was only one, as far as I'm aware,' Ellen said crossly. Her expression became pinched. 'You don't believe me.' She sat back and let go of Liz's hands. 'You always did that, you always treated me like I was lying.'

Liz was in the jaws of a flashback, back outside the bathroom door the last time she'd seen Ellen, when they'd started to bicker and snipe. She snapped back to the present. This time she would not let the moment unravel. She grasped Liz's hands again.

'That's not true. It's just that Dad's memory is so dear to me. This is such a big shock. I can't, I don't . . .'

Ellen rolled her sleeves up to show Liz the scars. Liz gasped at the extent of the staggered criss-cross silvery-red lines that stretched from Ellen's wrist right up to the crook of her arm. There were fresh wounds and bandages around her precious wrists. Liz reached out, horrified. Her fingertips hovered over them, afraid of hurting her more.

'It helps, believe it or not,' Ellen explained. She tapped a temple. 'The pain in here doesn't go away, but when I have something to look at that shows how much I hurt, it helps me to deal with it. It makes what's inside here real. It takes the pain outside my head. And I know it's wrong, but when I'm in the moment, I get relief from watching my dirty blood drain out of my body, because new, clean blood takes its place.'

Liz bent her head and lifted one of Ellen's precious arms to her face, holding it against her skin, kissing it. Ellen pulled it free, stood up and walked to the window.

'But if you knew Dad had died, why didn't you get in touch?'

Ellen stared. 'I'd too much to lose by then. I'd a life of my own. There was no way I could have answered your questions about where I'd been without risking getting Jack in trouble.'

'Jack?'

'He's the person I owe everything to. He's the reason I'm still alive. He saved me from myself. I knew that if I did come back, even if you'd agreed not to ask me any questions about where I'd been, the press would never have let me alone. They're still writing about me. If they had got the true story, it would have been the ultimate betrayal of Jack. All his work would have been for nothing.'

'Why? Who is Jack?' Liz asked, wanting to understand. She'd hero-worshipped their father.

'Jack is . . . my angel.'

Liz tried to rub some warmth into the tops of her arms. It was so cold. The hotel might be the best in town, but right now it felt old and draughty. 'But I still don't understand. Derek had your uniform, your shoe was found up in the mountains . . . ?'

'We staged all that,' Ellen said. 'Derek helped me to get away.'

Liz swallowed. 'What?'

'Derek brought me a change of clothes so I wouldn't be recognized, and planted the shoe in the mountains because of all the talk of a serial killer.'

'Derek knew?'

Ellen nodded rapidly. 'I went to him like I told you I would the last time I saw you when we rowed. Do you remember that day?'

'I remember.'

'I wanted you and Derek to break up so badly back then. I thought you were the only one I'd ever be able to tell what Dad was doing to me. But you were spending all your time with him. Maybe I was a bit jealous that you were so happy, too, when I was in such agony.

'I told Derek he was ruining your life, and, by proxy, mine too. He said he loved you. I told him that where love goes, hurt follows. Dad was always telling me he loved me, and look where it got me. Derek said I was fucked in the head. Those were his exact words.'

Liz shook her head.

Ellen shot her a strange look. 'You still doubt me. You used to say I was a pathological liar.'

'No, I don't think that now. Go on.'

'Derek asked me why I was being such a "bitch", and

that's how it all came flooding out. I told him everything Dad had done to me. I told him I wanted to die.
He said he'd help me to run away. He took my uniform,
and he gave me an old pair of his jeans, a T-shirt and
coat, and a cap. He put my old clothes in the Henry
Norton's grocery bag that I'd been carrying with the
stuff Dad wanted me to get after school. He cut my hair.
He brought me to see a garda he said he trusted, who
gave me the money for the ferry to Holyhead, and drove
me there. I was out of the country before I was even
reported missing. By the time my picture was faxed to
the ports, I'd made it to continental Europe. That's
where I met Jack.'

'But why didn't Derek tell me you were alive after
Dad had died? Why didn't you get in touch?'

'If it's any consolation, Derek wrote to me many
times begging me to tell you. But I had a new life. As the
years went by, my reasons for staying away got more
complicated, because of Jack. Derek's last email made it
clear he was going to tell you. And when I met Derek
again, last Friday, he showed me the Henry Norton's
bag he'd kept all those years, and told me he had my
uniform still, so I *couldn't* get out of telling you what
had really happened.'

Liz stood and walked over to her sister and hugged
her tight. 'Did you marry Jack? Are you a mum? Does
Conor have cousins? I want you to tell me everything
about your new life. All about what you do now, too.

You've obviously done very well for yourself if you can afford to stay in a place like this.'

Ellen sniffed. 'Jack's dead. We didn't marry. It wasn't like that. He was already married. His clients became like my children. But even his passing hasn't affected my work in his memory. It keeps him alive.'

'But what did Jack do?'

'I already told you, he was an angel. It's hard to explain, but I can show you,' Ellen said. She reached to the ground for her bag and put it on her lap. 'Close your eyes,' she told Liz. 'The reason you're so cold is because I switched off the heat. When you get to my size, you don't need any extra help in that department. But I've got something that will make us both feel warm again. Go on, close them.'

Liz did as she was told. A second later a sting on her arm made her eyelids spring open.

Ellen jabbed a second syringe into her arm and removed the first.

'Ow . . . what are you doing!' Liz shrieked.

'I prefer to do it myself, though Jack always used a machine. He called his first one his "Thanatron". It's Greek. It means suicide machine. He was only able to use it twice, though, because they took away his medical licence, so he could no longer get access to the drugs he needed. That didn't stop him. He was a genius. He called his second invention the "Mercitron". You needed a mask with that one, to release the carbon monoxide. It worked the same as connecting a hosepipe to your exhaust and trailing it inside your car.

'That's how we met. I contacted him to assist me into the next world, because I was too big a coward. I wanted him to take my life for me. But his machines need the client to press the button or flick the valve switch. I couldn't even do that. He talked me around. He said all I needed was a new life, not the next one. He even offered it to me. I became one of his disciples, so to speak. Thanks to him, I know what it means to be divine, to be omnipotent, to be loved more by strangers than my own family. You wouldn't understand unless you'd had someone look into your eyes the way they look into mine. The trust, the subjugation, the gift to me of the most precious thing they possess, even when what's waiting on the other side might be the flames of hell. Afterwards I lie with them – wash them down, and hold them as all mothers do their children. What better way is there to die than as if you were being born?'

Liz slid off the bed and started to push her legs, trying to back up. They were like lead. 'What?'

'It's the sodium thiopental – barbiturates. The first one was saline. The sodium thiopental will just calm you down. Some describe the sensation as a Nirvana. The third injection is the last. It contains potassium chloride to stop the heart, and pancuronium bromide to prevent your muscles from spasming and jerking.'

'Why did you come back?' Liz asked, trying to think

straight through the haze. She had to wake Conor and get him out of here. Ellen was a foot away from his neck, and her horrific bag of tricks was now sitting on the bed.

'A journalist contacted me and told me he was going to write a big story unless I paid him off. He'd hacked into Derek's email and got my contact details, and from that he was able to hack into my account and find out about my private business . . . Jack's business. He said it was the story of the decade, and told me I'd have to give him what he could get for it from a news corporation to stop him running with it. I agreed to come back to Ireland and meet him. Secrecy is the only way we can exist in most of the world. We angels are not about to trade up our lives to go to prison. What would happen to all the souls we have to save?'

'You'll never get away with this,' Liz said. Her words were slurred.

'I already have.' Ellen moved to the wardrobe and opened the door. The movement caused Paul Bell's lifeless head to slump on to his chest. 'Murder is a meaningless word for us. The greatest gift you can give someone is a life free of pain.'

Liz tried to bolt for her son but everything was out of kilter. The room was swaying.

'Not much longer,' Ellen said, watching. She tilted her head and gave a strange smile, then headed for the bathroom door between Liz and the door out on to the corridor and opened it. Liz could see an arm dangling over the rim of the bath. She opened her mouth to scream, but no sound came out.

'Don't worry about him. He's already passed. He's a reporter, too. I wasn't expecting either of them when I went to the house that had belonged to the one that tried blackmailing me. I'd brought the solicitor in the boot of your car, Liz, and I'd kept her under sedation in a bedroom while I quizzed her to find out if she'd told anyone else. I had to kill her because Derek had told her about me. But I couldn't do that until I'd established if anyone else knew. I got Amanda in without being seen, through the grounds of the old convent.

'It turned out to be a blessing in disguise, because while I was hiding out waiting for my opportunity, they thought Amanda was dead and they decided to dump her body. I'd cut myself – it's become a ritual now when I'm with a subject – and he just presumed the blood was hers without even looking for a wound. I hid out in another of the rooms while he argued with the guy who's in the bath.

'I felt bad that they took her out of the house alive, because I pride myself on making the passing painless,' Ellen said. 'I was glad of the chance to punish them, knowing I had to kill them anyway because they knew too much. Today, I rang Paul and told him I wanted to meet in my hotel room. I told him I was going to pay him to keep quiet. Jack was always afraid of some weirdo summoning us to a hotel room with an ulterior motive, so I always carry a gun, that's how I managed to persuade Amanda to get into the car in the first place, on Friday night. But when it came to my meeting with Paul Bell, the weapon jammed and he and his pal were able to wrestle it off me. They drove me to the mountains and almost killed me, but they didn't have the balls, and the promise of money got me safely back to my hotel room again.'

Liz tried to move her eyes to Conor, but even they had turned to stone. Nothing moved. She was locked in the prison of her body.

'When I met them, I let them think I was playing along, got them to tell me everything, who else knew. They tried to turn Jack's work into something evil, when it's holy. He was a God. Don't worry, Liz. There'll be no pain. I'll give you the fatal dose once you slip under. Not long now. And I'll visit Derek again before I go. It was too risky when I was there earlier. The only other one who knows I'm still alive is the cop from all those years ago. They're the last people I need to send on their way. If the press find out I'm alive, they won't stop sniffing until they find me. That would be a catastrophe.'

A rap on the door made Ellen turn quickly.

Liz's eyes moved to Conor.

'That'll be one of them now,' Ellen said, quickly. 'Can't have you acting all weird on me and giving the game away.' Hurrying over to the wardrobe door, she banged it shut, then roughly started to push Liz through into the bathroom, where she piled her on top of a very dead Niall Toland.

65

Within a few hours, Jo had relocated the incident room to her kitchen, which quickly filled with the core members of her team. She wasn't leaving her family exposed again, not until she'd worked out where she'd gone wrong on the case. Cuddling Harry on her lap, she organized a set of crayons to colour in a picture of Dora the Explorer, while spoon-feeding him some alphabet spaghetti – his favourite.

'Doesn't Dora have a little cousin called Diego?' Joan asked, giving Jo a wink.

'I only love Dora,' Harry answered, giving the page a kiss.

'Bless,' Joan said, putting a hand to her heart.

Jo kissed the top of his head, nuzzling his blond curls with her face. She promised herself never to let a case come before her family again.

Foxy carried five mugs with spoons jangling inside and a teapot to the table. 'Can you get the milk and sugar?' he asked Aishling, who was surveying Jo's framed family snaps on the wall.

'And biscuits,' Joan said.

'Derek's been discharged from hospital,' Sexton said, finishing up a call on his mobile. 'Alfie's going to have him charged this afternoon.'

'What with?' Jo objected. 'Amanda wasn't murdered, and they haven't got any of the missing women.'

'With attempted arson, attempting to wipe out his family, oh, and with extortion,' Sexton said.

'Can you find out if Alfie's interviewed Liz yet?' she asked. Harry turned to check her tone, unsure if he was being scolded. He looked so deeply into her face it gave Jo a jolt. With one reassuring smile, he went back to colouring, and Jo acknowledged yet again that she was going to have to tone it down. She sighed.

Foxy slid a mug over to her, out of reach of Harry's hands. It didn't matter, as he wriggled down to the floor, telling her he wanted to watch *CBeebies*. After settling him in another room, Jo returned to the team, reaching for her mug.

'Right, where were we?' She took a sip and looked at them expectantly over the rim.

'The techies have been going through Derek's email. It looks like Alfie does have a case of extortion against him,' Foxy said.

Jo tilted her head.

'But not against the other residents of Nuns Cross,' Foxy went on. 'Derek was blackmailing Mervyn. That's

402

where he got his hundred grand. Liz's car was towed from the hospital car park. It had been sitting there with no sign of an owner. I had it checked for tampering, because I presumed you'd have wanted that to be done, too.'

Jo nodded. 'Excellent deduction. How did you get on?'

'They found some device linked to the starter wire that would have caused an explosion', he said, 'if they hadn't accidentally cut the starter wire in the process. They must have done it while Liz was in the hospital with Derek. The same sort of device has been used before by mobsters, so I couldn't work out how Liz could have crossed people like that until I found out Derek had taken on Mervyn. Derek's brakes had been cut, by the way, which explains his crash.'

'If Mervyn and his crew were putting the squeeze on Derek, if they wanted their money back that badly, maybe they started the fire at Amanda's office,' Jo suggested. 'You need to get on to Alfie, Sexton, and tell him no visitors for Derek.'

'He's already had one,' Sexton said nonchalantly. 'Any bickies? I'm starving.'

He looked up. 'Don't worry, Jo. First off, it was a woman. She said she was Derek's sister. And secondly, Liz recognized her.'

Jo pounced. 'Liz showed up at the hospital?'

'Yeah, sorry, I forgot to say.' Sexton pulled a face.

'Anything else?' Jo asked, glancing from face to face.

'You'll love this,' Sue said. 'Helena Moriarty, the woman entitled to the newspaper reward is the mother of Niall Toland's girlfriend.'

'You're kidding,' Jo said. 'How did he think he'd get away with that?'

'Helena claims it was only because of Toland that she was so interested in the story of the missing baby in the first place, and that that was why she acted on her suspicion and phoned in the information.'

'Oh, and Hawthorne was looking for you,' Joan piped up.

'Makes a change,' Jo reacted.

'The lab results turned up something in Amanda's blood he hadn't foreseen.'

'What's that?'

'Enough sedative to stop a horse, and a rare one. He said he's only ever heard of Jack Kevorkian using it.'

'Jack who?'

'You know, Dr Death. The guy who killed his clients for cash.'

'You mean euthanasia?' Jo asked.

'Correct.'

'Sexton, get on to Hawthorne ASAP. Find out the exact name of the drug he's talking about. Then contact the medical team monitoring Derek, and tell them they need to run tests for its presence in his bloodstream.'

'Are you saying that you think Derek's sister is trying to kill him?'

'I'm saying we presumed that Ellen was dead after we found out that it was her blood in the room.'

Rory arrived into the room. 'Mum, Dad rang. He's got the all-clear. They've given him a list of things to watch out for, and they want him to come back if he shows any signs of the symptoms, but he said he feels fine. Nothing's broken. He's just sore.'

'I'll collect him,' Jo said, standing.

'No, I offered for you but he said he wants to go and see someone first.'

'Who?' Jo asked.

'He said you'd know. He said it was a blast from the past.'

Jo stood up so quickly her chair upended. 'Ring him now, Rory. Ask him where he's going?'

'I don't have to . . .'

'Just do it,' Jo snapped.

'No, Mum, I don't have to because Dad already told me. He's meeting someone called Angel in the Shelbourne.'

'Ellen,' Jo said.

66

Conor opened one eye, and estimated the distance Anakin Skywalker would have to travel through space and time to rescue Princess Leia chained in a dungeon in the City of Flies. The queen fly wanted to put worms in Babia's nose to turn her into a fly, too, but Skywalker realized what she was trying to do. He ran really quickly at the queen fly and jumped on her back. She started screaming and thrashing and trying to slam his back against the wall, but Anakin grabbed her spare injection from her bag on the bed, and he stabbed it into her neck, making her scream. She fell on her face and dropped the injection she'd been carrying and he stabbed that into her, too. His leg was trapped under her, but he managed to free it and get into the bathroom where Princess Leia was making sounds like a crazy woman. She was lying on top of a huge, ugly green spider. Maybe there were flies in her mouth already, Anakin thought, and if so, all flies would have to be burned underground to stop them spreading. Anakin reached for Babia's arm and she made a noise that sounded like 'Water'. Anakin turned the taps on and filled a glass and held it to her mouth. She drank like a woman who'd just fought a million evil droids in a desert, and then she poured the rest of the glass over her head.

'More, son,' she said, 'more, more,' and Anakin kept filling and passing over the glass until she started to get her strength back and sound more human and less fly-like. But then a door outside burst open and General Oogway – a good guy – called his mom's name.

67

'What happened?' Dan asked Liz, limping up to Ellen's body. 'I heard shouting from outside, and the door wasn't locked, so . . .'

'My sister came back from the dead,' Liz answered. Her speech was coming back slowly. She still sounded like a stroke victim.

Dan cleared his throat. 'You OK, son?'

Liz glared. 'Can we get out of here? I don't want him traumatized any more than he's already been.'

'What happened?' Dan asked the kid.

'I HATE injections,' he said, 'and earrings, needles for sewing, and safety pins, anything that could make someone bleed. Mostly injections, though . . .'

'He's in shock,' Liz said, flapping. 'He's got . . . issues. I don't want to have this discussion in front of him.'

'I really, really hate needles,' the kid said. 'Brooches and badges do it, too. They totally freak me out.

'There's a goner in the wardrobe and another one in

the bathroom,' the kid went on. He leaned towards Dan, and said with emphasis, 'Bodies.'

Dan limped to the bathroom door and looked inside. He headed to the wardrobe door and took a step back. 'What the fuck . . . ?'

Liz was pacing. 'My sister worked for Jack Kevorkian, helping people to take their own lives. She wanted to take her own life from her teens but couldn't go through with it. She said our dad abused her, but I don't believe it. She invited us here for a big reunion to explain why she's been missing for the last twenty years, and then to tell me that she wanted to take her own life. She said these men were her clients. I was trying to talk her out of it, but I couldn't stop her.'

'No, Mum,' Conor said. 'The fat lady was here with the dead guys when we arrived, and she tried to kill you, so I killed her, remember?'

'What did I tell you?' Liz snapped. 'Go.' She pointed to the corridor.

'No, it's all right, you can stay,' Dan said. He fiddled with his watch and handed it to the boy, showing him the stopwatch function.

Conor started timing himself to run the length of the back wall.

'So what's the truth?' Dan asked her.

'OK,' Liz said. She put her hands to her mouth. 'I killed her after she'd bumped off the other two and tried to kill us.'

'Mum, don't be a dick, the guy said he wants the truth,' Conor said, bolting past.

Liz looked panic-stricken.

Dan shot her a pull-the-other-one look.

'I did it . . . in self defence.'

'Actually, General Skywalker should get the credit,' Conor said cheerfully.

Liz shot a look of sheer terror at Dan. 'What are you going to do?'

He didn't get a chance to answer. They both turned at the sound of a hard single rap at the door. It was followed instantly by a shout, 'Gardaí, open up!' and then it crashed open.

Somehow, in the commotion, Liz managed to cock the gun she'd taken from the man in the bath, held behind her back, and pointed it at Dan.

'Don't be stupid,' a woman's voice said from the doorway. She was pointing a gun too, at Liz.

Liz fired to show her she was serious; plasterwork from the ceiling came spattering down in clouds of grit, and when the dust cleared she was pointing the gun at Dan's head.

'Put it down, Jo,' Dan said, extending an arm towards the door.

Jo took a second to size up his request and then dropped her weapon. She told someone out of view standing beside her in the corridor to back up.

'You know her?' Liz asked.

'She's my wife. I knew your sister, too.'

'Ellen was going to kill you,' Liz said, sliding down the wall and sitting on her hunkers, still pointing the gun at Dan. 'He's just a kid,' she said about Conor, who was under the bed.

'It's all right, I know, I believe everything you've told me,' Dan said.

'What happened?' Jo asked.

'Liz came here to meet her sister, Ellen,' Dan said in a flat, unconvincing tone. 'Two of Ellen's clients were in the room and already expired when Liz arrived with her son. But, it turns out, Ellen just wanted to say goodbye.'

'Actually, that's not the way it happened at all,' Conor said, putting his hand up from under the bed.

Jo's stare moved from Dan to Conor to Liz before settling back on Dan. She watched him hang on her decision as she made up her mind. 'That's what it looks like to me, too. Open and shut. Some cases are better that way, end of.'

Liz put down the gun. Conor rolled out from under the bed, and Dan bent down to retrieve the gun before helping Liz to her feet.

Wednesday

68

'Where do you want me to start?' Derek asked Liz. He'd been moved out of intensive care and into a high-dependency unit, where Liz visited him first thing the following morning. He was propped up against pillows. In a chair alongside his bed, the heat of the ward was making Liz feel groggy herself. She'd slept soundly for the first time in months, and attributed that to the heavy dose of barbiturates still in her system. Derek cupped his hand over hers on the bed.

'Start with where you were all day Monday, after you left the hospital,' she answered, slipping their linked hands on to her lap.

Derek glanced around uncomfortably. 'I thought the only way to get Mervyn and his crew away from you and Conor was to disappear. I thought if I brought the phone, they'd have some cop on their payroll who'd tip them off. So I left it in the hospital. I needed to make Amanda's basement ready for you and Conor to move in. I thought once you two were safe, I could lure

Mervyn out and make it look like he'd been killed in a gangland slaying. I bought a gun from one of the men who used to work in Mervyn's Meats and was none the wiser about me being sacked. But I made the mistake of telling Tom about what I was going to do, thinking he'd supply me with Mervyn's whereabouts. Instead he double-crossed me, just like he tried to blame the porn he downloaded on me. He told Mervyn where I was.'

'Tom's not who we thought he was.'

'Who is? Amanda thought I was the one blackmailing her.'

'Paul was blackmailing her too?'

'He'd threatened to tell her boyfriend's wife about them. She presumed it was me because I'd sussed the affair when I'd worked with Tim on the restoration job. He was her plumber back then.'

'No wonder she was vindictive enough to send the letter warning the department not to pay out.'

Liz poured herself a glass of water from a jug sitting on Derek's locker and sipped. 'How did Ellen know where to find Amanda on Friday night?'

'She'd tagged her location on one of the social-networking sites. I had gone to town anyway to meet Ellen because she'd been in touch to tell me she was home for the first time in twenty years and wanted to talk. I thought she'd want to talk about how we'd break the news to you. But she wanted to know who else knew that she was alive. I explained nobody, except

Amanda, and I told her why. I needed a lawyer to tell me if I could face prosecution over my role in helping Ellen to flee all those years ago – if I was going to go to prison for wasting police time. I thought I was entitled to some free advice from Amanda because she still owed me money. Ellen wanted us to go and persuade Amanda to come to her hotel room where we could talk properly, but I didn't want to see Amanda because of the way she'd treated me earlier. She was even trying to contact me on Friday night to continue the row. Ellen already knew that Amanda was right around the corner from where we were. "Four-squared" was the app she used to explain how she'd found it on Amanda's Facebook site.'

He winced. Liz could see how much pain he was still in. He'd had a major kidney infection on top of an internal bleed, and that had caused his collapse. According to the doctors, he was lucky to be alive.

'Ellen promised me she was going to contact you,' he went on. 'She asked me for some more time to get her head around it. She said she only needed twenty-four hours. I agreed. She asked me for a car to get around in, just to make a quick trip to see all the old places and put her demons to rest. I drove her to your car, and gave her the spare key that was on my key ring. She asked me if I'd ever heard of a journalist called Paul Bell. I couldn't believe that she knew him, and she couldn't believe it when I said he used to live right next door, but that his house was empty now.'

Liz dropped her hand and crossed her arms. 'Why didn't you tell me Ellen was alive? You know what I went through. How could you not have told me?'

'Every day that passed it got harder. I thought you'd never forgive me for what you'd already been through. I couldn't risk losing you. I was trying to get her to tell you. I thought it would be better that way. I was glad when she said she was going to tell the truth. I never trusted her, though. I always thought your life would be better without her in it.'

'Did you know what she was doing?'

'No, of course I didn't. The only reason I ever contacted her was for you. She gave me an email address to stop me phoning.'

'Why did you wash your clothes on Monday morning?'

'Ellen had a bad cut on her arm, and I got blood on them helping her with a new bandage. I didn't want to have to explain to you whose blood it was.'

He paused. 'How are you coping with it all?'

Liz shrugged. 'How can I grieve for someone who I thought was dead, and who wanted to kill my son, my husband, and me? I was overwhelmed when I saw her alive. It's not every day that the sister you presumed was gone for good shows up. How am I? I'm still here to tell the tale. I'm sorry for hitting your head and wanting to kill you. If it's any consolation, I wouldn't have been able to go through with it. And I'm wondering if

Conor's condition means that by some miracle he's managed to skip the prospect of lasting damage as a result of what he's been through.'

Derek reached for her hand again. She gave it. 'I'm sorry for keeping you in the dark,' he said. 'I thought I was doing what was best. I mean it.' A pause. 'Don't leave me. They're offering us a new life in Australia on the witness-protection programme. I won't go without you and Conor.'

'How would we sell the house when nobody's buying?'

'The state would buy it.'

'Really?'

He nodded.

'But what about his scholarship?'

'They'd pay for that, too. Anything that we had lost or were about to lose as a result of the move is covered. So there'd be no pressure on Conor to get the scholarship. We'd have our choice of school out there.'

Liz felt the weight on her shoulders start to lift. 'What about Jeff, his friend?'

'It's a virtual world, Liz. I bet they can work out a way to outwit the bad guys and stay in touch.'

'If we were going to start anew, I would need to change one thing about us.'

'What's that?'

'I don't want to spend the rest of my life hiding who Conor is. I want to be able to talk about him to you without feeling like you think he'll grow out of it.'

'I wouldn't change a hair on his head. If the hospital rang me and told me there'd been a mix-up at birth and that they'd given me someone else's baby, I wouldn't be able to exchange him for my own blood. He's the heart of me.'

Liz eyes began to fill. 'We've been under so much stress. I need to stop beating myself up about whether it was something I did, or some problem with the pregnancy, or because I got him the six-in-one jab, or didn't love him enough when he was little.'

'You know what I think?' Derek said. 'There are so many parents in the same boat as us, maybe the species is just evolving because it's a virtual world. Who needs language now we can witness everything first-hand?'

'I love you,' Liz said.

'Does that mean we can still be a family?' Derek asked.

'No more secrets?'

'I promise.'

'I'm sorry I believed you could have hurt anyone, and I'm so sorry I hurt you.'

Liz leaned across the bed to kiss Derek just as Conor entered from the corridor. 'Ahem,' he said loudly, making them both laugh.

69

All the talk about Ellen Lamb's career had put Maura to the forefront of Sexton's mind again. He'd come to Deansgrange, the graveyard where Maura had been buried. It was the first time he'd been back since her funeral. After walking around for the guts of an hour, he knelt on his hunkers in front of the headstone, staring at it in shock. Firstly, because there was a headstone there at all, which he hadn't ordered or paid for – the last time he'd been here was for her funeral, and then he'd only had time to arrange for a modest wooden cross. The other thing causing his jaw to constrict was the sight of the name 'Patricia' engraved on the granite. That was the name at the bottom of her suicide note, too – but it wasn't her real name, and was the reason he'd become so convinced in the three years since that she hadn't taken her own life. His eyes dropped to the other details on the inscription. The information about the woman he'd married and buried in this spot was correct. The surname was right, and the birth and death dates. The surviving family members' names were correct, too, but, for the life of him, he could not work out what the hell was going on.

Water from the supermarket flowers he'd bought on the way spilled down on to his shoes.

'Shit!'

He jumped up and rubbed the toe of each on the back of the opposite trouser leg.

'Sorry, love.' She'd always hated him cursing. Maura only ever used 'fudge' and 'sugar' when she got stressed. She didn't drink alcohol, either. She was a bloody saint.

It must have been Esther, her mother, who'd commissioned the stone, he decided, leaning forward and placing the bouquet carefully on the pebbled surface, rubbing his hands together.

The water had soaked through to his socks. *Bloody chilblains to look forward to on top of everything else,* he thought. *What the fuck was going on?* he wondered as his teeth started to chatter. It had always been biting cold in this cemetery, at every funeral he'd ever been to here. Today's squall carried a fine drizzle, adding nicely to the sense of gloom.

He stared out over the sea of gravestones. Maybe it was the exposure to the elements that did it. The graveyard had no natural barriers. Maybe it was all the marble, or maybe it was just too many bones. Whichever way, the place was depressing as fuck.

'I brought you those,' he said to the grave. 'Cheapo,

like the plonk and the chocolates I always got you. I don't know why, because I'd have given you anything you wanted – you know that, don't you? So where did those other ones come from?'

He scratched at his stubble as he realized that Maura's grave was also looking very well maintained. His gaze moved over the shrubs evenly spaced in pots. New, all of them. There was even one of those eternal candle thingies burning away under her name. He knelt down and picked it up, and turned it upside down for a closer look. It was powered by a battery, screwed in by a little nub that could only have been there twenty-four hours, based on the level of rain there'd been the day before. No way would it still have been lighting after that. He put it in his trouser pocket, trying to make sense of everything.

The flaw in his theory was that Maura's mother, Esther, always got in touch when she came down for a visit. She lived up in Belfast. She'd been down four times that he knew of – for the funeral and the anniversaries. Each time, he'd met her at the train station and had driven her here, declining to go to the grave itself, which he found too painful. He'd brought her for a little meal and brandy afterwards. But she'd have mentioned buying a headstone, wouldn't she? Anyway, only family were allowed to erect headstones, he was sure. Esther was the closest thing to a mother Sexton had had himself; his own had passed away years back when he'd been just a kid. He'd even let the old dear have a little cry on his shoulder.

The last time she'd asked him 'Why?' as she always did at every meeting. Maura hadn't been depressed, that anyone knew. She'd had plans for the day, for her life. It wasn't that she hadn't had friends. Just that most of them were hippies travelling the world, and unable to get in contact easily, or get back home because they were too broke.

He pulled out his phone, flicked it open, and dialled Esther's number, pacing away from the graveside as he did so. He needed to think on his toes during this conversation so as not to set off any alarm bells. Esther picked up straight away, as he'd expected. She didn't really go anywhere any more.

'Hello, Gavin. I've been meaning to ring. Thanks for everything on the anniversary, love. You made it so much easier.'

Her voice was wobbling already. He was sorry he'd rung.

'I've been better, Esther, to tell you the truth. I'm here at Maura's grave now. That's why I'm calling . . .'

He heard Esther draw a difficult breath on the other end.

'The headstone . . . when did you . . . It's just, I want to contribute. I would have done it. I just hadn't got my head around it yet.'

'What headstone?'

Sexton fell silent. He stopped in his tracks ten-odd graves from Maura's now, his back to it, pressing the space between his eyes.

'There's a headstone on Maura's grave where the cross used to be. Are you telling me you had nothing to do with erecting it?' he asked.

'No, of course I didn't. I'd have asked you about anything like that. Who put it up?'

Sexton rubbed a hand over his face, trying to think of a way to backtrack. He didn't want Esther to get all alarmed. She was the type who'd be on the next train, and that was the last thing he needed at the moment. He started snapping his fingers. 'Sorry . . . sorry . . . it's coming back to me now. I did order it. So long ago, I just forgot, that's all,' he lied. 'You know me, head like a sieve. I promise I'll ring you back tonight, when I've got my head straight. Sorry for worrying you.'

After some more cajoling, Esther calmed down.

'One last thing, doll, before I let you go . . .'

'What is it?'

'Did Maura mention wanting to be called Patricia again before, you know?'

Esther sighed. 'Why would she want to be called that? Why do you ask? What's going on, Gavin? You're making me nervous. Please tell me. I won't be able to sleep trying to work it out.'

'It's just something one of her friends said. I'll talk to you about it properly when you get down.' He'd have to, he realized, if she came to Dublin, she'd want to know why that was the name engraved on the head-stone as soon as she saw it.

'She never meant to do it,' Esther said suddenly, breaking down, 'it was all a terrible, terrible accident.'

Sexton paused. 'What do you mean?'

'Well, I keep having this dream. I can see her as clear as day. It's so sad because I can't remember her face when I'm awake. I look at photographs and I ask myself why I didn't notice a freckle, or the way she'd changed her hair. In this dream she says to me, "Mam, I didn't want to go."'

Sexton exhaled. 'I've got to go, doll. I'll ring you soon as I can. Try not to worry.'

He hung up, put the phone back in his pocket and turned to head back the distance to his wife's grave. What he saw made him stop in his tracks. A man was kneeling down, polishing the headstone with a cloth, and there was a new flickering red candle light where the old one had been.

Epilogue

Jo couldn't see a thing through the steam in the shower. Dan liked it extra hot, and she listened as the sound of his footsteps crossed the adjoining bedroom. Harry was asleep. Rory was in school.

Jo had learned a lesson she wouldn't forget about delegating. Other officers were preparing criminal files for the DPP on George, and the McLoughlins. The drug squad were pursuing their case against Mervyn and his cronies. Baby Hope was gaining strength by the minute. Niall Toland had been captured on CCTV in a florists purchasing the flowers that Paul Bell delivered and sealing their fate. Paul Bell's wife Jenny had been located and had claimed to know nothing about his recent pursuits.

Jo leaned against the tiled wall of the shower, waiting as jets of steaming water bounced off her skin, sending spears of heat through her body. The Perspex doors were open, Dan's spot directly under the nozzle free, and the door to their adjoining bedroom open.

'Happy anniversary,' she said as he drew closer. 'Only two days late.'

He slid the shower door shut behind him and buried his face in the nape of her neck.

'Jesus, what a week,' he said.

'It's over,' Jo said. 'And if it's any consolation this case has made me realize that judgement calls are where real justice is. Putting that kid into an institution would not be justice. He's a sweet boy.'

Jo moved behind Dan and started to massage his back. He leaned his neck towards the movement of her hands. 'I'm sorry I didn't tell you what had happened. I should have, in hindsight.'

'You're a man of your word. You protected your source.'

'How many people might I have saved from Ellen if I'd done what I was supposed to?'

'Those people would have found someone else to help them.'

'I just didn't think that I had a choice back then. Ellen was threatening to kill herself rather than go back to live at home again. She'd already tried it at least once: we'd found out about that hospital admission I told you about. I should have had her taken into care, and Liz taken out of that house, and made a paedophile atone for his crimes.'

'If he was one,' Jo said. 'Ellen was a disturbed girl, just as she was a disturbed woman. We'll never know if her problems resulted from her abuse, or if she was abused at all. You did what you thought was right. The fact that Derek lived under a cloud of suspicion for the sake of Liz's future is admirable as far as I'm concerned. What could you have achieved by forcing Ellen to stay? She said she would refuse to cooperate with any court case. She'd have been a hostile witness. It's hard enough to get abused girls to come forward. What kind of signal would we have been sending out if you'd forced Ellen into the dock? She wanted to get on with the rest of her life. She claimed she didn't want an abuser to dominate her future. She didn't want her abuse to ruin Liz's life.'

'Having a sister going missing kind of guarantees that,' Dan said.

'Yes, Liz lost a sister. But the alternative would have been losing a father and a sister.'

'You can't bury the past,' Dan said.

'If they hadn't confided in you, you'd have been none the wiser about what had happened to Ellen. People run away all the time. It's not a crime. What I still don't understand is why Derek kept the information from Liz. She was supposed to be his girlfriend.'

'Because there was no way of telling her why Ellen had gone without telling her what her father had done. He wanted to spare her that. He didn't think she'd believe it, and thought it would become a life obsession.

I risked my job, my reputation, my livelihood. I risked losing you by not telling you.'

'Because you know exactly the way the system works. Anyone who likes can walk in off the street and see who the anonymous victim's father on trial is. Every guard in the country can get the name, the address, the details. She'd have had to lead a different kind of life.'

'I should have told you years ago,' Dan said.

Jo didn't answer.

'I didn't want to make you culpable for my mistakes,' he explained.

'You want me to say you're right. I can't. It doesn't mean I love you any less.'

He leaned in and nibbled her ear. 'I'm horny as hell now you know all my secrets.'

Jo cupped his face in her hands and leaned hers towards him. 'Ditto.'

Dan stepped out first and reached for a bath towel, putting it around her shoulders.

Jo followed, but stopped at the sound of him opening the door to the bedroom.

'What's the matter?' he asked.

'Help me, Dan, help me! I can't see anything.'

Acknowledgements

Thanks to my husband, Brian, for the continued love and support when I most needed it.

Thanks to my editors, Cat Cobain, Brian Langan, Lucy Pinney, and Stephanie Glencross for making this book so much better. I know how lucky I am to have each of you.

Thanks to my agent, Jane Gregory, and the whole team at Gregory and Company for all the expert guidance.

Thanks to my family, especially my parents, Sheila and Eamonn, for helping with the children, and brother Gavin, who was a great sounding board.

Thanks to my pals, Siobhan Carmody, Carmel Wallace, Maria Duffy, Sarah Hamilton and Vanessa O'Loughlin.

Thanks to Victoria Smurfit for a particular conversation that got this book kick-started.

Thanks to Team Transworld, especially Eoin McHugh, Stephen Mulcahey, Madeline Toy, Helen

Gleed O'Connor, and Declan Heeney for all the support.

And last but not least, a heartfelt thanks to my first crime editor, Selina Walker, and first mentor, Cathy Kelly, for getting me started on this treadmill. I've never looked back.